Author Notes:

This retelling is based upon an actual event.
Many of the elements within are factual,
and some, equally, are not.

Acknowledgements page:

My sincere thanks go to my family and friends who have supported me over so many years. The original draft of this story began nearly twenty years ago, and it has been quite a journey bringing it to life.

To my publisher, Chris Day, and the Filament team — thank you for your guidance and commitment in helping me move this manuscript into its finished form.

I owe special gratitude to my uncle, Chris Willis, who has been a tremendous support and my patient, diligent first editor. You were a steady sounding board as I pieced everything together, and I couldn't have done this without your encouragement.

My thanks also to the team at Flipscript, who created the unique ambigrams and the bespoke interconnected design developed especially for this book.

On the subject of design, I am deeply grateful to Dawn Lauder, whose talent brought to life the other internal illustrations — each one crafted and refined with such care.

Finally, to my beta readers and friends — Leo Calcioli, Martina Cubbidge, Chris Mowen and Chris Woodhead — your support and thoughtful feedback proved invaluable.

To everyone else who has walked alongside me on this long road: thank you.

A new psychological drama, based upon an incredible true event

Warrick is locked inside a room with a spiritual shaman and his devout followers of an esoteric sect, with seemingly no way out. Thoughts of blood sacrifices and sex orgies heighten his experience, as he witnesses clannish dances and mind-boggling moral lessons.

He has to cleverly escape when threatened to remain.

He witnesses tense and sometimes volatile experiences of all that go on with various members within the circle of devotees when confronted by their spiritual shaman. Emotions run high and people's viewpoints are pushed to their limits, as they gear up for the finale of finally ousting their "chosen one" for the evening.

Will the interactive rings of the Divinities belief system, really hold the key to man's salvation...?

This may interest those looking for something out of the ordinary. The saga is enlightening, inspiring, yet mentally challenging. All that you thought you knew about the world about you is stripped bare for you to reimagine and reevaluate.

Modern concepts, narratives and twisted social trends are challenged throughout the book as spiritual enlightenment is weaved within its pages.

What people are saying...

An excellent, captivating read with lots of twists and turns. I like the surprise ending, which leads one to question: what comes next?
MC

This is outside of my usual genre, but even so, it had more in common with my genre than I thought it would, and in unexpected ways. An adventurous and thought-provoking book, that made me look at my own life and the people I surround myself with.
LC

The story drew me in fast. I loved the plot of this book. I have been fascinated by spirituality and the psychic realms since I was a teen. All in all, a fascinating read!
an unknown reader

I found this a genuinely fascinating and very intriguing story, not to mention extremely clever, with all the associated symbology, ambigrams and mysticism.
CW

The author — who, I must add, is a good writer — offers a wild trip into ideology, spiritualism, God, and a host of other subjects, mostly seen through the eyes of a shaman. And, you know what? It's compelling stuff.
"A thought-provoking trip into spirituality, ideology and human culture. Fascinating!"
— The Wishing Shelf Book Review

For my sister,

Jo

Other books by Stephen

NOVELS

What's the time, Mr Wolfdog (psychological thriller)

Brotherhood of the Serpent (A psychological thriller)

THE CHRISTOPHER DARING SERIES

Spirits of the Dead (Book 1)

The Forest of Riddles (Book 2)

The Secret Puzzle Box (Book 3)

NOVELLAS

Time for Obsession

The Figure in the Mist - a short ghost story

One Winter's Day in June

A Season of Hauntings

The Butcher's Apron

SCRIPTS

Anthony and Cleopatra - television script

(award-winning, TV pilot for a supernatural detective series)

Entrusted-short film script

(award-winning, short film script about a corrupt drug rehab)

For more visit www.stephenjwillis.co.uk

A psychological drama

By Order of the Shaman

STEPHEN J WILLIS

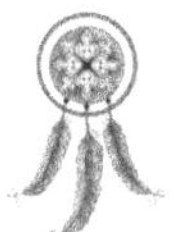

Published by
Filament Publishing Ltd
14, Croydon Road, Beddington
Croydon, Surrey CR0 4PA
www.filamentpublishing.com
+44 (0)20 8688 2598

By Order of the Shaman - by Stephen J Willis
ISBN 978-1-915465-90-0
© 2025 Stephen J Willis

The right to be identified as the author of this
work has been identified by Stephen J Willis
in accordance with the Designs and Copyrights Act 1988

Printed in the UK

Ambigram Illustration Designs
www.flipscript.com

Illustrator
Dawn Larder
www.theglimmertwinarthouse.com

Original Divinities and other internal illustration concepts
Stephen J Willis

Table of Contents

1.	Demonic or Angelic	1
2.	The Drawing Room	14
3.	Mind, Body, Soul & Space	19
4.	Devotees	28
5.	Gird One's Loins	37
6.	The Shaman	45
7.	Enlightenment	50
8.	Lord of the Dance	55
9.	Soul Cleansing	62
10.	Truth be Told	69
11.	Truth be Damned	75
12	Divinitas	82
13.	Defiance and Regret	94
14.	Abhorrence	106
15.	The Law of Ascension	119
16.	Respite	131
17.	Is or is not?	152
18.	The Spectral Realm	174
19.	Samsara	196
20.	A Crow to Eat	204
21.	Social Piranha	224
22.	Incorporeal Transcendence	238
23.	The Chosen One	257
24.	Guiding Light	270
25.	Rank	283
26.	Cult or College?	289
	About the Author	297

Looking back, it dawned on him just
how long he'd been searching,
though for what, he still couldn't say.
Perhaps tonight would offer him a glimpse of that
missing something.

~ CHAPTER ONE ~

Demonic or Angelic

'What do you mean it could be a satanic cult?' asked Warrick, peering back at the telephone handset.

His mother continued in rapid-fire down the public telephone earpiece.

'Yes... yes, Mum,' he acknowledged, trying to get a word in, 'but I hardly think that is going to happen to me, is it?' he sighed. 'I know, Mum, I know... But I've known these friends for a while now, and I think I would have sensed if they were into anything dodgy, you know?'

Still doubtful, his mother carried on, leaving Warrick to roll his eyes.

'Okay, okay,' he said finally, 'if I think it's too weird, or if I get asked to drink any goat's blood, I'll leave. Yes, I promise... yes, I am taking you seriously. Of course I believe you, and I know it happens, but not very often. Now, don't worry. I'll see you later. Okay? Good... bye, Mum, bye.'

Warrick replaced the telephone handset onto its cradle and looked down at the scribbled notes he had made around the edges of his newspaper. If he was honest, he wasn't even sure what a spiritual shaman was. In his mind's eye, he would picture an Indian guru sitting on top of a mountain, smoking a long pipe adorned in symbolic paint and gathering warmth by a crackling fire. Either that or a room full of devout satanic followers, dressed head to toe in black robes and chanting for deliverance from some fallen angel.

It was an ignorant, Westernised view, he knew, but such clarity in such a specific subject was not something he was accustomed to.

Warrick ruffled his crop of mousey hair and wandered out of the red telephone booth and back over to the lake he'd been walking around. Gliding majestically towards the reed-cluttered bank and breaking the orangey reflections cast down by the distant sun, two beautiful white swans decided to join the party of ducks by the water's edge.

The expansive waters, stretching out before him, were known as Victoria Park, wedged between Bow and South Hackney in London. It was too deep to paddle in and far enough across that you couldn't clearly see the other side. A natural calmness enveloped the area, and, for all intents and purposes, it could have been located within his rural Hertfordshire rather than within this tranquil East London parkland.

He looked back at the address he had written down and pondered. Why he had been asked to attend some spiritual soirée at the last moment, where some mystical guy — a shaman — was to take the floor for a night of unforgettable divine enlightenment, was anyone's guess.

His mother had passed on the unusual message when he had called home.

'Just you make sure you know what you are getting yourself into,' she had said. 'I know what you're like.'

Yet the idea still intrigued him. He'd never been to such an evening before. But anything that drew his attention away from the humdrum existence that he felt his young life had become was definitely going to interest him. His family and friends would, he knew, mock such an evening; it was what they always did.

He frowned at the conservatism of the middle classes, despite being brought up within their class system. Now nineteen, he had grown accustomed to the comforts that such a lifestyle could provide, but he also felt trapped, unable to wander outside its accepted social boundaries. So, this shamanic gathering was, therefore, beyond their idea of an evening's entertainment. However, on further reflection, he had to admit that, even for him, it did sound a little unusual.

Something about it nagged at him nonetheless. The last time he had witnessed something vaguely similar was in some cult horror film, where devil worshippers had gathered together for a night of moonlit, ritualistic sacrificing and sexual indulgence. Well, if he did decide to go, then at least there would be a chance he would get laid, he mused.

All the same, he doubted that any such nonsense would happen during this occurrence, as it was all too far-fetched for some urban location in West London. As usual, his mind was running away with itself in an attempt to distract him from the doldrums of a humdrum daily life — a habit he often considered would, if left unharnessed, lead him astray one day. Perhaps they, the middle classes, were right. At least being careful kept you safe, kept you out of trouble and kept a stable roof over your head.

But contradicting his thoughts once more, he reviewed his invitation; maybe this was his chance to do something exciting — an adventure of sorts. Perhaps he would finally see or meet someone inspiring — someone who would at least give him a glimpse of life outside of his boring bubble of existence.

That was the thing with Warrick — he was always on the lookout for something that might shed more light on the world around him.

To his parents' surprise, they once found books on ESP, telekinesis, and clairvoyance among his library books — not at all what they'd expected. Warrick was sure they would have preferred something grounded, like football, chemistry, or engineering, not this wishy-washy world of the supernatural and the occult.

He dreaded to think how they'd react if they knew he'd once slipped into the local church to learn about the laying on of hands — the invocation of healing and spiritual energy through touch. Looking back, it dawned on him just how long he'd been searching, though for what, he still couldn't say.

Perhaps tonight would offer him a glimpse of that missing something.

Playing before him and squabbling like school children, a gaggle of baby ducks fought over each other for the handfuls of broken crusts that they knew were still to come. An old man, sitting silently on a bench before Warrick, slid his hand back into his plastic bag and pulled out more bread to throw towards the awaiting hungry mouths. Warrick watched them bobbing beneath the water, cleaning themselves, and thought how simple and carefree their lives were.

The old man cleared his throat with gruff irritation. 'Poison — or so I've been told,' he said, with no preamble.

'What's that?' asked Warrick.

'The bread — it's supposed to be bad for them,' he continued without looking up. 'Can you believe it? People have been feeding bread to ducks for centuries, but now some of the PC brigade want it banned. Moronic sheep — the lot of them! Offended by this and offended by that — I'm surprised they can get out of bed in the morning without being offended by the time of day.

'Damn these flowery millennials and their fluffy outlook, and damn all this PC bollocks. I'm sure they spend more time stopping the world from progressing than actually helping it.' He shook his head. 'Some people are so easily led. I mean, there are leaders, and then there are leaders. And those people always seem to follow the wrong ones. Mark my words, they'll be setting up their own self-protection scheme before long,' and he sat thinking up a slogan. After scratching at his head, making Warrick itch, he lifted a grubby finger as if to announce his thoughts on the matter. 'Wait a minute... the... the T-P.O.D.S.,' he said finally. 'The Protection of Delicate Snowflakes...' He laughed to himself, which brought about a wheezy cough.

Warrick offered a small acknowledging chuckle. Although he agreed, he was hesitant to fuel the man's obvious irritations.

Peering up at the sky and the ominous darkness of the rapidly approaching and angry-looking clouds, Warrick decided that it was time to vacate the tranquil scene. Besides, the bulk of the rush-hour traffic would be over now, and he could cruise relatively easily around to the other side of London.

Cutting through the stillness, Warrick watched a little boat come meandering silently towards him. It ploughed headlong into the resting ducks that suddenly scattered and took flight where they could from the oncoming attack. To his far right, a cheer arose from a small jetty, where two young boys sat on the adjacent bank, stealthily operating the boat's controls. Warrick smiled to himself.

Large spots of rain started falling rapidly from the heavens above, and he had to run to his car. Just in time, he pulled the handle and jumped into the driver's seat.

The brilliance of a lightning flash pierced the rapidly darkening sky, and a heavy rumbling of thunder shortly followed.

After switching on the windscreen wipers, Warrick cleared the inside screen of its misting surface using a worn cloth that had seen better days. Through the torrential rain, his eyes locked onto a poor mother and her little girl running desperately for the protection of an old coach shelter that sat just in front of him.

Panting, the two boys from the jetty joined them briefly, hovering there with their small boat before tearing off again.

Crying, the little girl pointed down to her ice cream that had fallen from the cone. Warrick leant forward, feeling uncomfortable, wishing he could help. The mother tried to comfort her, but, being upset, the little girl resentfully threw the remaining cone down to join it. Ignoring this, the mother grabbed the little girl's hand, and they, too, made a run for it across the car park. Warrick peered blankly at the fallen ice cream, staring as it began to slide down into the tiny stream of rainwater and disappear into a watery path and out of sight.

Deciding to finally leave, he reached for his seatbelt and started the engine. Then, digging under his seat, he pulled out his old A-Z road map and began plotting his route.

With his phone battery flat and the car's built-in satnav stuck on an "Update Error" screen, he had no choice but to go old-school.

He wavered on either driving across the Regent's Canal and onto the A10 main road or heading over to the A12 to pick up the A406 North Circular. Deciding on the latter, he memorised the basic route and put the map to one side.

Finally getting onto the road he wanted, Warrick was irritated to see a queue of traffic building up ahead.

He should have taken the A10 instead. But within moments, a workman in a fluorescent vest and plastic helmet waved him into a second lane.

Emerging from the slalom of roadwork cones, Warrick's mind drifted back to his earlier conversation with his mother. She'd told him that his friends, Rumi and Sumera, had called. They were sorry for the short notice, but they wanted to invite him to meet their shaman, who was making a rare appearance. They weren't quite sure why they'd thought of him specifically, only that it had felt like the right thing to do — that they'd had a "feeling".

All he had to do was wait outside a big old Edwardian house, and they would introduce him, since no one else knew he was coming.

Warrick was intrigued, but one detail continued to nag at him. His mother had mentioned an odd request: if he agreed to go, he mustn't tell anyone else. Rumi had, apparently, said that he didn't want it to sound "cultish," but the gathering was a closed group of sorts, and privacy was paramount.

That concept lingered in his head like an itch he couldn't scratch. Warrick had heard about cults and weird spiritual gatherings, and he couldn't quite figure out why the invitation intrigued him so much. He never saw himself as gullible or easily led. Usually, he dismissed things like this as half-baked nonsense — people sitting in circles, banging on bongo drums, trying to invoke invisible spirits.

He had almost talked himself out of going when he reminded himself how bored he was with his life. Only minutes ago, he'd been complaining about never meeting anyone interesting. And now, when such an opportunity arrived, he was hesitating.

Reaching the A406 North Circular, the traffic began to thin, and he pressed down on the accelerator.

Gazing up at the road signs, he caught himself slipping into autopilot, heading home out of habit.

He sighed. He felt adrift in life, directionless in his role as a trainee security technician — a job he hadn't chosen so much as fallen into.

It was the kind of job that someone else always seemed to want for him. "You need to get a trade" was the most promoted phrase. Working as a tradesman was the last thing he wanted to do. Not that he was a snob, but it wasn't the sort of environment he felt comfortable in. From his current experience, the conversations were limited, and the alpha-male mindset was something that he found both irritating and amusing. Watching a regular guy you were working with suddenly turn into a cocky *Jack the Lad*, as soon as a few men got together, was curious to behold.

Anyway, just because many of the other family members felt comfortable in such workplaces didn't mean he had to follow suit.

But Warrick, not wanting to disappoint anyone, had simply gone along with it, an almost apathetic, even defeated, decision, despite his protestations. At the time, it felt easier to comply than to risk hurting anyone's feelings. After all, they meant well. So, somewhere along the way, he'd assumed it was the only path open to him — for now, at least.

Modelling had been suggested — mostly by his girlfriend, who insisted he had the cheekbones, boyish charm, and the poise to pull it off. His long eyelashes and demure grey eyes, she'd said, could seduce any lens. His height wasn't quite catwalk standard, but it gave him an edge. His lean frame, often credited to a fast metabolism — or, by less generous friends, to reckless weekends clubbing — he attributed instead to regular gym visits.

He knew he was attractive, but the idea of pouting through photoshoots, changing outfits, and wearing make-up every day didn't interest him. It didn't feel like a real purpose — just more performance.

Sometimes he wondered if he ought to lean into his more philosophical side. He had other wide-ranging interests: the cosmos, archaeology, and even palaeontology. But whenever he brought them up at home, they were usually met with blank stares or politely doubtful smiles.

Still, for reasons that he barely understood, their approval mattered more than he liked to admit. Maybe it was just habit — trying to live up to expectations in a family that clung to stability, predictability, and the idea of a "normal" life. A job, a house, and a 2.5 family. He would shudder at the thought. But sometimes it felt like letting himself down was the price of keeping the peace.

As the traffic slowed near the Hanger Lane gyratory — where the A406 met the chaotic A40 — Warrick reached over, untangled his frayed phone charger, and examined the connector. It was done. He tossed it into the footwell.

Glancing at the map spread across the passenger seat, he followed the curve of the roundabout. Not long now.

Again, he thought about what the evening might bring. He wasn't even sure if a shaman was good or bad — or what one actually was. It all sounded a little too "cultish," too "un-middle-class."

And yet, despite his scepticism, a rebellious flicker stirred inside him. A small thrill danced at the thought of stepping off the expected path. Why shouldn't he venture out and discover the world for himself? He hadn't made any life-defining decisions yet — hadn't even started his life, really.

Meeting a spiritual leader might be absurd... or it might be the first step into something he didn't even know he was looking for.

Something had shifted inside him. The weight of monotony eased slightly. Intrigue had taken root. Excitement followed.

He pulled over to check the map one last time. The rain had all but stopped. He flicked off the wipers.

Warrick rechecked the address he had jotted down on his newspaper and, realising he was on the correct road, found the house number and parked up. As he was early, he sat there for a while, nervously picking at his nails. He reminded himself that if he saw anything remotely dangerous once he'd entered or noticed any signs of entrapment, then he should politely leave immediately or perhaps say that he had to go, as he had friends waiting outside. This way, he would not appear to be too vulnerable or completely alone.

Watching through the windscreen, various people arrived and entered through two large, ornate double gates. They seemed pretty ordinary — no cloaks or symbolic regalia. Mind you, there was the possibility that they could change into satanic outfits once they had entered.

By 7:15 p.m., his friends had still not arrived. And by 7:30 p.m., Warrick decided to get out of his car. They were now 45 minutes late.

Shutting the car door, he crossed the road beneath a slate grey sky, somewhat begrudgingly. Strangely, the streets appeared almost dry at this end of London. It was almost as if it had never rained; just a fine mist seemed to drift about lazily in the evening air. Warrick put it down to the build-up of wind that was now spiralling leaves and bracken into mini cyclones. A nearby willow ruffled its branches against one another, and its fallen pink blossom swirled about in the air for a moment before being chased off up the quiet road.

As he approached, Warrick looked up at the expensive-looking house. It seemed huge. The building sat isolated, dominating all others on the road.

Leaded stained-glass windows gave it an air of authority, and the thick climbing ivy that grew between them indicated their extreme age.

He peered in through the open black gates, where two entrance pillars flanked a double front door. A gravel drive ran up to the entrance, complemented by a central fountain that featured two vicious-looking dragons, both spurting water. Surrounding the house and grounds stood a seven-foot wall, whitewashed and topped with gold-tipped black spikes. Reaching out a hand, he ran his fingers over the house number that was set out in elegant calligraphy.

'Sixty-six,' he murmured slowly. After the last six, he became aware of someone's attempt to wash away the defacing scrawl of an additional number six. 'Six...six...six,' he repeated to himself. 'Well, that's a good start.'

Adorning the pillars that supported the wrought iron gates stood two winged serpents — supposed guardians of the house and its inhabitants. And again, Warrick thought about the various horror films he had seen in the past. More often than not, they had involved strange religious groups and secret underground sects. Some involved devil-worshipping and weird practices, sometimes concerning animals and the probable harvesting of adrenochrome from young children in terrifying, macabre sacrifices. And now that he thought about it, one of the last films he had watched even featured the Goat of Mendes – the devil himself. It had scared him half to death as a kid. He remembered a big country estate with winged serpents on the entrance gates and a secret wood-panelled room with a sacrificial altar guarded by men in long robes and swinging incense holders.

Warrick's stomach knotted as he looked from one pillar to the next and paused, staring back at the winged serpents, wondering if this was a sign of good or bad fortune. Involuntarily, he gazed towards the heavens.

His hesitation lingered as he questioned what he was doing. It was not that he was scared, as there was even the tiniest thrill of adventure lurking in his bones. It was the apprehension of the unknown that most tugged at him.

What if they overpowered him — he was just a young man, a late teenager, after all. Perhaps now was the time to draw on his tradesman persona, to summon his inner alpha male. He inwardly smirked at this thought. Who was he kidding? Society might acknowledge him as a man, but standing here beneath the rapidly looming twilight, he felt unmistakably like a boy again. A small wave of nausea rose in him; what if he was making a dreadful mistake?

So, torn in his decision, he turned back towards his car, playing for time, but in doing so, almost walked headlong into a couple that had approached from behind him. They excused themselves and, passing Warrick, walked up the shingled driveway with their umbrellas extended, protecting them from the fine rain that had started again. They stopped short at the two large front doors. Flanking them, two burly men dressed all in black looked down at them, and they smiled back politely. As the doors opened, a tiny woman, smartly dressed from head to toe in an elegant grey and maroon trouser suit, walked into view and looked down at her clipboard. She peeled back the top sheet and thumbed through the list of names on it, looking back at them expectantly. The man holding the umbrella lifted his left hand, and the woman looked down to see an expected symbol embossed on his signet ring. After a nod, she let them enter.

Warrick rubbed subconsciously at his left hand. So, this was a secret group, after all. But he had no ring — how was he to enter? He peered up and down the desolate road, but there was no sign of his friends.

'Well, you wanted an adventure, and now you have one,' he murmured to himself.

He clenched and unclenched his fists as the nervous tension all but pinned him where he stood. Then, noticing that the bouncers were now watching him, a burst of adrenaline seemed to make up his mind for him, and he set off, albeit reluctantly, towards them.

~ CHAPTER TWO ~

The Drawing Room

As Warrick approached the large black doors, the two bouncers stepped sideways, blocking his entrance.

Finding his voice, Warrick spoke, trying hard to mask the nervousness that resided there. 'Erm, I think I'm supposed to be meeting some friends here.'

The ominous-looking bouncers looked at each other and stared back down at the innocent young man before them. But before they could speak, the door behind them opened. The small woman from earlier stepped between the two towering men. She had a kind face, but looked ridiculously tiny in comparison. Her dyed black hair, pulled back into a high doughnut style, enhanced her already bony features. And judging from her pale, waxy skin, Warrick estimated that she was in her late sixties.

Along with her grey and maroon trouser suit, which was stylised with a matching silk neck scarf, Warrick also noticed that it was peppered with many, almost indistinguishable, tiny black and gold symbolic markings.

Without wanting to stare, he quickly glanced at a few markings before looking back at her. The most repetitively used was that of the secular peace symbol.

It was mainly printed in black and appeared so often that it was more like a watermark. The other symbol was one he was not too familiar with. He had seen it on odd occasions, but its purpose was unknown to him.

At a guess, he thought it had something to do with ancient Egypt and was somehow related to life and the afterlife. It may even represent the life-force or the eternal nature of one's soul, although that seemed rather a deep symbol to put on a neck scarf.

And as if these fabric insignia weren't enough, the woman also had a gold-plated breast pin. This was a little easier to see, as it was much bigger and sat upright.

This, Warrick was sure, had something to do with duality — or Hermes, the messenger god — and symbolised the protection and guidance of others. Or was it more than that? A representation of higher consciousness? A path to ascension?

Perhaps that was why the woman wore it. Was she a protector?

A guide?

But then, why so many symbols? So much mystic insignia? Did they hold a collective meaning — a kind of coded message? Was it all just a coincidence — that she happened to wear so much of it, on this night, in this house?

Coughing, she gave him a confident smile and pulled out her clipboard.

Feeling more at ease, Warrick smiled back into her tiny grey eyes and straightened up.

On a golden chain around her neck hung her glasses, which she lifted from her chest. 'Name?' she asked firmly.

'Name?' Warrick repeated. 'Oh, no, I am not expected, but my friends told me just to come over. Actually, they did tell me to wait outside — well, I thought they did, unless they meant inside,' he babbled, and she raised her eyebrows.

Warrick tapped at his phone, which was still in his jeans pocket, wishing it were still powered.

'Really?' she replied, sounding both curious and confused.

'I've been waiting a while now, but they haven't turned up yet, unless they are already here?' and his voice trailed away — put off by her look of bemusement.

He looked at the bouncers, but they, too, seemed to stare blankly back at him. She took in a long, deep breath and peered over her glasses at him.

'Did you come on your own?' she asked.

'On my own?' he repeated, his stomach tightening, wondering why she had asked.

'Yes, on your own?'

'I did, yes... But, I am not on my own... Well, I am — so... no.' And he frowned, trying to judge whether he was saying the right thing. But her unflinching gaze unnerved him further. 'But saying that, yes, I am on my own at the moment — obviously, but, erm... my friends are supposed to be meeting me — out here — unless they are already... in there,' he stuttered, pointing at the front door.

'Yes, so you've said.' She looked him up and down, saying nothing.

Feeling stupid, Warrick half-turned to leave. He'd been reduced to a gibbering idiot by this diminutive 60-year-old woman. But perhaps this was a sign that his suspicions had been confirmed, as anyone who made him feel this uncomfortable must be representing something bad. Yet, despite awkwardly succumbing to her refusal of entry, he actually felt relieved inside.

'Have you changed your mind?' she asked, confused, lowering the clipboard.

'No, but I thought...'

'You thought...? You think too much.' Finally, deciding that he was harmless enough, she looked over her glasses at him and cleared her throat. 'Okay, let's take you inside to look for them, shall we?' And she gave him a warm and reassuring smile before retreating.

Warrick nervously followed, squeezing between the statuesque sentinel figures.

They made their way through a wooden-panelled entrance hallway and into a vast room, their footsteps echoing off the wooden floor and yet more wall panelling. Warrick assumed that it must generally be used as someone's elaborate sitting room. But not tonight, as it was almost entirely empty. All the furniture had been removed, apart from eight isolated and equally spaced out, unlit floor-standing candelabras.

Dominating the room at the far end sat a great chair, like that of a majestic throne. On either side of this were two giant black and gold tasselled floor cushions.

Mimicking the room's inner circumference was a second circle, curiously made of many pairs of shoes, socks and sandals. Odd — why was there a circle of shoes around the room with no owners present? Peering back to the far end of the circle, he noticed that there hung a large tapestry displaying two knights sitting on two fiery stallions amid a great battle. The rest of the scene was partly obscured as a giant chair sat directly beneath it.

'Just leave yours with the others,' said the tiny woman, indicating a space.

Peering down, Warrick stared at a space between two sets of shoes and paused. This was getting serious now. Why was it necessary to take his shoes and socks off?

Stalling, he looked back at her with what must have been a blank expression as once again she raised her eyebrows with an expectation of his unreserved obedience.

Feeling strangely coerced and rather foolish, Warrick ruefully looked down at his shoes and socks without question, clenching his fists to calm his growing anxiety. Once again, in his mind ran the perverse images of barefoot devotees summoning up dark forces and evil spirits in a circle of gleeful euphoria. Regret was beginning to simmer inside him now, and it was all he could do not to turn around and walk straight back out.

He breathed out heavily before deciding to just go along with it, and he began removing both of his shoes and socks. So, this was it; he'd committed himself.

~ CHAPTER THREE ~

Mind, Body, Soul & Space

Thoughts of smoky rooms holding séances and sacred group sex orgies flashed through his mind. And once again, visions of people shrouded in long, dark cloaks wheeling in half-naked and semi-conscious victims cluttered his thinking. What was wrong with him that he kept feeling and seeing such debasement? The mind was a strange beast, he thought, where it tended to imagine and assume all sorts of weird and wonderful things, although usually more along the lines of the macabre.

Warrick could also feel his heartbeats quickening due to his negative thinking, which was definitely running away with itself.

He looked closer at the nearest candelabra, and at two small dreamcatchers that hung from each of the two furthest candle holders. On the left one, miniature circles of different sizes, constructed with a delicate weave, sat around a translucent central theme, wherein a beautifully coloured and ethereal image of an Indian, in full shamanic regalia, stood embracing a lone wolf. On his right were the same arrangements of woven circles, but this inner translucent theme depicted an owl in flight, soaring through the night sky, where a full moon and a blanket of stars provided an enchanting backdrop.

Warrick glanced along to the other candelabras and noticed that they, too, had uniquely different, centrally themed images hanging from their two dreamcatchers. Some were even embellished with sparkling jewels that were strung together with glistening silver thread.

He was about to turn and move on when he noticed something else — a word or text cleverly embedded within the black ornate metalwork of the candelabra itself. The word was repeated over and over, creating a circle of repetitive words.

Crouching, he ran his finger over the wording and found himself squinting at the almost hidden text.

'Mind,' he murmured, and he looked up at the tiny woman, only to find she was carrying a curious smile upon her face.

Warrick stared out at the other candelabras. They, too, had a hidden word built into their ornate black framework. All in all, he counted four words. Over the eight-floor candelabras, each word was repeated twice. He read them out aloud, although more to himself: 'Mind, Body, Soul and Space.'

Each of the words had been cleverly created in the style of a unique ambigram, wherein the words themselves could be turned upside down and still be read in precisely the same way. If it were not for this quirky fashion of wording being only recently back in vogue, in books such as Angels and Demons by author Dan Brown, Warrick supposed that he might not have noticed them.

As he touched the top word, the actual circle of words began to rotate within a metal wheel. He spun the disc around and around, but again it read the same, so whether upside down or not, the word was identical.

Once again, he peered out at the other candelabras. Presumably, their words, too, spun if initiated.

Warrick repeated the four strange words aloud — 'Mind, Body, Soul, Space' — then turned to the woman.

She smiled sweetly. 'When merged, they are known as *The Divinities,*' she said proudly.

The woman then flicked through various pages on her clipboard to arrive at an image, printed on the board itself. She then spun it around to display an interwoven collection of rings.

Warrick leant forward; he realised that they were not just basic circles, but the actual words again, now harmoniously amalgamated into one iconic image.

'*The Divinities*,' he murmured in fascination.

'Exactly. It is a wonderful symbolic analogy of the mathematical *Borromean rings*, or *knot theory*, wherein if only one of the inner rings is removed or broken, it then releases the other two. This, therefore, represents the interplay of our three inner key elementals of: Mind, Body and Soul — all encompassed within the outer ring, representing *Space*.'

Warrick nodded, coming to terms with how much intelligence had been forged into the actual ideology of this unknown shamanic following.

She gave a forced, polite cough. 'Simply put, he — that is to say, Man — is a combination of factors. He is made up of different parts that all interact with one another. Thus, we have our first and most basic law: the law of divinity.'

'Oh, I see,' said Warrick, starting to grasp the concept.

'Mind, body, soul and space,' she repeated, her voice now softer in tone. 'One without the other, and we no longer have a human being before us.'

Warrick pondered this. 'Yeah... I guess so,' he replied, eventually. 'But why?'

The woman thought for a moment, the end of her pen tapping against the clipboard as she did so. 'Man is a composite; that is to say, the sum of the interplay of the postulated collective.'

Warrick's mind went blank. 'Erm... the what?'

She smiled apologetically. 'That is the deeper meaning, but if you break it down, it makes sense. If one were to collect together the four component parts, and project an interaction of them all, one would find themselves with that which stands before them: Man.' She took a breath. 'In the *grand beginning* of all existence, an original idea or concept was born out of the static state of pure knowing. And from that prime conception, life was then brought into being, so as to fulfil such an interplay.'

Warrick shook his head, amazed. *How did people think up or work out all this clever stuff? How would one even go about creating such a powerful belief system?* It seemed beyond him. *A higher purpose, perhaps — some sort of spiritual calling?*

When Warrick was a child, he was thrown out of Sunday school for repeatedly questioning various key points during study periods. After making a clay model of Adam, one afternoon, he asked how it was possible to create Eve from a tiny rib, stating that the clay model would be too small.

He reasoned that if he couldn't do it with plasticine, then surely God couldn't do it with a simple rib — otherwise, women would be too small. This earned him a stern talking-to about flippancy and challenging a well-known belief.

Similarly, he didn't quite understand the spontaneous act of ammonia bringing life forth from the sea. He considered that if this were true, fully formed people would be emerging from the sea on a regular basis, completely naked. This observation invited a clip around the ear for being insolent.

Yet the arguments and questions continued, much to the dismay of the staff. It was soon considered that he had asked too many questions for his own good — that he was clearly heading towards a troubled life. He was obviously a defiant child, one who would never learn to do as he was told.

And as he was not about to stop challenging his elders anytime soon, it was perhaps not the right place for him.

Warrick, much to their confusion, was rather pleased.

So here he was again, being asked to accept, on faith, someone's belief system. Were *The Divinities* purely guesswork and speculation, or were they based on proven, verifiable experience?

They were impressive, no doubt about it, but all the same...

There was so much noise out there, especially on the internet, that it was hard to know *what* to believe. For Warrick, people as a whole seemed to just follow trends, believing what their friends or opinion leaders suggested was true, rather than seeking out their own truth. How quickly people would jump on the bandwagon to hate certain people, celebrities, or subjects they knew nothing about bothered him. These were not the kinds of ignorant social circles he liked to be part of. In fact, he found this reactive kind of mindset rather dangerous.

He leaned in to re-read the circle of repetitive text that displayed the word: "Mind".

'Mind, Body, Soul and Space…' he muttered again. 'But why *Space?*'

The woman looked at him in curiosity.

'One *is* a *soul*,' and she pointed to a candelabra that contained the word *soul*, 'trapped *within* a *body*,' and she point to another candelabra, 'and using his *mind*,' and she pointed to the nearest candelabra, 'one can eventually transcend into, and thus conquer, infinite *space*,' and she indicated the final and furthest candelabra.

'Oh, I see,' replied Warrick, trying to imagine the sequence of events.

He lifted his hands to inspect them.

'It's just a vehicle,' she said, indicating his body. 'Once it dies, you pick up another.'

Warrick's eyebrows rose with this new concept.

'I thought we were supposed to *have* a soul…'

'*Have* a soul?' she guffawed. 'And where do you suppose that you are to keep it — sitting at home quietly glistening in an empty jam jar?'

Warrick shrugged.

'My dear boy,' she continued, 'you *are* a soul; you don't *have* a soul — like one keeps a pocket hankie.'

'I suppose it makes more sense,' Warrick replied, with a false chuckle.

'There is no *suppose* about it, *you* are it, the spirit, the being, the genie in the bottle — it is only a *body* that you are trapped in, and not some ornate ruby-enriched Eastern oil lamp.'

She gave him a genuine smile. 'You have probably gotten used to it being incorrectly assigned.

And don't even get me started on that ignorant *Darwinian man-comes-from-mud nonsense*. A *spontaneous combustion* of natural elements, my...' she stopped herself. 'It's fiddlesticks, and it is all far too complex not to have some intelligent grand design at the back of it all. If only he had started out with the life of a mono-cell that divided and subdivided — then perhaps further life-forms might have some sensible credibility. Look here,' she went on, but now facing him head-on. 'Mind,' and she indicated to the area above his head, 'Body,' and she grabbed at his shoulder, 'Soul,' and she pressed a finger dangerously close to the area between his eyes, 'and Space,' and she swept her hand about the empty room.

Warrick felt a strange and inexplicable excitement rear its sleepy head ever-so briefly, before lying back down again.

But the fact that it did rear its head and did carry a tiny thrill of knowing piqued his interest. Something about what she had said unlocked something deep inside him, had opened some distant truth of which he could not quite confront or was ready to fully understand.

The next thing he knew, he was still staring unfocused at the circled "Space" ambigram. The woman had already continued walking toward the end of the room, where two French doors stood open, and was waiting for him.

Wonder and mysticism had now unexpectedly encroached upon his growing fear and anticipation. He glanced about at the other hanging dreamcatchers as they too swung gently in the evening breeze. Although all were slightly different in structure and theme, they still carried a resonating air of ancient magic. A tiny buzz of intrigue diluted his nervousness.

Then laughter from beyond the open French doors broke his momentary trance, and he looked back at the tiny woman who simply stood there watching him, her arms crossed. Having his attention once again, she beckoned him with her index finger, as if to share a secret.

She did not smile when he approached her but just eyed him with further curiosity. Despite her size, Warrick still felt like some tiny amoeba under the wary gaze of a giant microscope.

A draught of cool air sailed across his face and into the room as he paused in the doorway. He looked around at the various types of people, all of whom were happily chatting. His friends, however, were not there, and he wondered if they would actually turn up at all. Hopefully, they had not left him alone, at the mercy of an evening that might ramble into the unknown.

~ CHAPTER FOUR ~

Devotees

Barefoot, Warrick, too, stepped into the garden, walking directly underneath a large interlinking marquee. The grass was cold but not wet, unaffected by the patchy weather. Above him, a gently billowing, soft, cream-coloured fabric roof lightened the rapidly darkening evening. This was enhanced by gently twinkling white lights that ran around its perimeter and was then further complemented by more lights artistically entwined around the outer pillars. Similarly, like the small woman's neck scarf, these pillars also featured a similar array of mixed black and gold symbols delicately woven within the creamy fabric that adorned them.

On this occasion, he even noticed another symbol he recognised — the Omega.

If memory served, it was said to mark the end of all things... or perhaps it pointed to something far greater — the divine itself, the Alpha and the Omega.

He shook his head in amazement. It was another seemingly random piece of insignia — wasn't it?

Wherever he seemed to look, other symbols appeared to jump out at him. He even glanced upon an elegant symbol tattooed onto a woman's wrist as she reached up to procure a drink from a passing waiter.

The tattoo was of three interconnected circles — rings of sorts, all encompassed by a fourth. Seeing him staring, she lifted her wrist to give him a closer look.

Warrick realised what it was. '*The Divinities,*' he offered, reading the small name above, written in italics.

The woman, although more of a pretty girl up close, inclined her head before locking eyes with Warrick. She sipped the golden liquid, leaving a thick layer of orange lipstick upon the glass, which Warrick could not help but notice was almost the same shade as her copper-coloured hair.

'It's just as divine,' she said dreamily, looking at the drink, 'like an elixir for the soul.'

Warrick lifted his hand to take a glass, but at the last moment decided to retract it. The woman gave a short grunt of amusement before ending the interaction with a flirtatious pout of her lips and sauntering off to join her awaiting friends.

Without her pretty face and slim frame to carry it off, Warrick was certain that such an aggressive crop to her luscious hair would probably not have worked as elegantly upon another.

Although still a little uncertain, he continued to look around the meticulously landscaped garden and was relieved to see that the bulk of the people were actually normal. They were not adorned in cultish cloaks and perverted sexual attire, but were, on the whole, rather sensibly clothed. They were dressed in clothes that naturally befitted their social and cultural backgrounds. In fact, they seemed a somewhat pleasant and peaceful group, with an age range between the early twenties and the mid-seventies. It was obvious that he was the youngest one there.

Feeling more relaxed, he smiled to himself and acknowledged a mild annoyance at his own far-fetched assumption of joining some covert and dangerous off-beat sect.

But upon a second glance around the grounds, his certainty wavered, as a single figure-a solitary man-individuated from the rest of the group, by his general demeanour, sat alone on a far bench.

This thin and fragile-looking man was peering out towards the others, as if from purgatory. The bench upon which he cowered was situated within a pretty and colourful section of the garden, full of vibrant flowers, and where another blossom tree hung with a depleted array of dainty pink flowers. Yet this man, this sorrowful figure, looked decidedly out of place in his drab and pastel-coloured attire. He appeared as if his stomach were churning over and over — as if he were beginning to wish he hadn't come. Subconsciously, the man wrung his hands together, before squinting down at his watch and staring back toward the empty room from which Warrick had stepped. The man gazed hopelessly, almost without focus, as regret seemed to flood his face and engulf him. He steadied himself by clinging onto the wooden seat itself, before pulling a handkerchief from his pocket to wipe at his running nose.

Warrick considered him for a moment. What would make a grown man so apprehensive? What was it about the room that worried him so? Was it something that he, Warrick, should also be concerned about, that he was yet to find out in due course? Possibly... Or was it something completely remote from this gathering, such as a personal issue — a heavy guilt, for instance — that this poor man carried? Maybe, but Warrick doubted it. Yet, on second thoughts, the man did appear unmistakably afraid — too afraid.

Warrick did not need another reason to be both further intrigued and cautious, as this served as a good reminder for him not to let his guard down. All was not clear as yet — there were definitely things about the evening that were hitherto unknown.

However, aside from this one oddity, the others were calm and in good spirits. Of the eight or so groups, four were sitting in small circles on the ground.

Two of the groups looked rather "new age" and stuck in the seventies, with their flowery clothes, beads, and ribboned hair. In contrast, others could easily be mistaken for business commuters or general family members. In fact, to his surprise, they all looked rather run-of-the-mill.

The tiny host squeezed his arm, grabbing his attention. 'Let me introduce you to a few people here,' she said, and began indicating to one of the hippy-type groups beside them.

'I'm sure it's gonna be him… so Jemima reckons…' Warrick overheard as he approached with the host, and the party of guests went quiet.

The tiny host then spoke. 'This young gentleman is new,' she announced, and they all turned to smile. 'This is Joyce,' she continued, and a nervous woman, surprisingly and incredibly much smaller than the host, smiled back at him through tiny round and rather thick glasses. She squinted out at him like a mole peering out of its burrow. After patting her thinning and badly dyed plum-coloured hair, she attempted to curtsy by lifting the edges of her matching purple skirt.

Warrick smiled back.

'Here we have Ruby,' the host went on, and Ruby raised her glass.

Warrick thought that she was another rather odd-looking woman, as she appeared to have an enormous bottom but barely any shoulders, which also made her head look much bigger than it probably was. And this was not made any better due to the fact that she had the biggest mass of curly and tangled mousy-brown hair he had ever seen.

Even the coloured ribbons and lace that she had attempted to twist about it to enhance it did not help, for Warrick, on second glance, thought she looked more like a poorly dressed Christmas tree.

'Elderflower is so very special at this time of year, don't you think?' she asked.

But before Warrick could answer the random question, the host moved on.

'And before I retreat,' the small woman continued, 'I would like you to meet Brigadier Johnson,' she announced proudly.

'Well, well, hello there, young fellow,' he replied somewhat brusquely, and thrust his hand at Warrick.

This tall man had a gaze that could freeze water. Ice-cold eyes of steel bored into him with not so much as a blink. He twitched his moustache as if daring him to look away.

Warrick felt him squeeze his fingers unnecessarily hard, and with a forceful shake, he asserted his self-importance.

But behind him, Ruby shook her mass of ribbon-laced hair and rolled her eyes, mimicking the word "Brigadier" with disbelief. Satisfied with his authoritative introduction, the man released his iron grip and withdrew into a nearby circle of guests.

Of all the groups in the garden, Warrick had to be introduced to this one. Although probably harmless, they were clearly all barking mad. And, Warrick feared, were the sort of people to be brain-washed into any old nonsense and pretentious hocus-pocus. He smiled at them all and, despite feeling vulnerable and awkward with his bare feet, decided to sit down, cross-legged, to join them anyway.

Once comfortable, he sat upright, only to notice that the woman directly in front of him was sitting as rigid as a statue. Only her weighty earrings, which tended to drag her earlobes close to her shoulders, caught his attention with their rainbow of coloured beads. With a milky-white complexion, in stark contrast to her multicoloured shawl and lemon-green blouse, the woman was pursing her lips together so tightly that they inevitably generated the only other colour upon her face.

She had also folded her legs unnaturally tight upon one another, so that she was perched with her back ramrod straight, and upon her knees rested her open palms, with their thumbs and index fingers touching. Warrick leaned forward, trying to see if she was still breathing.

Nudging Warrick, Ruby began in a whisper, 'Jemima is currently aligning her *chakras* — you know, the seven energy centres within the body — due to some recent negativity which had pushed her whole system out of sync.' Ruby then indicated down the centre of her body at each of the seven energy points.

Noticing Warrick's vague expression, she began explaining herself. But feeling somewhat embarrassed, Warrick struggled to watch as the woman started by pointing towards her groin.

'Let me see, first we have the *Root chakra*,' and she patted the area around her vagina, 'then the second is the *Sacral chakra*,' and she placed her hand over her navel.

Warrick felt himself going red, as if he shouldn't be looking at the areas she was indicating.

Unfazed, Ruby rolled up some of her fallen bangles and continued. 'The third is, of course, the *Solar Plexus*, which is here,' and she patted the centre of her torso, just below her rib cage. 'Next up is the fourth one, which is your *Heart chakra* — my favourite, as it represents love and healing.' She rubbed at the centre of her chest with a comforting smile.

Again, Warrick half-looked away, not wanting to be caught staring at her exposed cleavage.

'The fifth energy area is the *Throat chakra*,' and she pawed at her throat, stretching her chin skywards.

'Then the sixth, as you may already know, is the *Third Eye chakra* — essential, this one. It's good for psychic awareness and all sorts of mental energy and intelligence,' and she tapped at the centre of her forehead. 'Then last but not least, we have the *Crown chakra*.' She waved her hand mysteriously over the top of her head.

'This is where one reaches a kind of spiritual awakening — a place of calm serenity — like that of *The Divinities*, our own state of inner bliss, unity and wholeness.'

She turned to Warrick and smiled sweetly. Warrick smiled back, trying to gauge the tangible reality of such beliefs, and torn between wanting to accept the spiritual aspect of life and rejecting their entire cosmic energy movement.

Part of him wanted to laugh — not at Ruby, but at himself, for even entertaining the idea that chakras, energy centres, and divine awakenings might be real. It all sounded like poetic nonsense. And yet... wasn't that hypocritical?

After all, he'd read mystical books and tried his hand at psychic healing down at the local church. So what gave him the right to be sceptical now? Perhaps it was too ethereal and not tangible enough.

Another part of him — quieter, more reflective — leaned in. There was something disarmingly sincere about Ruby. Her voice, her eyes, even her calm presence radiated a peace he hadn't felt in a long time. Maybe ever...

He hated this mental tug-of-war between belief and doubt. He wasn't a hardened rationalist, but he did like things to make sense — and this didn't. Not yet. Not fully, at least. Still, the idea that something unseen and luminous might be guiding life stirred something in him.

Was it curiosity? Or just a longing to feel connected to something more? Questions, questions...

'Oh, and stop me if I'm wrong, Jemima,' added Ruby, pointing at her matter-of-factly, 'but even your six harmony points need to be realigned as well, I think you said?'

Similarly, using two hands this time, Ruby pointed down at her own body to indicate the six main points of focused energy; she pointed to either side of her chest, her rib cage, and finally to either side of her stomach.

'Three lines of body energy — the trinity of energy flows,' and she indicated the three lines of energy down Jemima's body. 'There is nothing more important than having harmony or unity with one's own body. It's always good to have a balanced flow of energy, you see. And I wouldn't put it past Jemima to start hunting for that healing crystal of hers, once she's back home. But for now, she is just preparing her *Crown chakra* — the top transcendence point — for this evening's spiritual event. Isn't that right, Jemima?'

Jemima gave a very subtle nod, leaving her multi-coloured earrings to sway back and forth — the only real proof that the woman was still alive.

Warrick, too, nodded in reply, but now with somewhat perplexed amusement.

'Look,' pointed Joyce surreptitiously, whilst nudging Ruby, 'he's doing it again. I knew it — I simply told you so, didn't I?' She then adjusted her thick glasses, making her eyes appear even larger.

'Oh, yes, Joyce, Raymond does look *rather worried,* doesn't he? Perhaps he knows he's the one going to be *chosen* for tonight?'

Warrick spun around, and there, in the half-light just beyond the perimeter of the marquee lighting, sat the solitary man he had noticed earlier. There was definitely something withdrawn about him. His eyes still surveyed the party of guests from a distance far greater than that of the garden boundary.

"Look, rather worried..." Warrick repeated in his head — the man looked positively petrified!

~ CHAPTER FIVE ~

Gird One's Loins

Raymond rocked back and forth ever so gently on the bench. He looked out at all the other barefooted guests and sighed.

'Hang on... what... what did you just say?' started Warrick, with a frown. 'Did you say chosen?'

Ruby burst out laughing. 'Ah, give over,' she said, giving a dismissive wave of her hand, 'you make it sound really quite sinister. It is for the greater good, after all.'

Between them, Ruby and Joyce continued to laugh. Warrick, in turn, smiled awkwardly back at them.

'Well, he is just a man,' said Ruby, re-tying a loose ribbon in her large mass of hair.

'Don't say that,' laughed Joyce nervously, waving down Ruby's comment, 'or he'll think you're some aggressive feminist or part of that religious Sacred Feminine movement.'

'No, no,' said Ruby playfully, patting Warrick's arm, 'I'm just teasing.' She turned back to Joyce. 'I'm no Sacred Feminist follower, you know that. Those types may well think that women are more sacred or closer to the divine than men, but we know better; we know the real meaning of the divine. And it's not just sex that will elevate man into that sacred plateau, either.'

Warrick baulked at this comment with a frown. Were they talking in riddles on purpose?

Joyce turned pink, her large, magnified eyes blinking rapidly through her glasses. 'Oh, no, wait a minute, we don't think that... no, that's just the Sacred Feminine's opinion,' she said quickly, 'not ours.' Warrick nodded with a polite smile as if he understood.

'But,' added Joyce, 'we are not knocking them. No, don't get us wrong, because the harmony of both the feminine and the masculine is absolutely paramount in balancing out one's sense channels.'

'It's The Divinities, dear boy,' interrupted Ruby, 'it's why we are all here. They are unparalleled and are the true path. They mark the native equilibrium of human nature. They provide the undeniable fact that men and women are both equal, and together we are in perfect balance.' She looked to Joyce for confirmation, but she was already nodding enthusiastically. 'So, we are not some tribe of Wicca witches or New Age God worshippers, you know. But that said... we... we do have our own methods,' she winced briefly. 'The thing is...' and she rested a hand upon Warrick's arm again, 'is that one does have to do what one has to do — it's survival after all. And there again, if one is chosen, well...' she tailed off with an unspoken gesture to Joyce.

Just then, a strong breeze blew in through the garden. The fabric of the marquee billowed up, rocking the entire roof, and everyone's clothes flapped wildly about them.

Ruby raised her hands to the wind. 'It's a sign, a sign from above, I'm sure of it. An omen of change, of new things to come — like a new broom sweeping the room.'

Warrick resisted the urge to laugh, so he benignly looked about as if trying to perceive this "wind of change." But as far as he was concerned, it was just as the weatherman had predicted: a strong easterly wind that would last until the early hours. So, nothing unusual about that.

But a cascade of conflicting questions still scattered through Warrick's mind. What exactly was a chosen one? And why did there need to be one?

Warrick looked about at the various clusters of people. And yet, it was incredible — they seemed normal enough. Well, most of them.

The kind of people you'd expect to see walking their dog, shopping for milk, or waiting for the number nine bus. But here they were, calmly discussing spiritual awakenings and chosen ones, as if it were just part of everyday life.

That was the unnerving part. Not the talk of energy or fate, but the ease with which they all seemed to accept it. Warrick suddenly realised he had no idea what any of them were truly capable of.

Who really knew what went on in people's minds? Serial killers and devout religious followers in close-knit cults always seemed normal enough — at least, according to their neighbours in TV interviews.

His mind was wandering again, and his friends had still not arrived. He wondered if they were waiting for him at the entrance. He should have stayed out by the front gates a little longer. Actually, that's probably what he ought to do now. Yes, that was a good idea — he'd make some excuse, go back in, pick up his shoes and wait in his car. But for some reason, something was keeping him there, tethering him to the evening's event. It was such an odd pull, a deep-rooted kind of reasoning. He looked back at the solitary man, wondering about his fate. Was he really this chosen one? And what would they do to him?

Perhaps there was going to be some sort of a sacrifice after all. But why did they think it would be this man?

What had he done to deserve such a thing? Had they been informed of a crime he had committed, or was it just that his "time was up"? But what if he was just a victim of circumstance? Or did they have some power bestowed upon them by this magical shaman? Maybe they were naturally psychic and had real spiritual abilities — maybe they had actually reached their sixth chakra, and had access to their Third Eye. Warrick contemplated the thought — perhaps only a true telepath could ever truly know such things. They, of all people, would see everything — and leave no stone unturned. Karma was such a fickle gift from Mother Nature, so again, maybe Raymond ought to be punished if he had been bad. Perhaps he was going to get what was coming to him.

Raymond took off his crooked glasses and pinched the bridge of his nose in an attempt to relieve the stress.

'Strange kind of cat, isn't he?' sniffed a new oily voice from over

Warrick's shoulder. 'He's chosen all right — I'd bet my wife on it.'

Warrick turned to find another odd-looking man gazing beyond him to the lonely figure still sitting on the bench. The man with the oily voice looked back at Warrick and smiled knowingly.

This man was completely bald on top, apart from a few determined grey hairs. Still, he had seemingly decided to overcompensate by strangely growing the sides of his curly hair outwards about four inches, making him look like some peculiar cartoon character. Warrick stared at him, wondering whether to laugh or not. It was like he, Warrick, had been inserted into a slapstick comic book, where all of the characters' key personality traits had been exaggerated.

'These parties bring them all to the surface, if you ask me,' the man went on, whilst still staring at the figure. 'I think it's the Telluric Energy currents, to be fair. I mean, they do have every event at a house that is situated on or near one.

Think of it...' He then pointed to Warrick, as if suddenly indicating some secret wisdom.

'The what?' Warrick asked, confused.

'You know, Telluric Energy, the underground electric currents, magnetic lines and flows of energy that almost govern where all mystic forces are drawn to.

They run invisibly up and down the country, and some places are real hotspots for psychic and mystical phenomena — maybe Stonehenge is on one, or they could be the causes of the odd UFO sighting.' Then he placed his hands out as if to feel energy rising from the floor.

'I can perceive it,' he whispered with his eyes closed.

'Right...,' frowned Warrick, looking between the damp grass and this strange new character's outstretched fingers. But Warrick's attention was still on the lonesome figure, '... so what does it mean, to be "chosen" then?' he went on.

'You mean to tell me you really don't know?' His eyes widened.

'Ho, ho — are you in for a surprise,' he replied with a hearty chuckle.

'Know... know what?' asked Warrick, not finding anything to chuckle about.

And the man continued in a murmur, barely opening his mouth. 'Well, there has not been one chosen for a good few years now, but this shaman carefully hand-picks one, once in a blue moon. So, it's quite something when he does. However...'

'But what for exactly?' pressed Warrick, looking back at the forlorn figure.

The man answered with an enigmatic grin, his eyes inquisitively looking over Warrick's face. And Warrick felt as if the man was trying to prejudge the outcome of his following answer before speaking.

'Ahem,' interjected a voice across the garden, intending to gain attention. 'Ladies and Gentlemen, if you please. I have a small announcement to make.'

Warrick turned around, breaking away from the conversation.

The tiny host was standing on tiptoe, again brandishing her clipboard. 'If you would start to take your places, as tonight's event will begin in five minutes.' She smiled curtly and disappeared back into the large room.

Séance, more like, thought Warrick dryly. As he turned back to the man to finish his sentence, he saw that he was gone. He was now left with yet another mystery — who or what was a chosen one?

And, unexpectedly, the earlier nerves of apprehension reemerged, to gnaw with renewed intensity in the pit of his stomach. This was it now; he was going in. An additional pang of suffocation seemed to tighten in his chest, giving rise to climbing panic.

They all bustled into the room, their whispering voices echoing in the empty space. One by one, they reunited with their shoes and sandals, re-forming the giant circle. And one by one, they sat down, cross-legged.

But as Warrick watched the circle taking shape, a fresh surge of anxiety hit him. He couldn't think straight. Part of him now desperately wanted to leave—but he could barely move. Fear was urging him to flee, yet some ridiculous loyalty to his friends held him back. But what was this loyalty? Did he even really know them? Clearly not...

They'd spent three years hanging out, and not once had they mentioned any of this spiritual stuff. Not that they had to — but still.

Maybe they couldn't. Maybe he hadn't been ready to hear it. Was he ready now...?

They'd been clubbing together, eaten out at restaurants, even shared a grubby adventure in a giant tent at Glastonbury.

But never once had they hinted at this sort of thing. And yet, now that he thought about it... he didn't even know what "this" was.

And they weren't even here now — not to guide him, not to explain what was going on—and that was bad manners enough. If he was being honest, he actually felt rather set up.

And so, through his conflicting thoughts, his limbs began to seize up, and he struggled to turn through the haze of unfamiliar faces. He felt himself buffeted back and forth in the hustle and bustle, as the others scrambled to their respective places.

Across from his predestined location sat Joyce, Ruby and Jemima, and they smiled back reassuringly. Within this frantic motion, their gentleness seemed to create a moment of calm, which instantly smothered his angry flames of trepidation, allowing Warrick to relax enough to finally sit down as well. He took a deep breath to regain his composure and looked blankly down at his shoes and socks, placed beside him, thankful that they sat so close to the main entrance.

The loud slamming of the garden doors made Warrick turn his head, and, regrettably, watch two heavily built doormen locking them shut, grinding the two huge bolts home and turning the keys in both locks. Noticing that they were now lit, the candles in the furthest two floor candelabras flickered in their holders from the draught. Then the two big men turned their backs before the tall French doors and crossed their arms defiantly, like burly bouncers blocking any passage out. Warrick felt his insides tighten even further. And, as if to reaffirm his concerns, he heard, for a second time, two more wooden doors slamming into their frames, as the main entrance doormen rapidly sealed the two large front doors.

Warrick could hear the bolts securing them well and truly shut. Following suit, the two men turned around, also standing with their arms crossed.

Nobody was leaving tonight.

~ CHAPTER SIX ~

The Shaman

A cold chill formed along Warrick's spine and spread up to his neck, making him shiver. He felt suddenly sick. His friends had abandoned him, and despite being part of this circle of exuberant people, he felt alone. What on earth had he gotten himself into?

His certainty wavering, he looked again around the circle of assorted people — his friends were definitely not there. Warrick searched his memory in vain. It was number sixty-six, they said, wasn't it? Or was it fifty-six? Panic leapt inside him as he desperately tried to remember. He pleaded with himself that he had not made a mistake, and that he was not in the wrong house. It could not be true.

Before he could worry himself further, the small woman, still clinging to her clipboard, walked into the centre of the room, her heels noisily announcing every crisp step in the enraptured stillness. Apart from the bouncers, she was the only one allowed to wear shoes.

She cleared her throat again and spoke excitedly.

'And now, the moment is finally upon us, and for some, it has been a long three-year wait. But that wait is now over; I have the honour to introduce our saviour and our guide. And I know of no other that enables one to plumb the emotional depths of one's very soul, like that of a Greek tragedy.'

Warrick inwardly rolled his eyes.

'Pray, let him flood you with light and beautify your inner native power, and may his words of wisdom embellish your karma with peace and serenity.'

Warrick looked for another to share his playful smirk of discontent, only to be greeted with a gormless grin from the thick-lensed, bespectacled man across the circle. Awkwardly, Warrick half-smiled in return and looked back at the speaker.

Excitedly, the host went on, 'Let the evening commence — as I give you... our shaman.'

She gave a kind of odd curtsy and hastened back out of the room.

There was an apprehensive stillness, as nothing seemed to happen for a moment. Then, suddenly, out of the silence, a tall, mixed-race, Indian-looking man, barefoot and dressed from head to toe in a long, flowing linen outfit, strode effortlessly towards the centre of the room.

An instant feeling of awe rose within the circle members, and a sense of suppressed jubilation heightened amongst them.

The shaman was a very handsome man with a fairly rugged build, and Warrick was sure that he would not go amiss as some leading actor in a Bollywood feature film. He appeared to be a mix of Indian and possibly English descent.

He stopped at the centre of the room and bowed gracefully upon the rapturous clapping. He brushed back his long, black hair as it fell before him. The thick, glossy mane was partially tied up and pulled back at the sides, complemented by a combination of golden beads, ribbons, and small white feathers.

The first thing that Warrick noticed was that the man seemed to have an indescribable calmness about him.

And as he began to walk about the circle, Warrick became convinced that this man was definitely like no other that he had ever met or encountered before.

The man's voice was deep and slow yet held a graceful gravitas which Warrick felt was strangely magnetic.

It was an unusual voice that seemed to convey authority naturally. There was no specific accent either; it had an almost neutral tone, neither Indian nor English.

The shaman gestured for their silence.

'Welcome — welcome one and all; I am very, very pleased to see you,' he began.

Slowly, he started to pace about the circle, looking at each and every one of the members, as if talking to them all personally. He paused in front of an elderly couple and smiled at them. Excited, they in turn both smiled back, and then at one another.

'Listen and listen well,' he continued, 'for you are all on the brink of greatness. But take heed: woe betide the man that douses his own fire of life, as it is he who thereby extinguishes his own dreams, desires and aspirations. And it is also he, and he alone, that must carry that burden until such time as he is willing to look back at his own neglect of responsibility for it.'

Warrick shifted in his seated position.

The shaman exuded a knowing presence that seemed to emanate from every pore. Each word was delivered with precision, and each was voiced with definite purpose.

As he smiled, a few of the women nudged one another, clearly enamoured. There was no question that he was the walking epitome of an alpha male. Warrick could understand the shaman's appeal, as he gave out a raw kind of sex appeal, a sort of innate procreative force. It was in the form of complete confidence and unwavering competence.

Yet there wasn't the slightest air of arrogance or self-admiration, only a sense of innate power. He just was.

Warrick looked on in awe. If there was ever a man to aspire to, then this shaman was undoubtedly in the running.

The shaman lifted a hand as if instructing a class of students. 'Our spiritual path does not take one away from that of the physical body but rather allows the spiritual to enhance the latter. Our sacred writings can unbind you from the past and the physical restraints of the body, your carbon-based corporeal forms. But bodies are of no real concern of ours, as our quest is that of the immortal.'

A cynical voice in Warrick's head guffawed, this coming from a man who looks like a Greek god and has the muscle mass of Tarzan.

The shaman continued, 'And despite our apparent allegiance to the ideologies of Gnosticism — the belief that the spirit can be unburdened from its bondage within the human form — we are, in fact, a totally separate body of uniqueness. Although our belief system is new, it is grounded in many ancient and sacred teachings that have come before. So, now we are out of the dark ages and the oppressions of religions of a yesteryear; we are free to carry out our quest for the true wisdom that has been denied us.'

The shaman bowed, and everyone clapped. A few of the women, Warrick noticed, were still staring at the man like love-sick teenagers. He didn't recall ever seeing his own girlfriend look up at him like that. Nevertheless, Warrick half-clapped, partly because his mind was still trying to play catch-up with everything that had just been said.

'One is either the originator of causality or one has become the victimised affected in this life. And this includes being causatively affected as one chooses. The choice of being a victim is a fool's escape from one's responsibilities.

You can blame only yourself if you look back far enough.

Until such time, he shall lock himself down in chains of his own making. And when he is ready, there is a way out waiting for him. He only has to pick up his feet and walk towards the lightness of truth. It may be a long and arduous journey for some, but the release of restraint from self is a reward worth everything. Some sacrifices must be made.'

He paused briefly in front of Warrick, whilst smiling gently at the woman to Warrick's right.

Mimicking, Warrick mouthed the word "sacrifices" to himself in wonder. Blimey, this guy doesn't pull any punches, does he? What an opening line!

~ CHAPTER SEVEN ~

Enlightenment

As the shaman stood there, paused in mid-speech, Warrick saw various tiny mystical signs and symbols tattooed in black and gold on both the Shaman's hands and feet. Here they are again, Warrick pondered — like some sort of a motif.

Before the shaman moved on, Warrick was able to get a quick glimpse at a few of the images. The first was the symbol for Yin and Yang — the Chinese philosophy of balance, representing the harmony of both light and dark, as well as the feminine and the masculine.

The next symbol, which was the largest, was one that Warrick had not encountered before. It was the sort of sign he would have expected to see on some Eastern pendant or imprinted on some ornate and ancient artefact.

Not realising that he was staring, a middle-aged man to Warrick's left leant towards him. The man looked Eastern, as if originating from Pakistan or a similar region.

'It is the Adi Shakti,' he whispered, 'which is the original cosmic energy that is recognised in Hinduism. It sort of represents the dynamic forces which move through the entire universe.' Warrick nodded in acknowledgement.

As the shaman shifted slightly, Warrick noticed another symbol that he'd seen before. It was the symbol for gender, and in this case, it was used to indicate heterosexuality.

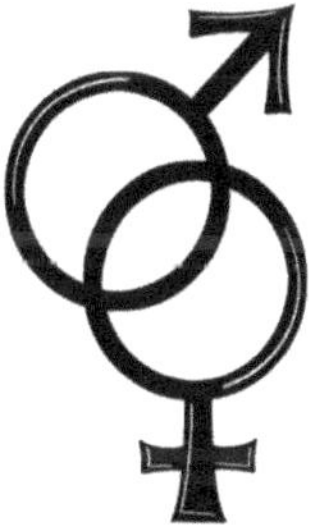

As the shaman started again around the circle, a slight chill ran across Warrick's neck, and he looked behind briefly, only to notice, for the first time, that the flickering candles also carried the same tiny symbols embossed upon them in black and gold. They're everywhere, he thought. Warrick was left wondering to what depths these symbols plunged this mystic's beliefs and ancient knowledge, and more importantly, what he had really gotten himself into.

'Man must awaken,' the shaman continued. 'He must cast aside the blanket of unconsciousness that smothers him into complete mystery and disinterest about his real existence in this life.'

As he spoke, the shaman became quite animated, waving and pointing, and swinging his arms about himself, creating shapes and patterns in the air to increase understanding, so that everyone there might grasp his words with visual concepts and further clarity.

'You, and only you,' bellowed the shaman, 'are the source of your own power, using inner love and compassion for others to expand your life, thus going where others will not, and where some simply cannot, and having the gratitude for what you've had, what you have, and what you will have. Therein, you open the door and the future is yours.' He opened his arms welcomingly before going on. 'There are natural laws of spiritual operation that hitherto have been untapped and long forgotten.

So, follow me and you shall find and release that invisible energy that lies dormant deep within.'

He closed his eyes with reverence, crossing his hands against his chest.

Warrick was uncertain whether to be impressed and overcome or simply bewildered and disillusioned. He felt the shaman spoke with a kind of poetic hypnotism. He appeared genuinely educational and yet, at the same time, conveyed a spiritual awakening. But despite trying to deny it, something deep within Warrick did feel aroused — it was sort of a treacle-sweet warmness that was spreading from the inside, something that he had not felt for what seemed an eternity.

The shaman had spoken with a force that Warrick was unaccustomed to. For some, an irresistible preamble it was not, but for others, it was like the man spoke from a great shrine, a pedestal that the others in the room could not see. Warrick had never heard a speech communicated with such significance and meaning.

What did he mean by "there are natural laws of spiritual operation," he thought? Was he talking about these divinities? Were there actually methods of teaching men to outmanoeuvre their existing mental reasonings? What was this blanket of unconsciousness that smothered man into complete mystery about his existence? Warrick's head was spinning; it was a head rush like no other.

Once again, the shaman looked around the room at each and every person; his smile was infectious. 'This brings us finally to that burning question that has sat with such trepidation upon your very lips this evening... is there or isn't there?' He smiled knowingly. 'Is there a special one amongst us tonight?' The other members began to murmur with excitement.

'I am pleased to announce that there is — and their presence will be made proudly known in due course.'

Once again, the shaman closed his eyes at the sudden clapping of his audience.

Warrick looked again towards Joyce and Ruby, and saw that they were distracted. They were both staring across the circle. Warrick followed their gaze and noticed Raymond, who only had eyes for the parquet wooden flooring. Absentmindedly, he appeared to be running his finger along the cracks of the floor tiles, seemingly unaware of the anticipation around him. He took off his glasses and wiped his brow. Something was clearly eating away at him.

For one crazy moment, Warrick got a ridiculous picture in his head of Raymond being the one being sacrificed that evening. It was a picture of him all tied up in a white gown, being wheeled in on a trolley, lying on his front with his head propped up, an apple stuffed in his mouth and surrounded with food — like a pig at a grand banquet.

Stop it, for God's sake, Warrick scorned himself, *or I'm going to scare myself to death.*

'So,' announced the shaman as if to conclude, 'we begin.'

He gave a loud and rapid double clap, as if to awaken everyone, and began striding about the great circle like a lion stalking its prey, pointing to everyone as he passed. His steps were wide and forceful, making his movements appear definite and intimidating.

Then, with the charisma of a stage magician, and in one fluid motion, he reached into his left sleeve and pulled out a long silver flute.

After a deep breath and a knowing smile, he began to play.

~ CHAPTER EIGHT ~

Lord of the Dance

It was a sweet, high-pitched tune that swiftly dominated all who heard it. Audibly mesmeric, the music practically had a life of its own. It seemed to swim and swirl about the room like silvery threads of light.

Warrick finally gave in, closing his eyes as the haunting theme tugged at his consciousness, caressing and beguiling him, like the tender touch of some elusive seductress. An unseen breeze added to the dreamlike illusion, and Warrick had visions of ghostly spectres freely flying about the cavernous space, weaving in and out amongst the swaying guests and shimmering through the flickering candles.

Aware of movement before him, he opened his heavy eyelids as the shaman began to dance to the melody, like one trying to entice children out of fear and into wonder. Then, with one hand holding the flute to his mouth, the other hand began to point out to the awe-struck audience that sat before him, tempting them into the middle of the circle to take part in the dance.

'And... release...' he said, between breaths.

Warrick stared on in astonishment, still listening intently to the magical sound. The little tune was as delicate as a soap bubble, yet so powerful that it seemed to echo not only around the room, but also, strangely, inside Warrick's head. It began stirring a sleeping energy deep within him.

The shaman continued to sweep about the room; his bare feet nimbly skipped across the wooden floor, with the air and grace of a ballerina.

Excited eyes followed his every move. He was like some enchanted pied piper.

After another minute of elaborate dance, the shaman came to an abrupt stop. He stood tall and erect in the silence, before finalising his performance by sweeping himself lower and lower to the floor.

Then he appeared to end his small ritual, curled over, face down.

There was another pause, and then he rose again, particularly slowly this time. When he had reached his full height, he clapped his hands together with a crisp snap and then spun around, this time to point firstly at a small, rotund man sitting on one of the giant floor cushions to the left of the throne.

On cue, the man began a melodic drumming upon a large West African dun dun drum perched upon his crossed legs. It produced a rich and thunderous sound, giving the impression that it was a much larger drum than it actually was. Boom — boom boom, pause, boom — boom boom, pause. The sound was repeated over and over, and seemed to reverberate against the walls and floor, making Warrick feel as though he were sitting in some giant cathedral.

Turning to the other side of the throne, the shaman pointed again—this time to someone seated cross-legged on a floor cushion.

Warrick studied the young individual, confused. He couldn't tell if they were male or female. At first glance, they seemed peculiarly asexual — neither masculine nor feminine — but perhaps they simply gave off both vibes, an entwining of energies. Their features leaned toward the pretty, even feminine, but something beneath, in bearing or attitude, felt undeniably boyish. Even when they smiled, he was unsure.

Still, Warrick found them... attractive, though in a way that unsettled him — a path which he had never run up against, nor had had to question, before. It wasn't an attraction he could easily define.

There was something masked here, a blur of signals — enticement laced with subtle danger. It felt less like desire and more like being pulled, drawn in without permission. It created an uneasiness that Warrick did not like. Despite the attraction, it did not feel pure or clean; it was as if the truth of the person was hidden behind a mixture of contradictory messages and subtexts. Warrick had never sensed such a conflict of sweet enticement and of beckoning danger.

Warrick hated that feeling — that sense of being seduced or manipulated without consent. The night had already pressed his limits, and this ambiguity added another layer he wasn't prepared for. Maybe this person was here to explore their identity or to help define their sexuality. Or maybe they were meant to challenge his...

He'd seen people before whose sex was hard to place — older couples merging into each other's likeness, or younger, prettier faces that defied quick assumptions. But this... this felt intentional, charged, as if their very presence was designed to destabilise the observer.

There was an energy to them, subtle but powerful. Not overtly sexual yet vibrating with magnetic pull. Warrick had to resist it, consciously release the hook that seemed to sink into his awareness. Whatever it was, it was a capricious and unauthorised seduction, or dare he say it, entrapment, of his attention.

Trying not to stare, he glanced away, then back. No stubble, no curves.

The eyes — too large, lashes too long. Was there makeup? Or just youth and softness yet to harden into masculine lines? Perhaps... No hint of a cleavage either, unless they were flat-chested. But with these current sexual trends, some did appear to use this as an excuse to exercise their curiosity into this void of ever-growing and manufactured sexual complexity.

A controversial line of thinking, he knew, especially these days; however, he was entitled to his point of view after all.

Whoever they were, their effect was undeniable. And Warrick, unwilling to wander into that confusion, or challenge his current heterosexual orientation, forced his attention back onto the shaman — just as the ambiguous figure lifted their tambourine and began to shake it softly, in rhythm with the drums.

Pleased with this added ensemble, the shaman worked his way back to the centre of the large circle.

Then Warrick heard it — the first voice. Then another and another, as people sporadically started to hum and chant from different places within the circle. Warrick was beginning to feel uneasy, especially as he noticed some of them starting to sway gently, half-meditating with their eyes closed and their arms outstretched.

Outside, as if adding to the chorus of building voices, Warrick heard the wind howling in the background. It had really built up now. Occasional creaks and groans from the surrounding wooden panelling also acknowledged the growing pressure outside.

'And release...' he started to hear repeatedly from different parts of the circle.

Warrick looked uncomfortably back at the shaman and noticed that he was now placing his hands before him as if in prayer, attempting to calm his mind.

His actions alone were spellbinding. All remaining eyes were on the shaman, and apart from a few, nobody moved.

Warrick watched as he swayed back and forth on the spot for a moment, pulling some invisible energy from deep within him to release it out into the candle-lit room. Upon throwing his arms out before him, a breeze simultaneously worked its way around the room, acknowledged by a flickering of the candelabra lights.

The shaman stood like some great warrior preparing his men for battle — the battle of their inner minds. He was going to cleanse their souls, and there was nothing but their own mental barriers to stop him.

Suddenly, again with great rapidity, he spun on the spot — his flute slicing elegantly through the tense atmosphere like a samurai sword. And before his watchful audience, he began to play once more, harmonising beautifully with the rhythmic drumming of the dun dun drum and the repetitive percussion of the tambourine.

The overpowering combination of the drumbeats, the high-pitched whistling, and the harmonic chanting of the followers was strangely hypnotic. The shaman's pace within the circle quickened, and he moved faster and faster, invoking the ever-growing feeling of euphoria amongst his followers.

Now back at the centre of the room, the shaman stood tall and resolute, a proud leader of men, and his commanding presence radiated out of him like a blinding light.

One by one, to Warrick's continued amazement, people started to get up and join in. They each had their own version of the dance, it seemed, all swaying, hopping, stretching and trying to release some inner demon from deep inside them.

'And release...' they each repeated, as they cast away their inner darkness.

All the while, the drumming and whistling were getting faster and faster.

People were getting up in twos and threes at a time now, and still the shaman played, stopping only to coax more and more spectators into the tumultuous clannish dance. He wielded the whistling flute around and around the dizzying, gyrating spectacle of the dancing men and women. It was a spiritual movement, like nothing Warrick had ever seen or heard of before. It was bewitching to behold.

Warrick let his spinning head fall back, and he stared unfocused upon the ceiling, only to notice the nightmarish reflections of the evening's event in the disturbing shadows cast up by the rows of flickering candles.

Warrick was beginning to feel lost and powerless. His negative and critical thoughts abated, and he was finally slipping into a sort of delirium as he became more and more entranced by the ever-growing wave upon wave of wonder in this spinning concoction of surreal visual and audio stimulation.

Over and over, they chanted: 'and release... and release...' It was becoming a choral cacophony of discordant sounds, all calling out at different times and different pitches. Warrick felt disoriented just listening and watching the orgy of limbs and mixed voices.

Making him jump, someone grabbed at Warrick's right arm and tried to pull him up into the dance — but he nervously refused. Then two others tugged and pulled at him, reminding him that he was the only one left to get up and join in.

The continual bombardment of grasping hands finally broke down his resolve, and he was eventually dragged to his feet with a resounding cheer. He stood there on the outside of what now appeared to be a tribal dance, struggling to throw himself into the mayhem. All the same, it was as if he were being drugged or becoming drunk, as the drums and the whistling seemed to get faster and faster still. It reminded him of being in the middle of a spinning fairground ride, with the added nightmare of some twisted house of mirrors — where people appeared in and out of focus, their faces large and small, laughing, singing, cackling, and jeering derisively and uncontrollably.

The pace and hysteria had reached such a zenith now that it was sickening, and Warrick doubted he could take any more without passing out onto the floor. Or worse, be trampled on and unnoticed in the stampede of madness. He just couldn't bring himself to join in. He felt dizzy, stupid and horribly embarrassed.

Then, with a resounding scream, like that of a native war cry, the shaman bellowed, 'ENOUGH!' And the music and chanting instantly silenced. 'You have done well; you may all return and prepare.'

Panting and sweating, the members lumbered back to their original seated positions. Warrick dragged himself behind them, dazed in the thick heat of candles and sweat-slicked bodies, struggling to find his original spot. As he hovered uncertainly, weaving between retreating shoulders and backs, he felt deeply out of place — and couldn't bring himself to meet anyone's eyes. Finally, he sat back down.

Then Warrick realised what the shaman had said: Prepare.

So... did he mean to say that was just the warm-up? But warm-up for what?

~ CHAPTER NINE ~

Soul Cleansing

After the hustle and bustle of everyone had abated and the final person had sat down, the shaman spoke from the throne where he now sat.

'As one of the guardians of truth, I have the pleasure of reminding you that tonight's journey towards inciting your spiritual renaissance here on Earth is wonderfully on track.' And the shaman clapped his hands in recognition towards everyone in the circle. Warrick waited until the rest of the room was also clapping before joining in. He wasn't entirely sure why he was clapping, but he felt it rude not to show willing.

'And so,' continued the shaman, getting rapidly to his feet, 'the cleansing begins...' He glided swiftly across the circle, stopping just before Warrick; then he turned and pointed. And with a booming voice, he projected: 'Stand... up.'

The sudden command and authoritative use of his voice seemed to shake Warrick, and for one stomach-churning moment, Warrick thought that he was talking to him. He almost felt compelled to stand from the shaman's unreserved intention alone. But thankfully, the woman to his right promptly stood up. She was a timid woman, neatly dressed in sensible beige and brown clothing. She gave the shaman tiny, brief, nervous smiles, between occasional facial twitches.

But despite this shy demeanour, Warrick found her rather sweet and could see her working behind the counter of some country post office.

'You have something to tell me, do you not?' the shaman asked. And then he mimicked the woman's body actions and motions. Warrick was wondering if he was trying to put her under some sort of trance, as she swayed ever so slightly on the spot before she spoke. 'Eh... ahem,' she nervously began, 'I guess there's no use hiding it from you, is there?' And the shaman shook his head politely.

'I'm sorry, I really am,' she went on, 'although I did put it back, didn't I?

'Yes, there is that,' he said and smiled. Warrick frowned with confusion. And the shaman continued, 'Yet despite this moment of mild complacency on your part, you managed to keep your integrity and are all the better for it,' and they both smiled at each other.

Warrick sat there bewildered, wondering what sort of coded conversation they were having.

'But other than that, I am glad to see that you have helped out rather handsomely in your community, and for this I commend you.' And again, they both smiled at each other. 'You may sit down,' he finished.

'Why, thank you,' she replied with a sweet, appreciative smile, and sat down.

The shaman stepped sideways to the woman next to her and repeated his impersonal greeting. 'Stand... up,' he ordered, and a very pretty woman with a shaved head stood up — her green, triangle-shaped earrings swinging from their long, thin chains.

For a brief moment before speaking, the shaman glanced about her, as if looking at some aura that Warrick struggled to see. Then he drew himself up to his full height.

'Children are all students of nature and of life, and as a parent, you carry that dependability to guide and instruct them. This does not mean dominating and overpowering them with your own self-righteous intentions. For when you override someone's decisions and intentions with your own, you will crush their own self-determined drive and decision-making efforts. In effect, you render them useless. They then no longer rely on their own judgement, but instead they rely on yours; thus, they are defenceless in a world of social interactions.'

The woman's body sagged on the spot. Despite being very attractive and socially vibrant on the outside, Warrick felt that beneath it all, she was really rather sad on the inside. And she knew very well to what the shaman was referring.

'You have acted unknowingly selfishly and have mistakenly cushioned your son, soaking him in a crudely surreal and flowery environment in an attempt to protect him from supposed harm — and thus, as you know, he has folded. Deny this at your peril.'

'I know I am a useless mother; I know I am. But he can't cope on his own — he needs me,' she answered, beginning to get upset.

'Yet the downward spiral still turns,' said the shaman. 'If you keep doing what you are doing, you will destroy your son completely, and may eventually emasculate him.' The shaman mimicked the downward-trending action of a spiral with his right hand.

The troubled woman pounded her palms at her temples. 'I just did what I thought was best — like any good mother would.' And she looked about the circle at the other women.

'I daresay, but you became lost in the world of the middle classes — a world of fear, hidden control, home comforts and supposed security, where you felt compelled to adapt to your environment, and are driven to be accepted by your friends and thy neighbours. Whereas what is contrariwise is the real reality.'

Warrick wished he would speak more normally, as, although he could understand the shaman's words, it took him an extra few moments to do so.

The woman sighed loudly. 'I don't know where I am any more,' she moaned.

'Oh, I'd say just behind your right eye by the look of it,' casually replied the shaman.

The woman instantly stopped and looked up at him. Then she appeared to be orienting herself inside her own head, as Warrick watched her eyes move about in the most irregular fashion. It was as if she were trying to look for an invisible fly that was moving about on her face.

'I wouldn't worry about it too much,' the shaman went on, 'it's where most people appear to be located. I'm not sure why, but we'll get you out in good time.'

And strangely, the woman started to calm down. 'A spirit residing in a body is as peculiar a sight to behold as a fully rigged ship in a bottle. Most odd,' he added, somewhat amused.

Warrick suddenly felt quite strange, as he also tried to locate himself inside his own head. It was bizarre; the thought had never even crossed his mind before.

'But let us look again,' the shaman asserted, 'what is the definition of a student?'

The woman turned the corners of her mouth down in a mysterious expression.

'A student,' he went on, 'is the willing participant in the receipt of knowledge.'

But the woman did not look amused or impressed. Yet, despite Warrick thinking that the definition was spot-on, he thought she looked rather smug and supercilious upon hearing this insightful news.

'This is not a digression, I might add, but an education — and I pray you embrace it and not reject it, for presently you seem neither able nor willing to recognise the truth when it is presented to you.

You are unaware of what it is you resist, even when presented with fresh, factual information. Therein, knowing best is not a trait worth clinging onto.' And he looked up at her through a furrowed brow, encouraging her to see her shortcomings.

For a while, she said nothing, and they just stared at each other vis-à-vis.

She looked away, thinking about what he had said.

'Willing?' she repeated.

'Willing,' the shaman said again with a smile. 'Not enforced... but willing.'

Quietly, the woman gently cried. Warrick sat forward, his chin resting on his hands.

'But I have warned him,' said the woman, 'what men are like — especially his father. I warned him how bad men can be, but he just won't listen; I'm only trying to protect him. He needs my protection. I don't want him to end up lonely like me,' she persisted through more tears.

'No,' said the shaman, 'he needs to be freed and to learn firsthand, not by your own experiences. He needs guidance and education, not control and domination. Your experience includes your own distorted hang-ups and issues with men. This is a polluted view of the world that will only tarnish and misguide him from what he would otherwise experience for himself. Your past veil of emotional scars is not necessarily a good platform upon which to educate him.'

The woman seemed to be spinning inwards into her own madness.

The shaman then spoke openly to the circle of listeners. 'Now, realise this; by her constant and relentless nullification of her son's opinions and beliefs, and her enforced summations of what she believes he is or stands for, she has crushed his confidence and self-esteem.'

The shaman swung his arm around the circle of watchers, pointing at each person. Nobody spoke.

'You now live on your own, do you not?' he continued.

The woman nodded regretfully.

'And yet you still want to feel wanted and useful, I see?' The woman's mouth opened in surprise. 'You cannot replace the love of a missing partner by controlling your son's life. You must see that death is both an end and a beginning. And so, you must now usher in a new beginning.' He opened his arms widely.

With a deep sigh, she agreed and wiped the tears from her face. 'Yes, I suppose. It's not the sex I miss, but the companionship. I need to allow that into my life again.'

The shaman looked back at her sympathetically. 'Life is simple. Mental gymnastics are not a prerequisite for a happy life. Thus, both your son and you need a quiet mind, free from the noise of other people's pre-programmed ideologies, desires and aspirations.'

Warrick sat there amazed as the shaman stripped down this woman's past considerations quicker than any counsellor could do after months of therapy.

'You're right, you're right; I know you are. I'm so stupid,' she said, attacking herself. 'And my mother would agree, if she were sitting here now.' She looked upon him with a genuine smile of thanks.

But to Warrick, there was suddenly a slight resurgence of the woman's spirit. Somehow, more of her, rather than just her somewhat insecure persona, appeared to be sitting there. She seemed to be emanating far more presence, whereas before, Warrick felt as if she were the sort of person that nobody really noticed was there at all, regardless of how pretty she was.

The shaman smiled back in return and told her that she may also sit down.

Despite the insightful provocations of the shaman's techniques, Warrick did feel his brain was becoming a tad under pressure, as this shaman seemed to be talking almost in riddles and in a way that made his head hurt. He appeared to speak with such precision of truth that the conversation appeared, at first glance, to feel quite heavy.

But in actuality, once one got to grips with the shaman's style of vocal delivery, it was instead the powerful blow of truthful facts that tended to smack one between the eyes, as opposed to his display of the dramatic.

And speaking of which, he hoped that he wouldn't be expected to discuss such personal matters in front of this room full of people, scrutinised for all to see. There were a few private things that lingered in the dark corners of his own mind, and he intended for them to stay there. In fact, he would bury them for good, given the opportunity.

Until then, Warrick could only wonder what on earth would happen to the chosen one.

~ CHAPTER TEN ~

Truth be Told

Fascinated, Warrick watched as the shaman moved from person to person. He seemed to know everything about everyone. They were all defenceless against him; he was able to penetrate their minds as easily as dipping a spoon into jelly. Old and young, sinner or saint, he addressed everyone equally.

The next man shifted uncomfortably in his seated position as the shaman approached. 'And you, stand... up,' he repeated in the familiar booming voice.

The tall, middle-aged man got up, sweeping his greying black fringe apprehensively out of his eyes.

'I'm not particularly impressed — as you can imagine,' said the shaman, before indicating to the woman sitting next in line beside him. 'In fact, I think on this occasion we ought to just cut to the chase — so to speak. Do you not think?'

'What do you mean?' replied the man, to which the shaman simply lifted an eyebrow. Again, he spun around to address the group. 'People, listen well and let this —,' and he pointed openly at the man before him, '— be a lesson for us all. Injustice and incidental misdemeanours are one thing, for they too will weigh the individual down, and one by one, they are the nails in their own coffin. But intentionally selfish acts of the flesh, of this nature, are nothing less than traitorous acts of adultery. A fool's game is no game.'

The woman next in line to the man threw her hands up in the air. 'You what?' she screeched.

'Silence!' sternly interjected the shaman, lifting his hand, and the woman resentfully bit at her lip.

'Now look…' pleaded the man to the shaman, and he raised both his hands as if to inhibit further probing and exposure.

'Oh, I don't think so,' said the shaman coolly. 'Now, the question is, do I tell your wife or will you?'

The same woman next to him took in an audible deep breath. 'I knew it, I knew — you cheating bastard!' she screamed, and she started punching at his legs and waist. 'I said all along, didn't I?! Didn't I? What is wrong with you… you stupid, stupid man?'

The man swung his attention between the woman and the shaman. 'Wait a minute — just wait a minute, will you? Let me explain,' he replied, trying to grab her beating arms. 'You said you didn't love me anymore.' He turned to the shaman. 'She did! She did!' he pleaded. 'She said she didn't love me anymore. Honest to God, I've tried everything!' The man looked quite desperate.

'But I do love you,' the woman interrupted, 'I do,' she wailed.

Then the man's voice started to break. 'But you said… you said that you'd fallen out of love with me… that we had drifted apart, and that you didn't like me like that anymore — that you… you just wanted to be friends.'

'But I didn't mean it, I didn't mean it!' she moaned.

'Enough!' commanded the shaman, and they both looked up at him. 'Do I tell your wife or will you?' he repeated.

'Look… just give me a minute, okay?' the man answered.

The shaman surveyed the man with much interest before turning to the upset woman and continuing.

'As you suspected, he has been having an affair with the woman at work.' The shaman then looked back at the panicking man before him and peered further into his surrounding space. 'Julia, I believe.' The man closed his eyes as the woman wailed.

'See, I knew it... I knew it — you are a bastard! Look what you've done — you've ruined everything!' And she stood up to attack him.

Several people gasped as the woman, now standing, appeared to be pregnant. The woman to the right of Warrick crossed herself as in Christian prayer, and he heard her mutter, 'What a mess,' as she squeezed an unseen necklace beneath her blouse.

The pregnant woman, poised aggressively, was rubbing her stomach. 'What am I going to do now?' the woman shouted, pointing to her stomach. 'And it's all your fault!'

'Enough!' boomed the shaman, and his voice seemed to hit them like a shockwave. They both stopped and looked back at him again.

Half upset and half annoyed, the woman shouted at the shaman, 'Look what he's done — he's ruined everything! See what men are like!' Addressing the circle of watchers, she pointed an accusing finger at her husband. Then she turned back to hit out at him once again, 'You men are all the same... You just can't be trusted, can you?' The man cowered away from her.

'You!' commanded the shaman, pointing at the man, '...sit down.' The confused and disoriented man sat down.

'Well, aren't you going to do anything?' questioned the angry woman at the shaman, bringing her hands to her waist.

'Enough,' replied the shaman. 'I hardly think you are in a position to throw up too much objection, in the current circumstance, to be quite honest.'

'What do you mean by that?' she snapped.

'Oh, I think you know.'

'Know what?' she said tartly.

The shaman said nothing, but began looking about her, seeming to be searching for something. It was as if he were searching for an invisible force field that surrounded the woman.

Warrick sat forward and squinted, hoping that this would help him to see whatever the shaman appeared to be looking at. But no, he could not see anything — no aura, no signs of enlightenment, nor any sort of tell-tale cosmic spiritual light. What was he looking at?

'Now look,' the woman started defensively, 'I won't have any of your mind games used on me.'

'Oh, it's too late for that, I am afraid,' replied the shaman, and he smiled confidently.

The woman wailed again, burning with rage at this outrageous suggestion. 'This is... is... intolerable!' she shouted eventually.

Drawing herself up, she squared up to him, her fists clenching and unclenching. She mouthed incoherently to herself as she prepared her inner dialogue. It was clear that the woman was psyching herself up to hit out at the shaman with some unmerciful accusation.

Then it came — both brutal and vicious. 'It's like... it's like... mental rape! Yes! That's what it is, it's mental rape.'

Pleased with her knife-slicing retort, she peered smugly about the circle of onlookers, although her chest was heaving with anxiety.

Continuing with twice the vigour, she raised an accusing finger. 'It shouldn't be allowed. If people only knew what goes on in here — brainwashing — that's what they'd say; they'd say it was brainwashing.' And she continued to wag her finger at him.

'These are harsh words,' calmly answered the shaman, 'especially from somebody who regularly turns up at these events, of your own accord.

And in fact, occasionally helps to set them up, I believe?' The woman showed agitation.

'However,' continued the shaman, 'currently, with the web of lies that you have cleverly weaved about yourself, I'd say your brain probably needed washing.'

Her eyes widened with indignation, and she looked to her husband for support, but he only had eyes for the shaman.

'Well,' the shaman continued calmly, 'let's break it down and have a look at this, shall we? The only reason that you are wrongly firing off at me is that I am preparing to declare what you are closely guarding.'

'Closely guarding? Closely guarding!' she shrieked. 'How... how dare you! I absolutely refuse to be spoken to like this. I will not be bullied or mentally abused by you like this — or by any man, come to that.'

'Silence!' boomed the shaman, unflinchingly. And the woman was quiet for a moment. '*"There is none so hated than he who speaks the truth..."* — once uttered a wise and ardent disciple of Socrates: Plato.'

Yet the remark was ignored with a dismissive wave.

He took one step closer to her. Yet with nervous defiance, she started up again.

'Well,' she sniffed, 'what have you got to say for yourself now?' Once again, she raised her hand, but this time jabbing repetitively at the air before her with an extended finger, as if to reinforce her following sentence. 'Cos' I've — done — nothing — wrong!' She grinned triumphantly. 'Go on... prove it,' she continued defiantly, crossing her arms.

But Warrick could see that beneath this façade, she was really quite apprehensive about something. And considering the people that had gone before her, he could not help but wonder what she, too, was sitting on to make her so vocal and aggressively defensive.

The shaman peered at her again, but more intensely this time. He seemed to scour the entire space directly about her. Concentrating hard, he seemed to be looking deeply into it for something Warrick could not see. It was almost as if each time he spotted something, she would relocate it in an attempt to hide it, and he would then have to find it all over again.

Once more, Warrick squinted, determined to see at least some speck of information, some clue as to what the shaman was searching for. Then, for a brief moment, Warrick thought he saw something — a flicker or ghosting of an image. Had he imagined it? Did he really just see a faint image, like a washed-out moving photograph? Or had he made it up, mentally dubbing it in, because he was so desperate to see some sort of hidden vision floating about the woman?

After a moment, the shaman seemed to find what he was looking for, and he readdressed her with a penetrating glare.

'Ahh,' he uttered softly, looking incredulous, 'done — nothing — wrong?' he repeated.

Straightening up, he lightly tapped his fingertips together. At the same time, Warrick felt the circle of watchers tighten and lean further inwards towards him.

A small but curious smile curled at the corner of the shaman's mouth, and he nodded imperceptibly, understanding now making itself known. 'What a delicious lie,' he breathed.

~ CHAPTER ELEVEN ~

Truth be Dammed

The woman stopped moving. She looked cornered. Her jibing, leering aggression had now ceased. As if defeated in battle, her body sagged. Her brief "tête-à-tête", her dance with the devil — as she may have deemed it — had not worked. Even her brazen attempt to outmanoeuvre this master of the mind, this magician of mental imagery, had failed. He was too much, too powerful, and too smart.

Distracting them all, a thudding, scraping sound caused Warrick to look up at the window. Outside, the wind seemed to be picking up again; it howled around the rattling windows and doors, the blustery gusts now whipping about the branches of one of the nearest trees. Its uppermost branches were now knocking and dragging themselves across the leaded panes of glass.

Warrick sat back, dumbfounded, and looked back at the agitated woman. How did this man know such things? What was this skill, this ability? And, just as importantly, could he learn such mastery of another's mind?

It was interesting that he did not appear to use this incredible ability for personal gain. He was, in his unique way, helping people — unburdening them from the chains of their own making. He had somehow worked out a way to mimic or read the mind of the person sitting before him. And actually, Warrick had to admire these brave people for being willing to let this guy carry out such an intrusive undertaking. It couldn't have been easy for them; they must have known what they were letting themselves in for.

Another thing Warrick noticed was that the shaman didn't discriminate. He seemed to care little for who sat before him or what their past held. Unlike the self-centred and critical people Warrick had grown up around, the shaman embodied openness — a refreshing change. Warrick was beginning to understand why people embraced such an extreme experience. The shaman offered something rare: a chance to reclaim integrity, and for those weighed down by life's chaos, even a glimmer of hope.

Warrick, by contrast, felt his upbringing had been tainted. The people he'd known — family, neighbours, small-minded acquaintances — had painted an unfair image of the world. They scoffed at his curiosity, mocked his embrace of multiculturalism, and labelled his desire to explore new paths a betrayal. They believed they knew what was best for him: sameness, stability, and staying put. To them, being different was a flaw — the mark of the deluded or unstable. Dreamers didn't matter; they just got in the way and stirred things up. Change, they warned, was dangerous. It brought confusion, upset the balance, and introduced ridiculous fads. Comfort zones existed for a reason.

Those attitudes had always irritated Warrick — and, if he were honest, made him quietly angry. Not because he thought he was special; he didn't. If anything, he was too hard on himself, though he had little reason to be. Still, deep down, he knew there had to be more than this grey, obedient life. There had to be something greater — a place where he could truly make a difference.

So now here he was, sitting cross-legged at the mercy of a powerful shamanic leader, patiently waiting for his turn to be publicly exposed. It seemed unavoidable now. The doors were locked, and the burly bouncers were not to be crossed. Well, he had wanted some change in his life, and here it was.

What a perfect example of a self-fulfilling prophecy... wherein he had created that very position in which he now sat. There was no one else to blame.

The shaman was slowly pacing back and forth. 'This lie is one that you can ill afford to use in my presence. And yet, you know this, but you challenged me all the same.' He shook his head. 'That said, you do have some interesting skills, which I must admit. But you do not use them wisely. Instead, you have redirected them to defend and to hide yourself — and your... your misgivings. And, all the more curiously, you do not use them to enhance and expand yourself — or those that you hold dear.'

The shaman turned away from the woman and pondered her dilemma. Occasionally, he would turn back, letting his eyes rove about her outer self. Finally, he spun back around to face her, a moment of realisation sparking in his eyes.

'My dear woman, I have it! You seem to have somehow inverted your energies, reversed and introverted your power. As powerful as you clearly are, you are using this divine energy to block, inhibit and hide from others your actions of a time long since passed. Reclaim the path of The Divinities, and start by telling me all.'

The nervous tension of the group heightened even further, as the force of the words seemed to hang in the air like a dense fog.

As if waking from a slumber, the woman gave a great burst of resurgence, as if she had been given an electric shock.

She looked outraged. Sheer panic and the threat of exposure flashed about her in waves of anxiety. Her widened eyes darted about her like a lone animal trapped in the wild.

And she, too, looked around herself at something that she clearly felt only she ought to see.

'I... I could sue!' she blurted.

The shaman shook his head. 'Do you know why there has been an increase in insurance companies and law firms over the years?' Perplexed, the woman shrugged.

'It is because greedy companies can feed off the growing victim mentality that surrounds us. "Look what you did to me! I have my rights! I will sue you for what you have done to offend me!" Such staggeringly low responsibility, do you not think? Alas, this present society has been educated to believe that they have the inalienable right not to be criticised — or, at the very least, not to be offended. A generation with no backbone will fold in on itself. So, tell me, are you now a victim?'

The woman, looking visibly confused, shook her head.

'Good,' said the shaman softly. 'Will you now acquiesce?'

The woman turned away, closing her eyes, and reluctantly shook her head.

The shaman sighed. 'Then so be it,' and he continued undeterred, with a repetition of his most recent question. 'Do I tell your husband or will you?'

The worried husband interjected, 'Tell me what? What? What haven't you told me?'

Ignoring her husband, the woman had already turned bright red and shook as if she was going to explode.

Warrick, like many others, fidgeted with trepidation at the prospect of more forbidden news about to be revealed.

Exasperated, she eventually shouted, 'It's exploitation, that's what it is! It's not right — all this... hocus-pocus. I've got a good mind to call the poli...'

'Silence!' bellowed the shaman, before she had time to finish. And the room fell silent — in earnest this time. 'You see, you cannot lie to me. You can hide nothing, as I see everything.'

The woman appeared to be locked into a tormented battle between screaming, accusatory obscenities and collapsing in an overwhelmed heap on the floor.

'Well?' he prompted.

But the woman just stood there, tight-lipped and still locked into some inner conflict, as her husband shook her with urgency.

The shaman sighed, before turning to her anxious husband, 'Alas, I am afraid that the child that your wife is carrying is actually fathered by your brother, Owen.'

The silence that preceded the outcry was practically tangible.

'Nooooo!' wailed the woman in despair, and she instantly burst into tears. She tugged at her hair and dug her fingernails into her face.

Warrick heard more gasps around him.

'You what?' shouted the husband, jumping to his feet once again. 'And you... you had the audacity to scream at me — calling me a... a bastard!'

For a moment, Warrick thought that the man was going to hit her.

'You sick slut — you disgust me. Why him, for God's sake? Why him? I... I don't believe it, I just don't believe it, my own brother.' And he paced in circles, with both hands holding his head. 'I trusted him; I confide everything to him — he's... he's supposed to be my best mate. I still don't believe it.' He stopped now and then in an attempt to make sense of the reeling confusion and disbelief.

'Why?' pleaded the wife at the emotionless shaman, 'but why?' she repeated.

But the husband answered instead.

'Why? What do you mean why? I should be asking you that, for Christ's sake. How long has this been going on? Clearly some months, by the looks of it,' he said, answering his own question.

Warrick thought he sounded more disillusioned than angry.

'I'm sorry, I'm so, so sorry,' she cried, holding her stomach.

And the two of them stared at the unborn child.

'It just happened,' the woman continued in a quiet voice. 'I don't love him. His comforting became — became...' but she trailed off.

Then suddenly, much to Warrick's complete surprise, they both hugged each other. And then the man, too, began crying. Warrick thought that if that had been his wife, he would have been out the door, drawing up divorce papers before the night was through.

Unmoving, the shaman silently watched them both for a moment as they cried and apologised profusely to each other. He seemed to be allowing them time to briefly absolve and resolve their current familial breakdown.

Then, as quickly as it had exploded into being, the sudden crisis seemed to rapidly abate.

Warrick, thinking that it must have something to do with the sudden release of truth, looked back at the shaman in amazement, but he just appeared content with the outcome.

'You may both sit down,' he finished with a brisk nod, and nonchalantly continued around the circle — his job merely halfway completed for the night.

Warrick was somewhat reluctant to move on with the shaman, as he felt he was owed more of an explanation of the last drama. He had too many unanswered questions, and he thought he was only catching the final juicy, dramatic and climactic scenes of a soap opera.

Regrettably, his brief ache for the gossip was short-lived, as the shaman had moved on. But had moved onto what... or rather, to whom?

81

~ CHAPTER TWELVE ~

Divinitas

Clapping his hands sharply, the shaman withdrew from the next person in line and instead turned his attention to the circle of people in general. At the same time, wooden shutters began closing over the windows to the walls and the rear French doors. People in the circle started turning their heads this way and that, shifting and looking concernedly at one another, all clearly as startled as Warrick. Once the final blackout was completed, the two people responsible returned to the darkness of another room.

Once again, Warrick felt himself squirm with uncertainty. As if that were not enough, the main lights began to dim until they were extinguished completely, leaving only the flickering floor candelabras as the sole source of light. Warrick felt his hands starting to sweat as he stationed himself upon the wooden floor.

The shaman smiled around the circle. 'Oxford, England, 1424. A time of significant change; a time of theological thinkers and bold postulators. Men of influence and vision came together to embrace that faraway outpost of the untenably unknown — that invisibly intangible, yet unescapable, world of the demiurge. Or, in layman's terms, our great and mysterious creator of all that is and all that is not: God.

'These men, in their foresight, opened the door to both esoteric and academic studies in a field that has plagued man down the ages. They had the decency, the courage, to allow others to now theorise and hypothesise, conjecture and speculate, about one of the great enduring mysteries — the great unknowns...

'In other parts of the known world, battles were being fought and kingdoms conquered. But not in Oxford, not for scholarly men or those seekers of truth. And nor, it seems, for the founders of the Divinity School. For here, their teachings of the divinities and theology are yet another example of how persistent the quest for spiritual answers has been.

'Let's not quarrel over biblical inferences, Babylonian scriptures, or Cuneiform tablets; the search has been an ongoing one. So, who are we really, and where are we going? Can the Seer's College answer these burning questions for mankind? Well, let us first start with a few basic tenets. Let us open our own door to other-worldly possibilities and see where it takes us.' Putting his hands together, as if in prayer, the shaman closed his eyes briefly.

Once again, Warrick sighed, feeling that he was attending an advanced class on spiritualism. Shouldn't he be taking notes or something? He was never going to remember all of this. In fact, he didn't even think he understood half of the words that the shaman had used.

His vocabulary appeared to be huge.

'Divinitas,' continued the shaman, 'better known to us in English as The Divinities, is the orchestrated interaction of the base elements essential to human survival. The roots of these Latin terms are there for you — for all of us. They are our beacon and our strength. Stray from them — from their light of truth — and you stray from the road of righteousness. Survival means living within the cosmic law of these fundamental truths.

One must strive toward The Divinities — toward all they represent.

'You are not born of mud or merely a cluster of cells, though your body may appear to be. You are so, so much more, and possess so much power, so much potential, that it can feel almost unobtainable to rekindle such a state of being once again... but it can be done.'

Smiling to himself, the shaman then pointed to the ceiling, and on cue, a bright light flickered above everyone's head. Warrick turned from the sudden brightness, as his eyes had become accustomed to the soft yellow ambience. The projected beam displayed an intricate interplay of white rings upon the parquet flooring. It was a giant image of The Divinities themselves.

At first glance, the entire image appeared as some squirming entity of illumination, as if each of the inner rings were alive with crawling insects. But in fact, each of the interconnected rings of light revolved around the other in a never-ending gyration, like that of a clockwork engine, the ambigrams' wordings travelling in their designated circles. And rotating around these, in the opposite direction, so turned the outer ring. It was rather hypnotic.

'All ye sinners,' began the shaman, 'so the priests and ecclesiastical representatives of God would have you believe. But why? Why cast such demeaning assertions to all that walk through their houses of holy protection? Are you all really to be dammed to some cauldron of boiling fury, some underworld of disrepute, where the guilty can never rise again, to be banished into perpetual darkness?'

The shaman circled the room as he spoke, addressing the wide-eyed onlookers as if he were casually pondering the fate of mankind over a light brunch.

'It appears to be a universal theme. But why such ideologies? Why such theories about mankind? None of us is perfect and none of us has not made a mistake. Ever done something that you regret? Hmm? Therefore, by default, does this make you a sinner — make us all sinners? Perhaps...'

The shaman paused, as if letting everyone in the circle take a moment to absorb this new line of thinking, this subtle cross to bear.

'And so, is it because this really is a universe full of miscreants, free to roam and free to cause chaos wherever they roam? Or is it that, once-upon-a-time, you were free thinkers and free beings, merrily going about your own business within this great universe, until one day you disagreed with those powerful enough to enslave you?' The shaman tapped his bottom lip as if to question such a notion. 'If so, if you were some galactic overlord with a gigantic inferiority complex, where would you put such people, such rebels and miscreants and any such oddities that flaunted their resistance to the status quo? Well, in a universe full of revolving planets, I should think you would banish them to the far end of some remote galaxy — would you not agree?' There was a general murmur of agreement.

'A planet that could sustain life and thus distract such troublemakers forever and a day. Perhaps where they could live out the rest of their days in a perpetual circle of lies, unknowingly trapped within a body each time, in a never-ending loop of mystery, and, with their memories wiped between lives, they would never know the difference. Around and around they would go, getting weaker and weaker, less and less aware. The perfect prison without bars.'

The shaman turned a full circle with his arms outstretched, as if indicting the world at large. 'But the final rub, the final and inevitable question is: have you ever wondered why you were on this planet?'

Warrick shook his head, as if clearing a confusion. What? What was that last remark? "Have you ever wondered why you were on this planet?" Such a deep concept made his head spin. He actually felt a little nauseous, as if he suddenly wanted to get off some perpetual fairground ride. This was now getting ridiculous. These highfalutin ideas were getting out of hand. How could he not be from this planet? He looked down at his hands, turning them over. He was born here, in London.

What was the point the shaman was making? But wait, his body had been born in London, but where had he — this soul, this spirit been born? Did it have something to do with this talk of the cosmos? Was he actually and factually lost in the complexities of the physical universe, when in fact, he ought to be striving to return to his native spiritual one? Or was he just missing the point entirely? Warrick seemed to have so many questions that it made him giddy.

So, in the main, what was this man, this shaman, actually saying? Was he, Warrick, on this planet because of something he had done or agreed to? Was he truthfully a prisoner, a captured troublemaker? Well, if anything, that made more sense than just being part of some organic protoplasm line, he mused. Or could it be that he was down here by mistake? Anyway, he thought that it was generally agreed that Earth was a one-off planet in a vast universe of billions of other planets. But even that thought now seemed ridiculous. How could they be alone in such an infinite amount of space?

Space... it was one of The Divinities, wasn't it? Not forgetting its connection to the other three, the inner: Mind, Body and Soul, too.

Warrick sat there trying to make sense of it all, trying to piece this gigantic jigsaw puzzle together.

He stared at the image rotating on the floor, pondering this new notion, as here was Space and within it was the composite of Mind, Body and Soul — in essence, himself, in human form. So, was that the point? Was he, too, trapped within a space... was this what this was all about? Or was he supposedly trapped within a body, within a space?

Warrick rubbed his face with both hands, overwhelmed by the torrent of new ideas and the creeping sense that everything he'd once believed might be a lie.

He needed some air — some space. He looked at the bouncers. Well, he wouldn't be getting that for a while. Taking in a few deep breaths, Warrick decided to calm himself. It was all just a point of view after all, just someone's opinion of how life was; that was all it was. There was nothing to worry about. Nothing was actually going to happen; it was like some intense belief system. He still had his own mind and could make his own decisions. He would simply take on board what was real to him and then... and then take up his own path — wherever it may lead.

As if reading Warrick's mind, the shaman gave a slight cough to indicate he was about to continue with his speech. 'I am not alone in pointing out this spiritual journey of enlightenment, as others, too, have paved the way out of this lie, this deception, this delusion, this so-called way of life on earth. Seek out other truthers, if you must, as well as other ologies, leaders, or foundations. But only you know which path you should take — and only you can ascend it. All I can offer you is the workable truths of these carefully constructed Divinities. The path that I have constructed will enlighten you and free you. You will be awash with hidden truths that you never even knew existed about yourself and the universe.

We can even enlighten you as to how some mystical belief systems are surprisingly riddled with mental booby traps, so that the person loses themselves within a circle of perpetual contradictions, nonsensical and non-sequitur evaluations, and with no real solutions. All these answers are there... for you. The Seers College of Divine Enlightenment is always open, and our foundation is your foundation. Embrace the raw power of The Divinities and they will set you free.' Warrick's mouth fell open.

There was a click, and the projector's light went out. Plunged back into the ambient glow, Warrick squeezed at his temples. It was becoming too much, too unreal. But after that display, what was real? Was this all a load of mumbo-jumbo, or were there actually small elements of truth? Or, in fact, was it all true? It would have been so easy to cast it all aside and just dismiss everything as nonsense. It was the sort of thing his current family and friends would do.

Warrick looked back around the ring of people. Were they all being brainwashed — or enlightened? Warrick found himself wanting to believe, to learn more about the mysteries of the universe, but how could he? It was just so far-fetched.

His cynical side was once again flagging up the warnings of being gullible and suggestible — but was he? Yet how could he expect to know about such mystical states of being in the grand scheme of things, anyway? Then again, great scholars and wise men had been hinting at something otherworldly for centuries. The Egyptian tablets, the Indian Vedic scripts, the mysterious Dead Sea Scrolls, and other grand religious manuscripts were perpetually scrutinised for their profound knowledge and secret teachings. So, was this it? Had this shaman finally accumulated all of their great wisdom and figured it out?

And was this, then, the naughty planet after all — for all the naughty souls, the cast-offs, the prison of the long dead, an outpost for the rebels and miscreants of the universe, to be kept away under perpetual lock and key? All ye sinners...

Mind you, there were enough of these nutters scattered about the planet to warrant such a claim — some of the political elite, for a start. And yet, the only way to become free of this so-called prison planet was to do so with the aid of these Divinities, or use another of these spiritual paths, created by others, the shaman had mentioned existed. In essence, with the knowledge of The Divinities, he, Warrick, could possibly break out. In effect, although more speculative, if he could not break out with a body, perhaps he had to do so spiritually, without one.

Warrick thought about some of the past sects that had followed cult leaders into an early death. Group adulation, group massacres and self-sacrifice. Was this what was going to happen here? Is this what they had been building up to? Were they all to commit group suicide? By poison, perhaps? Was he never to see his twentieth birthday? Or were they to sacrifice one of the followers instead and make him divine as an example?

Warrick looked across the large room to Raymond. As before, he was blankly staring ahead at the parquet flooring, his fingernails still tracing the cracks between the wooden slats. Warrick felt for him.

Closing his eyes, the shaman lowered his head and fell quiet. After a moment, he stretched out a hand, flicked open his fingers and proceeded to move around the very centre of the room, as if detecting or perceiving an invisible energy. He appeared to be reading unseen emanations from people as he moved. Now and then, he would pause in front of a person and take a moment to consider them.

People shuffled in their seated positions, some becoming worried, while others became excited. One by one, as the shaman passed each and every person, they relaxed further into their seated positions. Some of the more sceptical and resentful of the group also slumped, to some degree, appearing more docile.

And strangely, Warrick would occasionally see more vague and highly transparent images, social interplays of people connecting with their past. Each time the shaman stood before someone, an image or two from their memory would start up above them, as if being replayed. The shaman would watch the "mini-movie" with great interest. Sometimes he would raise his hands as if to slow down or rewind the memory. Now and then, an image would run as if under the influence of a thundercloud, darkened and somewhat electrically charged. If there was something in the moment that displeased the shaman, he would somehow reach out and highlight that segment. Upon being perceived and acknowledged, the darkened image would abate, and sometimes even vaporise into smoke and disappear entirely.

Warrick stared on in utter astonishment, wondering if anyone else could see what he was looking at.

Approaching Raymond, the shaman paused, his fingers tapping lightly at the air, as if he were playing an invisible piano. As he did so, both he and the seated man twitched and fidgeted, as if both were affected by one another. After a moment, the shaman moved on, leaving Raymond to hold his head as if something were going on deep inside. Another strange breeze drifted around the room, and both the shaman's linen outfit and long dark hair rippled before him. Unaffected, he continued around the circle like a mystic healer, remotely reaching out to invade their personalised universes and to delve within their complex minds.

Once more, the external wind created the electric atmosphere that kept the room in its heightened state. And a few times, the window latches above Warrick threatened to throw themselves dramatically open. Warrick could not help but wonder what could have happened to the marquee in the garden. He could imagine that, with such aggressive gusts, the illuminated marquee would now be soaring above London on its way to the Emerald City, like the spinning house from the Wizard of Oz.

As the shaman blindly swept past Warrick, he stopped and retraced his outstretched hand. The very tips of his fingers appeared to stretch out even further this time, as if he were picking up some sort of radio signal. Keeping his eyes closed, he turned to face Warrick before lifting his second hand. They both traced around in the air before him, as if tentatively sensing an unseen mystical energy. The shaman's face was a mask of secrecy, with only the slightest indications that he was intrigued with whatever it was he was detecting.

Warrick swallowed as panic began to build. He could feel something different in the air, like a tiny breeze hovering over his skin. A certain something was definitely moving about him; it was as if he was being caressed by unseen hands. It was not a sexual or even a physical experience. It was something much higher, more finely tuned frequency, and — dare he think it — an almost ethereal and spiritual experience. What on earth was this shaman doing?

The bubble that had slowly enveloped them both had created a temporary cocoon in which they appeared to be uniquely connected. Warrick felt himself slipping into a very relaxed state of mind, where invisible clusters of mental matter seemed to be drifting away from him. It was the strangest feeling. He could see nothing moving, but his space was becoming lighter and, rather oddly, cleaner. Was this how the shaman cleansed another person — another soul?

After the final invisible barrier had lifted away, which Warrick was not even aware existed around him, the shaman dropped both his arms, and the connection gently withdrew.

With his eyes still closed, the shaman seemed to take a moment to gather himself. Everyone in the circle was either staring at Warrick or at this mysterious shaman.

Warrick, however, was finding that he was now experiencing a new level of awareness. All about him, the people and objects appeared more sharply in focus. For the first time, he seemed acutely aware of his own body, of his heart beating, the gentle pulse of blood flowing around his veins. Clarity of hearing, too, was heightened. If he chose to, he could tune in to the breathing of the woman to his right, the shuffling of the man seated two positions to his left, or the gentle drumming of someone's fingers against the wooden flooring at the other end of the room. And, now that he attempted it, he could even focus his attention upon the minds of others. It was subtle and unobtrusive, but still, if he focused, he too could begin to see the very faintest of images that surrounded the person on whom he placed his attention. What was going on? What was happening to him?

With a deep breath, the shaman started up once more and continued around the circle. Once or twice, he paused again, but no one received the same level of attention that Warrick had experienced.

As Warrick looked about, there were still people staring over at him with immense curiosity. Some, with their heads cocked to one side, seemed to be considering him, with an undisclosed and uncommunicated pondering about who he really was.

Returning to the section of the circle where he had begun his perceptive wanderings, the shaman stopped and opened his eyes.

He gazed about the group with an expression of excited awe. He seemed particularly pleased with himself.

The shaman tapped at an imaginary watch upon his bare wrist. 'Time, which is so misunderstood, appears to be running away with itself. Let us, for now, at least, move on with the proceedings.'

At the other end of the room, Warrick watched one of the bouncers crack his knuckles together.

~ CHAPTER THIRTEEN ~

Defiance & Regret

Almost opposite Warick in the circle sat a young, tattooed man in his mid-twenties, whom he had not noticed before. The man stood up resentfully upon the expected command and folded his arms defensively.

'So,' enquired the shaman, 'you still defend your actions, do you?'

'I do,' replied an Irish accent, who clearly knew what the shaman was referring to.

'What a shame, what a shame.' The Shaman placed his palms together in front of his mouth, his fingers lightly tapping at his bottom lip. He continued in his deep and confident voice. 'Angry people sit on lies, don't you know?'

Resentment welled up in the Irishman's face, turning it scarlet.

'And rather remarkably, lies are also used by people wishing to control or deceive others. An interesting fact, is it not?'

But this time, it was not the Irishman who moved, but Raymond. Something about what was just said caused him to cough and jerk his body upright involuntarily, and everyone turned to look at him, including the shaman. Embarrassed, Raymond looked back at the floor. And now it seemed that he was attempting to hide his efforts to control his breathing, which, to Warrick, were becoming more and more erratic.

Irritated by the interruption, the naturally pale-faced and redheaded Irishman looked back at the shaman. 'I fight for what I believe in; I thought you of all people would understand that,' he spat angrily.

Warrick was itching to see what response was on the Shaman's face, but had to make do with reading between the lines, as the Shaman swung his arms behind him, one holding the other, with his back towards Warrick.

'I don't believe you are proud of your past street fighting back home,' said the familiar soft, deep voice of the shaman. 'Despite how well you feel, you disguised yourself.'

And yet again, Warrick witnessed another mouth open in incomprehensible surprise, and he had visions of some macabre and demented masquerade face mask hiding the Irishman's vengeful anger, as he screamed insanities at a fire-bombed wall of police shields.

Following a moment of confusion, the man stumbled over his words, unaware that he was scratching at the figure of a naked woman tattooed in red upon his right forearm.

'Yeah, but... look, it's simple, the Catholics and Protestants are... are known for their disagreements, aren't they? You can't blame the people. It's the way life is, and will always be — you just have to accept things. And anyway, religions are known as the cause of nearly all upsets and wars and all that! So, what have the people got to do with it?'

The Irishman lifted his arms with an air of injustice before going on, stabbing at the air with a protruding finger. 'It's freedom of speech — that's what it is. It's no different than people who fight and picket in the streets for more money or lower taxes from the government!'

As he spoke, the flickering candlelight beside him grew restless, causing animated shadows to dance upon the panelled walls. His emphatic gestures etched smoke patterns into the air.

He finished with a poor attempt at a smug grin.

Warrick shook his head ever so slightly, unimpressed by yet another defensive person.

The room remained dim, as the group's anticipation grew, its stillness broken only by the low rustle of breath and cloth.

The atmosphere wasn't softening — if anything, it was deepening.

'What utter nonsense and useless misdirection,' replied the shaman slowly. 'You, like all men in your position, are using violence as an excuse to put the other man down. It is a way of enforcing your self-proclaimed righteousness, so to speak. Forcing others into submission who do not and will not adhere to your beliefs is itself not freedom of speech, but an act of war—based dictatorship at its lowest level. Nobody likes being made to appear wrong, and this is one way, albeit violently, to make it so.'

There was a pause, where the Irishman glared at the shaman, as if baiting him into a new battle. The shaman, however, looked on in pity at the man.

The shaman raised a finger to indicate a further point. 'And, it is a fear of the unknown — like an unknown virus. If you and your enemies were truly religious in your chosen beliefs, then you would be following, even to some small degree, a moral guide of sorts. Every respectable religious group has one, you know, unless ill or corrupted judgment has overthrown their true ecclesiastical beliefs, thereby breaking down the spiritual bonds with their parishioners.'

The Irishman retorted with his fists clenched: 'What do they know, anyhow? But to be honest, I don't trust organised religions,' he said, putting quotation marks in the air with his fingers. 'They can't be trusted. So, in fact, I ought to be an atheist!'

A wave of unease circled the room, and the Irishman's last words seemed to hang, suspended like dust motes in sunlight.

Yet the shadows danced on, silently distorted around the room, quietly echoing the angry confrontations — some perhaps more spiritual than political. Warrick felt the room tighten, as though the walls themselves disapproved of his claims.

'Interesting comment,' answered the shaman. 'Glib, but I did not expect anything less. But one cannot place all religions under the same banner of distrust. What are their codes of conduct or doctrines? Do they deliver what they promise? By their actions you shall know them — and not through the eyes of a handful of vengeful, disgruntled, and bitter ex-parishioners. And tell me, what do you think a religion would be if it were not for organisation?' The Irishman frowned.

The shaman continued, 'It would be chaos, would it not? Something for which, curiously, you seem intent on exacerbating? However, observe that from out of that chaos, we get order — thus.'

The shaman brought his palms together and then raised them, levelling them out sideways through the air.

The Irishman gritted his teeth, seeming to lose ground. 'Don't you assume anything; I help out in my own way. I don't need a religion to tell me what I can and can't do — they're all as bad as each other!'

Before he could continue, the shaman waved his hand through the air and silenced him.

'Alas, I disagree, as firstly, a sweeping critical assumption is pure ignorance and blind arrogance. That is the voice of the people, not of the person. For if you look closely, you will find that this is not the case for all. And secondly, fighting, looting, and violently attacking all who oppose your aggressive scaremongering is not an effort to either help or educate your fellow man, and nor will it gain his trust. Can you see that?'

The man defiantly held his glare again, before dropping his head for the first time.

Once again, the shaman peered in and around at the man's invisible aura. 'Have you heard soccer fans confess that football is their religion?'

The man shrugged in mild agreement.

'People use the term rather loosely, do they not? How many people do you know who read a daily newspaper — religiously? Their belief is their daily fix of so-called world news.'

He paced slowly in front of the Irishman, arms loose behind his back. Someone in the circle coughed, awkwardly.

'They believe, sometimes without question, that some editor, no matter how biased or bitter he was on the day that he wrote his little article, represents the true voice of the nation. That this printed information must be true, or they wouldn't print it. Such dangerous power over the people, and in the hands of so few.'

The shaman's gaze lingered momentarily upon the man, who shifted under the weight of it.

'Especially as just a tiny elitist group actually controls the world news. Or do you think that one man, one newspaper, or one elite group, really ought to command the will and collective mind of the people? I think not.'

Warrick was aware of himself silently agreeing to this.

'Social media, regardless of the format or platform, is not a social pillar on which to base your life. You see what they want you to see. The real world is in colour and not in black and white print.'

He held up a hand — not scolding, but instructive.

'But, the kicker is, it is you who decides your future and your goals, you who carry your religious beliefs, you who follow your own ethical guidelines and your political stance — not some preprogrammed body of editors or tyrannical overlords.'

There was a silence now. Not one of comfort, but of absorption.

'Cut and paste — you do it, I do it, and newspapers and TV stations around the world do it — but with impunity. Responsibility is sharper than any axe. Misuse it, or deny it, and your own blood will run dry.'

The man became confused. He seemed to be gathering his thoughts, now challenging his past preconceptions of the world around him. He shook his head at something he was thinking about and even gave an involuntary chuckle, as if realising the truth of some inner lie. He looked back at the shaman, almost as if in question.

A ripple of calm seemed to be emanating from the shaman as he lowered his voice. 'I do, however, admire your guts and your determination, although your past behaviour has been... interesting. Religious intolerance it is not — but a form of communistic barbarism it is.'

A silence rang out, wherein Warrick was only aware of his own breathing. The Irishman said nothing, but let his unfocused eyes rove about the circle.

The shaman peered around at the invisible space about the man, pondering his following sentence. 'Deep inside, you are a man of honour and self-respect, and you must not lose hold of that — for if you do, you will fall.'

The Irishman looked back up at the shaman in disbelieving reverence, as the light of truth fell upon him.

The shaman smiled kindly. 'It is the irony of being your own executioner, I am afraid. A prisoner of your own mental making — and more often than not, you will be incarcerated by yourself and by your own acts of cruelty and insanity. By your hand be it.'

The Irishman was beginning to show his remorse. He was breathing heavily now, occasionally blowing out deep breaths, trying to hold himself back from tears.

'You must reflect on your actions — you are simply living a lie, and hiding your nervous tension behind the barbaric actions of such a group. It is nothing short of reckless irresponsibility. It is the same group behaviour as that of mindless football hooliganism. In truth, I do not believe you are truly of the mob mentality — are you?' The man shook his head.

'You got lost in the moment of daring rebelliousness and the supposed power of the masses. A group mind is not necessarily a sane mind.'

Now nodding his head, the man's resolve began to crack, and he gently started to cry. His body shook quietly. Nobody in the room moved a muscle.

It was unbelievable; here again was another person releasing built-up emotional shame and regret. Warrick stared at the shaman in amazement. Just how was he able to do this? What was such an ability? For he was breaking down the very fabric of their misspent lives and exposing the very falsehoods that they were building their lives around. He tore down lie after lie, stripping them from the dream world that they had grown so accustomed to believing was now real. He did not want them to live a lie anymore; he wanted them to be free from it all, the restraints taken off. Their lies lay scattered before them and torn to pieces — exposed for the untruths that they were.

Emotionally unaffected by the final outcome, the shaman commanded him to sit down. The crying Irishman now obeyed without question. Sitting back down, he took the tissues offered to him by the person who had gone before him.

It was beyond words, thought Warrick, that just a few minutes ago this brute looked ready to lash out at the shaman and the world about him. Yet here he was, the once resilient and — by some — admired hard man, reduced to tears, re-examining his shattered moral compass.

The shaman slowly turned to address the group. 'These lives you have been living, these games you have been playing, are an insult to your vast power. They are too small and too insignificant. Imagine here, if you will...' he indicated to the floor beneath his bare feet, '... an imaginary town of people, of livestock, of shops and of poppy fields.' He opened his arms before him, sweeping them around the floor.

The earlier light from before projected another image upon the floor. A small, animated 3D town began to take shape. Everyone sat up to a kneeling position.

'See the people going about their daily lives, the dog drinking from the pond, where the fountain glistens life into the pool of water. See there, the priest walking amongst the churchyard where bodies of those who have passed have been laid to rest. Two children run through the poppy field, reaching out to the flowers as they pass. An old man sits outside the local pub to enjoy a pint of beer and to read the local newspaper. And see here, some tradesmen are unloading their van, just as a woman dressed in a power suit struts past with her morning coffee — haha — frowning upon their scruffy attire. There are even two mothers rocking their prams in the park, as two more children travel upon the roundabout ride.

And here comes Mrs Jones from the butcher's shop, only to ride away on her bicycle.'

The shaman circled the image on the floor, transfixed by what he was seeing.

'Shakespeare once implied that all the world was a stage, and that all the men and women were merely players.

How very true the statement was. And here it all is, played out before our very eyes.' The shaman swept his hand over the illuminated scene. 'And this stage is your entire life — your game — and you are the player of this game. And, inevitably, thus we are nothing short of gods, looking down upon the chessboard of life itself. We manoeuvre our bodies, our cars, our children, all to play a game upon this stage.'

He gestured to various onlookers.

'Ask yourself, what game are you currently playing? What have you decided for yourself that your life will entail?'

Again, he pointed to various people before sweeping his hand across the moving image.

'And here it is, all laid out before you — the game of life, of which you — are — all — in — control!'

Again, Warrick took a moment for himself. He stared at the glowing town, mesmerised by the moving figures below. Was he ever really in control of his life? Even in those moments when he thought he was — choosing friends, making plans, falling in love — was it truly him calling the shots? Or had he just been nudged along by invisible hands, like one more piece on the board?

His career path, for a start — it had always felt like a somewhat resentful affair, as though he were being coerced into toeing the line. He remembered his school career meeting: how his teacher had calmly talked him out of becoming an actor, or a writer, or even a computer programmer.

"Programming is a fad," she'd said. "Artificial intelligence will eventually run everything". "Writing is not a proper job, and you can't make a decent living, and acting — well, that's for other people — not for the likes of you. Ignore your drama teacher; he would suggest you're good, wouldn't he..."

At the time, he'd believed her. Trusted her. Let her words steer him.

And yet, at the end of the day, he was the one who'd nodded along. The one who'd naïvely accepted without too much resistance. The buck stopped with him. He was starting to understand.

If he kept blaming others for the direction his life had taken, he was only giving away more control. To accept otherwise — to believe that his fate lay in the hands of others — was to hand them the reins all over again. He must grab back control of his life, not to blame others or make any more excuses.

Wow, he mused, *listen to me — getting all philosophical, now...*

'Pause!' commanded the shaman, and the image stopped moving. 'Now, look before you. See how small this game is that Mrs Jones is playing?'

Warrick squinted at the woman on the bicycle.

'A god in her own right, in her own world, upon her own stage, who has lost sight of the game itself and has become a chess piece — a mere pawn within her own game. The game has taken over, and she now thinks that she is that little body peddling down the road. No, no, no! You must stop this madness!' The shaman addressed the image of the little woman. 'Mrs Jones, my dear woman, what on earth do you think you are doing in there? You must awake from your slumber and rejoin those of us who have retreated out of the chess pit to play the game from outside. Step back and view the game from afar — as it ought to be played.'

Warrick blinked, as if waking from his own slumber. His head was spinning again. He was beginning to feel light-headed and slightly detached from the physical world around him.

He tightened his hands and squeezed parts of his body to remind himself that he was still there, still earthbound. He felt like a hand sliding back out from a tightly fitted glove. He was definitely still there, governing his body, but he now felt as if he could do so with less effort, more as if he were directing a marionette with invisible strings.

The shaman continued to talk to the little woman. 'Don't worry, my dear, we'll get you out of that body — that foolish head — one way or another.'

The room was silent. Warrick caught the eye of the timid woman next to him, and they shared an uncomfortable smile.

'Play!' Commanded the shaman, and once again, movement began.

As Warrick looked about him, everyone's eyes were on the village of people, all going about their busy lives. They were like small, animated plasticine models, carelessly walking about — blissfully unaware of the truth. The animation was clearly on a loop, as they went around and around, repeating the same action and the same journey in their preprogrammed little lives. Over and over, the loop played, and around and around they all went.

Warrick sat back, finally getting the message that the shaman was trying to communicate. Warrick curiously eyed the people in the room. How many of them had also understood, had gotten the message? For these little people in the animation represented all of them.

It also represented everyone Warrick knew; in fact, it represented everyone he didn't know as well. It was the same the world over. How many people were stuck in a loop? They were lost in their own game, going around and around in life, wondering where they were going, wondering who was really in control, and who was pressing pause, play or stop?

As Warrick looked over at the shaman, he was taken aback, as the shaman was staring directly at him. The shaman smiled with a gentle nod. He seemed to know that Warrick now understood.

With a crisp clap of his hands, the illumination went out, plunging them back into the yellow candlelight, and the shaman returned to the centre of the room.

There were murmurings around the circle as people began whispering to one another. Some spoke in excited amazement, and others, still reeling from their realisations, just stared at their hands and felt out at the floor and their neighbours, checking how real their environment still appeared to be.

The shaman, pleased with the effect he had had, held a finger up to his lips. Without having to say a word, the room fell silent.

'The moment will soon be upon us all, for the chosen one lies close.'

Gasps of heightened excitement and people nudging one another continued.

Warrick watched Joyce tugging at Ruby's blouse, as the shaman continued to make his way towards the man that Warrick had noticed had barely joined in the evening's event. A man whose eyes had never really left the cold, wooden parquet flooring.

~ CHAPTER FOURTEEN ~

Abhorrence

Of all the people that sat around the circle, some would offer up their recent transgressions rather matter-of-factly. However, still there were some that sat there resolute in their reluctance to divulge their recent misdemeanours. But despite all this, the one common theme that rang out at the end of each brief conversation was one of relief and calmness. A sort of magic was happening.

Yet, as far as Warrick was concerned, he, too, was not immune to this social exposé, as he would also be scrutinised, his life laid bare, his inner secrets exposed for all to hear. It made him feel rather sick, and the urge to pick up his shoes and bolt surged within him. No wonder there were bouncers on the exit doors. As with the others in the room, a particular transgression floated to the surface. His teenage hormones had gotten the better of him when he was back at school, and his more boisterous and laddish side was rather proud of his accomplishment, but ethically, he still knew he shouldn't have done it. If the authorities ever found out, he dreaded to think what could happen. He'd have to hide the memory, somewhere deep down, or behind something less conspicuous. So, for the time being, all he had to do was clear his mind. Perhaps he could even put up a black screen to block anything from being seen…? It couldn't be that hard, could it? Maybe he could try to match the shaman's powers head-on, mind to mind.

In the meantime, however, as the shaman worked his way around the anxious crowd, only one still seemed to be in an actual state of fretful apprehension. Never had Warrick seen a man appear so perpetually in a state of abject nausea.

Fear and confusion emanated from Raymond as he sat floating in and out of a trance-like state. Again, he removed his glasses and blinked his eyes as if stretching them. He looked up to the ceiling and gave a deep sigh.

Warrick questioned that if normal people were being subjected to all these various tumultuous evaluations, what on earth would happen to *the chosen one?*

And so, being next in line and trying to delay the inevitable with his head bowed lowest of all, the next member was finally commanded to stand up.

Raymond seemed to physically shudder as he delayed in preparing himself to stand. Warrick could feel his fear; he understood completely, as he too felt the stomach-churning unease that grew nearer as he was addressed. The mere thought of anything even remotely embarrassing or humiliating only accelerated Warrick's compulsion to run from the suffocating atmosphere. But Raymond's delay only caused another repetition of the booming command. Regretfully, he slowly stood up, with his head still bowed.

The shaman tutted loudly, and, shaking his head, he began talking with slow and definite precision. 'Raymond, Raymond, Raymond, this will not do.' And Raymond rubbed his sweating hands against his neatly pressed trousers. 'I will not tolerate this anymore. I have told you over and over again, yet you seem reluctant to control yourself. Let me make myself very, very clear. You will not violate your sister's children anymore.'

There was an instant gasp of disgust and revulsion that rumbled through the room, and the anxiety escalated to another level.

Raymond's head hung even further with shame as he began to shake.

'Your ineptitude is abhorrent, and your actions are sickening. You absconded from your natural duties as an uncle, and my wrath for you knows no bounds.' The shaman shook his head. 'And you, a doctor... this is also an abandonment of your Hippocratic Oath! Was it not from Hippocrates — that Greek father of medicine — that we derive the principle "do no harm" as one of the basic fundamentals?'

Raymond looked up briefly, his expression a mix of hurt and anguish, but said nothing for some time as he tried desperately to piece together something both tangible and credible.

In the waiting silence, the shaman put his hands behind his back and patiently waited, his eyes boring into the man silently falling apart before him.

Shocked and perplexed, Warrick sat more upright in his seated position. What an accusation! To Warrick, the man appeared physically wounded from this, as if the words had stabbed at his very innards. *How on earth could anyone ever redeem his social standing after such a brutal personal attack? It was a horrifying exposé. But why did this timid man neither react nor say anything? Was this sickening outburst true? What if this spiritual magic man had made a mistake? How could this man let the shaman cast such wild aspersions and do nothing to defend himself or, at the very least, try to keep some degree of dignity? Shaman or not, could he not be held accountable for defamation of character?*

But the Shaman just stood perfectly still, waiting in the rigid silence.

Then, finally, Raymond began to stutter, as he blurted out the truth in the form of pathetic and feeble excuses.

But what first started as a confessed plea for help ended up with him hyperventilating into a complete mess and praying for sanity and peace of mind.

'It's not that I do it on purpose,' he began, 'I just...I just ...I can't turn it off! It won't leave me alone! One minute I am fine, and the next thing, I am suddenly doing something completely psychotic. It's like... it's like I see something or hear something, and then I don't remember anymore. Something takes over me — I swear... and I can't stop it. I hate it, I hate it! And I hate myself for it, but I don't know what to do! I'm sick — I am very sick, I know...' And tears ran down his face in earnest.

Warrick felt himself squirm from the confession. How could this man admit to such a revolting compulsion? To actually speak such an aberration out loud? He'd be flayed alive if the people on the street heard of such a crime. What mental madness was this? It was a new level of sexual degradation for the shaman to resolve somehow. But how did this shaman think he could help him? And why would he want to?

The man's doleful eyes peered out at the Shaman. 'You have to help me — you just have to. Please help me, and make it stop! Please make it stop!'

He was really crying now, and his body shook quite violently as he tried to explain himself further.

'It's like I go on automatic pilot; I can't seem to control it. Look, I know how this sounds, but it's true — I swear it's true!' And he pounded his right fist into his open left hand. 'I am a good man underneath — I am, I really am — but I only really come to my senses after the damn compulsion has run its course.' He paused briefly to grasp his heaving chest.

'Look, I know some of the more deluded people in my position — well, in more powerful positions — are trying to normalise and de-stigmatise this... this psychological condition, by rebranding a... a paed...' he stuttered to get the word out, 'as... as being a "minor attracted person" instead, but I am not like them. I'm really not! And... and I am *definitely not* for this movement to protect this disturbed state of mind. Oh god...' he sniffed heavily, 'even some of the LGBTQ community do not want to be associated with it — far from it. But I...I...'

He was blubbering so hard that mucus and tears were running down his face in equal measure. 'You have to believe me...please believe me! I'll do anything, anything, just make it stop, *please make it stop*!' He wrung his hands together in sickening desperation.

When he had finally finished pleading, Warrick noticed just how dreadful and pitiful the skinny man now looked.

The shaman swung his arms from behind his back to place his hands neatly together beneath his chin. Beseeching and barely able to breathe, Raymond dropped to his knees, half-crying, and prayed before the shaman in a crazed state. Again, nobody moved, not knowing what to say.

'Enough!' finally boomed the shaman with a resounding finality, and his voice seemed to ricochet abnormally around the wood-panelled room.

At once, Raymond withdrew himself from the floor and began to regain his standing position and rebuild his dishevelled composure. He adjusted his glasses and tried to control his breathing.

'I do understand,' said the shaman. 'Now, listen to me closely:

The mind is a very complex machine — but if you never learn to understand it, you will forever be a slave to it.'

The effect was instantaneous. Like a grenade had been detonated within Warrick's head, he suddenly felt as if the four walls, the ceiling and floor had just been blown wide open. The space around him expanded exponentially. It was as if someone had just mentally slammed a lump of wood up against the back of his head. *What did he just say?*

Warrick ran the sentence back through his head as the hairs on the back of his neck rose. *The mind is a very complex machine, but if you never learn to understand it, you will forever be a slave to it.* The weight of that concept alone resonated so deeply within Warrick that he felt the gears of his own mind shift into overdrive, becoming more receptive and more alert. It explained so much in his life.

An irrational urge to burst into tears instantly overwhelmed Warrick to a point where he had to steady himself against the parquet flooring. What had just happened? Had this latest truth bomb decimated some inner lie, eradicated some deeply embedded falsehoods?

Yet again, he felt a resurgence of his own self, a rekindling of some innate causality. Realisations, one after another, rolled over and over, clearing unwanted mental clutter, shattering fixed ideas and supposed identities.

He closed his eyes to help stop the swirling storm within his mind as it ran through multiple acts of refiling old memories, old ideologies, old beliefs. It felt as if his mind was trying to reboot itself after a mental update.

He knew something had been wrong with his thinking, wrong with the world... He could see it now. That he, like so many others, had grown up in a system of enslavement; not just of the social order of things, but within their very own minds. People had become so accustomed to social control that it was a natural step for them to allow their own minds to step in and assume a form of control of their own.

They had all allowed their minds to become almost autonomous — almost self-aware. What terrifying, yet eye-opening cognition...

Warrick opened his eyes, aware that he was now sweating.

For him to move on, he must not listen to the "noise", the "voices" or indeed the various commands that the mind would lay down for him to loyally follow. He must now review everything and not just react to questionable compulsions. He had been asleep at the wheel for far too long.

All this time, his mind had been working almost silently in the background, making certain decisions for him, pointing out his vulnerabilities, dramatising his idiosyncrasies and placing him on a path that it deemed appropriate. Well, not any more. He had to make the decisions from now on, not just abide by the automaticities of his mind. He — yes, he — had to rise up and take back command of his senses and in doing so, his destiny, and not allow some unregulated set of mental circuits to dictate the narrative anymore.

Warrick let out a steady breath, knowing that the evening was not over yet.

The shaman continued to study Raymond. 'Fortunately for you, I can give you further help. However, you must do exactly as I tell you, for if you refuse that help, then you will be perpetually under its spell. Past lies, falsehoods, confusions, bad decisions, corrupt computations, and misguided considerations now block your path and your thinking — and they will conceal your insanities well. But hear me now, like you have never heard me before: this... *this is your last chance!*' he finished, with no remorse.

The tension in the room was as solid as a concrete block. The words took a while before they fully registered with Raymond.

'Oh, thank you, thank you!' Raymond blurted out in a cascade of broken sobs. 'You won't regret it, I promise, I promise.'

Raymond placed his hands together as if in abject prayer, snivelling with gratitude.

The shaman took a step back, but did not release Raymond. At the same time, the room took a collective breath. It was the most controversial exposé of the night.

No wonder spiritual men, groups, and movements like this were deemed dangerous, thought Warrick. But they were only dangerous to those who harboured such dark and reprehensible secrets. If men in positions of power kept secrets this deep — or this corrupt — no wonder they would vilify the good, the ethical, the brave. They'd have no choice but to crush them... and elevate the bad. In doing so, they could hide their crimes safely — and redirect the truth.

The shaman pondered for a moment longer before facing his circle of more ardent followers. His gaze drifted from one face to another — weighing their readiness — then he spoke, calm but cutting. 'Listen well. What we see around us — these twisted new trends — they didn't emerge from nowhere. No. They've been carefully seeded. This doesn't happen by accident. It's a design... from the top. What we have just witnessed is not such an isolated affair.' His tone darkened, his words clipped and deliberate.

'There exists a cabal of predatory minds — well-dressed, well-positioned — who wear smiles like masks. They claim to care and they claim to help. They speak of safety, of progress, of freedom. But what they do... is actually corrupt. This isn't just moral confusion. It's a calculated illness. A contagion of the soul.'

He swept an arm toward the group, fingers stabbing the air as if pointing at invisible phantoms.

'They target the family unit because they know — instinctively — that it's where our strength lies. And so, they unravel it; piece by piece. Not with bullets, not with bombs. But with a promised ideology, repackaged as love, acceptance, or "modern thinking." Even slogans promoting diversity are manipulated to mask their more twisted agendas.'

A hush fell over the room. The pretty woman Warrick had met earlier blinked rapidly, as if trying to steady her breath from a climbing pulse rate.

'And while we sleep, they deconstruct the language itself. They upend original library definitions, so words now reflect their new ideologies. Schools, colleges and universities alike all fall under the same covert hammer of indoctrination. Redefining what it means to be decent. To be a man, to be a woman. *To be anything.* They confuse the young. They rob them of their compass. And we... we let them.'

'See!' hissed a bearded man with a modest display of chest hair, as he nudged his friend, 'what did I tell you?'

The shaman's voice rose slightly, his chest rising with each breath now. 'They tell us: it's progress. It's freedom. But is it? Is the sexualisation of children — their indoctrination into adult concepts — a mark of progress? Or a sign of how far we've fallen?

'Let us hope that this ever-expanding "new movement" of incoherent paedophilic sexual diversity under the guise of liberation does not creep as far into the populace as they would like.

Remember, one's self-integrity is paramount, and once a person loses this, their downward spiral into the abyss of degradation will be their fate.'

He paused there, allowing the words to settle. Somewhere to Warrick's right, someone shifted on the parquet floor. A few mortified faces looked across the circle to one another, with uncertainty.

'We are witnessing the moral disintegration of a species,' the shaman said. 'And those behind it don't want fewer problems — they want fewer people. This insane depopulation agenda masquerades as environmentalism. But it's not about saving Earth. It's about control.'

Warrick's throat tightened. He suddenly felt acutely aware of his own breathing.

'We should be expanding, growing, thriving. But they feed us fear. Fear of ourselves. Fear of life. *That* is their true power.'

The shaman stepped forward, passing close to the circle's edge. His voice was no longer calm — it carried a raw edge to it now, like the tremble before thunder.

'Civilisations have crumbled before. Entire continents — perhaps entire worlds — wiped out not by nature... but by neglect. By madness, by madmen... Don't let this be another one.'

He looked directly at Warrick — just for a moment — and something behind his eyes struck deep.

For the first time, the shaman seemed to be building emotionally. His voice was now raised as he began to direct his more passionate beliefs.

Outside, the wind continued to ensnare the Edwardian house and grounds as its unforgiving might whistled down the open chimney and clattered garden bric-a-brac against the darkened windows.

The shaman paused, his chest swelling and falling with incomplete thoughts and excited insights, before animatedly continuing with two outstretched fingers pointing at his face.

'Only by looking — with your own eyes, and not through the preprogrammed ideologies of the corruptness of these people — will you go free.

You must not listen to these purveyors of manipulation, but seek your own truth. Do not allow them to twist truth with lies.'

Again, he moved his body back and forth, gesturing and thrusting his hands about him to bring further comprehension. And surrounding him, more ripples of unseen energy gushed outwards, flooding the room, cleansing everyone in its unavoidable stream.

Two top window shutters finally swung open with a clatter, and the outside air rushed inside, whipping about Warrick like some apocalyptic end of days, the candles now fervently dancing and people's hair swirling about in the powerful currents.

Two people ran in from a darkened side room and began closing the open windows.

Warrick stared at the shaman, whose hands were now dramatically raised as if fuelling this intense message from the heavens. Warrick shook his head in bewildered disbelief; he had seen it all now. This man was able to summon the very core of his spiritual energy, bringing it to life within this very room. He had harnessed his inner power and brought it forth to reinforce his message to humanity.

Mimicking the shaman, people around the circle closed their eyes. For a brief moment, Warrick too let his eyes close. He wanted to sense this power — to feel its raw energy.

After the moment had peaked, the shaman lowered his hands, dissipating the electrical energy in the room. As he paced about, barefoot, the silence in the air was as charged and as crisp as if it had followed a lightning storm. Bringing both hands up to his lips, he began again, although this time he spoke with a gentle whisper.

'Although buried, you must search deep within, and you shall find the light that you so instinctively need to see.

'For without it, you shall falter, abandoned and blind.'

Here and there around the circle, various people nodded in agreement. The shaman turned back to Raymond, who, despite being part of the shaman's dramatic speech, still appeared disconnected and deeply withdrawn.

Oddly, Warrick was suddenly feeling a surprising sorrow for this man, despite the sickening actions of his crimes. *How was this possible? Was it because this man seemed genuinely and earnestly affected by some hitherto unknown dark force within his inner mind? Or was it some new compassion for his fellow man? Was he learning to love without prejudice, like the many great men who had paved the way for such spiritual and humanitarian futures for so many? Was this why he was here tonight—to learn and love unconditionally? Like a mother's love?* Even if this were true, the man's behaviour had still disgusted Warrick, and nothing could change his mind about that. But this did not mean that he felt the urge to debase his sensibilities and lash out with his own class of "justifiable" vengeance. Yes, the man's behaviour was undeniably wrong, and yes, he needed some sort of punishment, but what he really needed was some deep psychological help. But Warrick's tangled thoughts were interrupted as the shaman ploughed on.

'However,' said the shaman, 'although excuses and justifications do not actually alleviate the crime, it is nevertheless just that. And you are a dangerous man, despite the fact that, during your moments of sanity, you do not intend to commit such heinous acts. And until such an outburst occurred, such as you have just given, I feared that we had reached an impasse — but maybe not so.

'You are to report to me afterwards, as much further work is needed.' Raymond nodded pathetically. 'You may now sit down.'

The shaman's dismissal, although polite, was resolute. Through Raymond's look of dread and confusion, relief released him from the spiralling depths of sheer sickening disgust that had been overwhelming him, and he began to recover himself. He slowly sat back down, not daring to look at anyone.

The shaman dusted his hands, ran his fingers through his long hair, and slowly turned to address the room at large.

'A show of hands, if you will. Now tell me, is anyone here familiar with the Codex Gigas — The Devil's Bible?'

~ CHAPTER FIFTEEN ~

The Law of Ascension

A show of four hands rose slowly into the air. The shaman turned to acknowledge everyone for their admission. Once again, he raised a finger as if to instruct.

'The Codex Gigas, also known as The Devil's Bible, is a massive 13th-century medieval manuscript from Bohemia, famed for its enormous size and a full-page illustration of the Devil. It contains the entire Latin Bible, along with various historical texts, and is shrouded in legend, particularly the myth that it was written in a single night with the Devil's help. An impressive tome filled with information, but who does it benefit? What purpose does it serve?

'Similarly, others — such as *The Satanic Bible* — are collections of essays, observations, and rituals that demand allegiance to a highly specific belief system. Unapologetic ego, the glorification of lust, and the degradation of women — whether enacted within black magic ceremonies or not — offer little, if any, value in the authentic pursuit of spiritual freedom. Lawless, reckless fornication between strangers has nothing to do with the spirit, no matter how vehemently one may deny it to avoid admitting error.'

The shaman began to slowly pace as he continued to talk.

'And the idea that one should embrace their "darker side" or build their personality upon it is not spiritual wisdom — it is the romanticisation of past trauma and unresolved suffering, dressed up as empowerment.

'It is a coping mechanism, not a path to truth. To believe otherwise is often to operate from faulty or incomplete data.

'For those who, without self-righteous bias, genuinely feel this path works for them, so be it — but they must walk it with others of a similar mindset. This road, however, stands in stark contrast to the teachings of our Seers College and The Divinities.

'Let it be known: many belief systems masquerade as liberating when, in fact, they are dangerous and coercive. They are built not on empirical wisdom, but on the ever-shifting, surrealistic psychology of the modern age. They are a guaranteed path into illusion — into a maze of smoke and mirrors where deceit becomes doctrine.

'Such paths do not lead to spiritual elevation but rather to a fallacious descent into the materialistic swamp of moral decay. There is no workable truth here — only a reversal and perversion of the original wisdom from which these ideologies claim descent. Whether in the denial of God or the embrace of Satanism, one enters a realm more akin to *Dante's Inferno* than any spiritual sanctuary. And in those dark, descending circles — make no mistake — it is no comedy.'

The shaman paused, making eye contact with various people around the circle. Some nodded and some smiled in agreement. He continued to ambulate.

'That said, the opposite is also true. You shouldn't blindly follow negative opinions or social trends that attack people who are genuinely trying to help others through mental or spiritual work, just because it's fashionable to agree with the crowd or because you're afraid of standing out. Where is your courage? What does that say about your own ability to think for yourself — if it says anything at all?'

Warrick sat back and stretched, genuinely amazed at the constant flow of knowledge that the shaman seemed to have.

Not only did he strip down the fabled lives of those sitting around the circle, but he also had the foresight and overview to try to correct a multitude of worldwide beliefs and social trends. He appeared to view everything through the lens of logic and empirical information that he must have spent years collating. And to think there were other people like this around the world, who the imbecilic would simply attack and destroy out of either ignorance or selfish personal gain. The shaman and others like him needed to be protected and admired for their dedication to helping humanity rise above the mud.

'So what, then, can we use to help guide us? What tangible evidence do we have? From which pool of data can we build our research?'

The shaman paused again, looking about the room of pious onlookers. Whether this was rhetorical or not, Warrick could not tell.

Either way, nobody answered.

'For those of you not familiar with the Seers College,' continued the shaman, 'let me give you an insight into a few elements which you may find... enlightening. As a person strives for excellence or better survival, they will notice that behind them lies the path to negativity — a path that darkens upon every fateful step, a path shrouded in all that should not be. Whether blindly walked or unpredictably fallen, the murky shadows of such lower echelons will bring nothing but fear and despair, clouding all sensibilities and rational computations.'

As the shaman paused, Warrick closed his eyes, trying to assimilate the usual concentration of heavy dialogue. Wasn't the shaman just covering old ground here? Or was this him just hammering home the simple message: do or die in the pursuit of a happy life?

That, unless you paid attention to where you were going in life, you would never get there? This was the sort of thing that motivational speakers, the world over, would try to impress upon their ardent listeners.

'Thus,' the shaman resumed, 'the way to greatness is to ascend to higher states of being. And I believe that there is a law to this phenomenon, known simply as: The Law of Ascension.'

As before, the shaman indicated to some remote operator outside of the seated circle, and once again the lights faded, leaving just the gentle glow of candlelight.

Out of the centre of the floor, slowly rose the revolving, growing tip of a semi-translucent pyramid. On each of the four sides sat a solitary word: Divine, Soul, Survive and Truth.

'Here we have the top of our ascension pyramid,' began the shaman once again. As the pyramid turned, the shaman pointed to each word as it passed him, reciting it aloud. 'Each is a desirable attribute, and each is an undeniable truism upon acquiescence.'

Once again, Warrick tried to digest this latest insight into the teachings of the Seers College. Across the circle, he caught the eye of the young woman he had met earlier. She smiled at him, and he was reminded of her Divinities tattoo and the phrase she had uttered: "...elixir for the soul" — wondering if there was actually more to it.

After a small clap from the shaman, the rotating pyramid began to rise higher into the air, now displaying a second, lower section.

Once again, a new word sat at the centre of each side: Enquire, Mind, Adjust and Justify.

Fascinated, Warrick looked on. This was not a new concept of visual conveyance, as other great spiritual and philosophical pioneers had created similar charts and pyramids, all essentially trying to communicate the same idea. But if this was just another insight into the teachings of the Seer's College, then it was appearing more attractive with every quarter lap of their cross-legged circle. This school of real magic was becoming as appealing as Hogwarts.

The shaman chuckled. 'Prediction is a useful tool in a person's mental arsenal; see if anyone can predict where this will take us.'

Once the shaman gave another small clap, the rotating pyramid rose still further out of the floor.

Fascinated, Warrick caught the young woman's eye once again, and using facial gestures alone, conveyed how impressive it was becoming.

Four new words sat beneath those preceding them: Decline, Space, Agree and Hide.

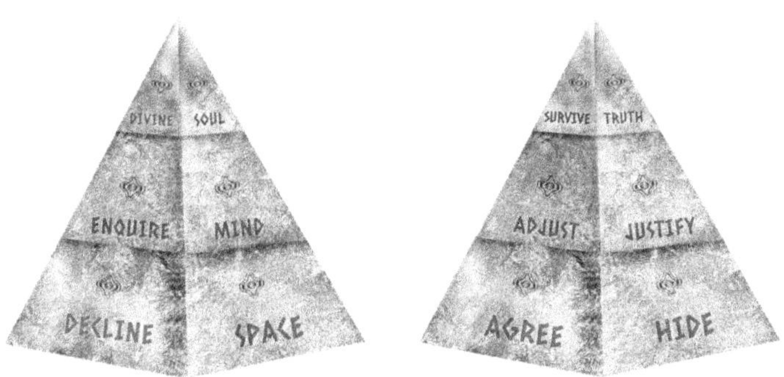

The shaman, like Warrick, looked around the circle for anyone daring enough to guess what they were looking at. No one, however, seemed to have the faintest idea, nor did Warrick. And even if Warrick did, the last thing he wanted to do was to draw attention to himself. The shaman even lingered in Warrick's direction, as if hoping for the seed of realisation. Undeterred, the shaman continued.

'Keep in mind, if you will, that we are dealing with not only the journey of ascending but also of descending. Constant willingness to uphold one's survival will fuel one's necessity to rise to the greater heights that await you. But see here,' he said, now pointing to the base of the pyramid, 'where one can fall through negation of one's accountability. Not a pleasant place...' he added, with a disapproving shake of his head.

With a final clap, the rotating pyramid grew out of the floor for a final time. As before, four new words turned slowly before them all:

Debase, Body, Succumb and Lie.

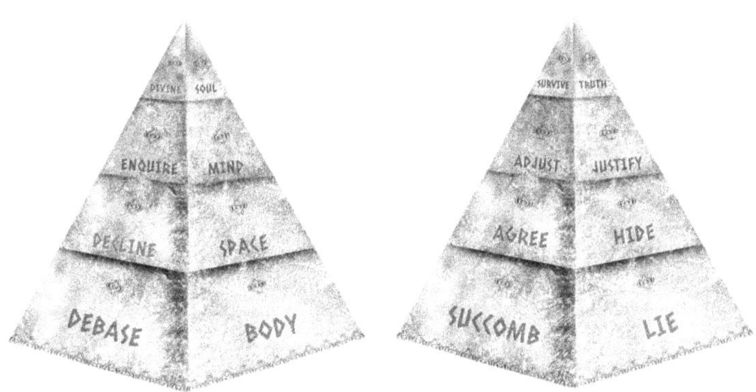

Around the circle, various people now seemed to grasp what this final step represented in this overall visual stimulation.

Warrick ran his eyes from top to bottom and back again over each side of the four-sided pyramid. Finally, it was making sense. It appeared to represent life in its most basic form. At its lower echelons, life was at its most vulnerable and undesirable, and as one ascended towards the topmost echelon, life was at its zenith and therefore most desirable.

With his hands clasped behind his back, the barefoot shaman sauntered around the rotating pyramid. He appeared to be letting people take in this now towering, visual, pyramidal guide.

'I give you The Law of Ascension!' The shaman bowed to the slowly rotating pyramid.

For a while, he did not speak, allowing everyone to take in this latest piece of enlightenment.

Warrick ran his mind up and down the various sides, seeing how each step could follow onto the next. How accurate it was, he did not know, but it was clear enough for him to determine the direction he wanted to travel. It was so simple, yet so powerful.

Why had no one pointed this sort of thing out to him before?

Still, was it really fair to fault others for what they hadn't shown him... when he'd never fully looked for it himself? The truth had been there, plain as day — only invisible to the eyes that refused to see. He leaned back, letting the rotating pyramid imprint behind his lids. Maybe this was the beginning of something, not just for him, but for whoever might one day cross his path. Maybe it was his turn now... to offer what he once needed most. Yes, he concluded. It was now his turn to carry the flame of truth and continue to enlighten others, to help share the wisdom of the ages. It would seem that the shaman had borne this mountain of truth for far too long on his own.

'And thus, as you can see,' began the shaman again, 'we have the dichotomy: good versus evil, survival versus non-survival. At the bottom, we have an inversion of all that is natural and pure. Now ask yourself, in which direction are you travelling? Not forgetting that to do nothing is just a slow decline into the abyss of nothingness. Reading insightful passages by some wizened sage is but a step in the right direction, but without action, without some positive intention to improve, tell me, will you truly change? "There but for me, go I" — as the alternate saying goes.'

Warrick stared at the revolving pyramid. If his family could only see him now, maybe they'd begin to understand — to glimpse the other side of life they'd never dared entertain. He used to think they were simply too comfortable, too invested in the daily rituals of their small world to ever stretch beyond them. But maybe that wasn't fair. Maybe it wasn't just apathy — maybe it was fear. Fear of losing their footing, of stepping beyond the safety of the familiar.

Even if it were presented to them with verbose pomposity via their revered government or trusted media outlets, they would still be blissfully unobservant. In fact, he was sure they would ignore — even dismiss — such radical or socially unacceptable views. But now, for the first time, he found himself wondering why. Had life worn them down so gradually that they no longer noticed? Had they simply been taught not to question?

He let out a soft breath. Maybe they weren't blind by choice. Maybe they were just waiting, like he had been, for something — or someone — to help them see.

And then there were those — the ones stranded somewhere on the lower levels of the pyramid — who would likely mock or outright reject any notion of a "Law of Ascension."

Some might even attempt to get it cancelled altogether, simply for challenging a worldview that didn't match their own. How strange, he mused, that people could be so threatened by others searching for deeper truths, as if the pursuit of meaning itself were an affront.

But maybe it wasn't malice. Maybe those loudest in opposition were already sliding down their own unseen descent. If so, their perception would have narrowed, their awareness dimmed, and any remaining spark of critical thought dulled by reflexive outrage. Anything that questioned accepted narratives — no matter how thoughtfully — would be flippantly dismissed as conspiracy theory or pseudo-philosophy, not because it lacked merit, but because it was inconvenient.

And yet, Warrick thought, wasn't it their rigid certainty — their refusal to consider anything beyond the social script — that might actually deserve scrutiny? In essence, it would actually be their bigoted points of view that ought to be invalidated.

Warrick stopped himself before carrying on. He was starting to sound like some of the people around the circle, wondering if that was a good or bad thing.

The shaman was now silently pacing back and forth as if in great deliberation. Then, on overhearing two women whispering something out of Warrick's earshot, the shaman chuckled.

'Let me answer that for you both, and perhaps for the rest of the room,' he said to them. The repetitive symbol you see above each word represents a key of sorts.

To what — I shall let you decide.' He gave a playful wink towards Warrick's side of the circle.

Contemplatively, Warrick considered that there was both a feeling of calm and yet a sense of building curiosity for this side of life that he had never been introduced to. What was happening to him? What was this shaman really doing? Trying to wake him up from the monotonous existence that he had been indoctrinated into believing was his lot in life? Well, it was working.

As if changing the subject, the twinkling of gentle lights began to emerge above their heads. Warrick recognised various star constellations and the wispy mystery of the Milky Way.

The shaman turned full circle, smiling up at the beautiful illumination. 'Ah, heaven's *mirror* — as the famous journalist, and dare I say, explorer extraordinaire, Graham Hancock once remarked.'

Warrick stared up at the starry sky, wondering if it was this beautiful closer up. In reality, if he were truly a spirit, encumbered by a body, and able to exteriorise himself without the body keeling over, thinking it had been abandoned, then did that mean he was free to roam the universe at large, seeking out new life and new possibilities?

The shaman took in a deep breath as if preparing for a long sentence. 'The Egyptian pharaoh, Akhenaton, was once rumoured to have been the first to try and assert that man was more than just mere flesh and bones, and that man had abilities way beyond the stars. He believed that they needed to live as gods among gods, existing as immortal beings, and not merely as those of the animal kingdom. Around 3,500 years ago, this information was kept from man by those wishing to enslave him, to banish him from the dizzying heights of spiritual attainment.'

The shaman looked back at the circle of onlookers and redirected his rhetorical questions. 'Just think, if you were a pharaoh, a prime minister, a president or, indeed, a reigning monarch, how do you govern a body of men that have the same level of powers that you do?' He paused again, gazing longingly back up at the stars as if it were the sky outside. 'Easier, is it not, to have them a little less able, a little less powerful — or, say, a little less knowledgeable than yourself? And therefore, it would be easier to govern — or should I say, control? A curious point of fact. Alas, it is the same old story.'

The shaman looked to the circle once again, before giving one of his knowing smiles, pointing dramatically around the entire group.

'So, you may ask, how do you rekindle your own lost and diluted powers from an age of eternal banishment and concealment?' Once again, he tapped playfully against his bottom lip.

Warrick held out his hands before him, aware that a tiny electric current now seemed to reside there. His whole body practically buzzed with the concept that he could have within him, untapped powers, and that this shaman and his Seer's College may actually hold the key to its release.

Could it be true that they had finally mapped out a path from which to ascend from the mortality of man to the ethereal spectrum of the spirit?

A cold thrill lingering in his spine crept up his neck like some euphoric aphrodisiac. Was this shaman even from this planet?

Once more, the shaman paced, his arms behind his back as if pondering his next piece of insight. The room remained in enraptured silence. The only sounds were of the wind howling outside and of the guttering candles flickering shadows against the parquet floor.

A few shooting stars shot beautifully across the faux night sky, their sparkling tails streaking with an enchanting radiance amid the universal bed of starlight. Here and there, people oohed and aahed.

Then another light, now yellow with a hint of blue, began to dominate everyone's attention. It was coming from a far wall that was previously in darkness. Squatting beside a large brick fireplace, one of the background staff members was igniting the grate log fire.

'So, what of aliens?' asked a female voice on the far side of the circle, making everyone turn. Her accent was distinctly West Country — soft and curious. She was staring up at a giant orb that was gently pulsing above her. 'You know, where do they fit in? Are they spirits too — but just in different bodies?'

But nobody answered, for the shaman had vanished.

~ CHAPTER SIXTEEN ~

Respite

Around the room, various wall sconces began to glow, bringing warmth and light back into the room. The crisp, clean steps of the tiny host introduced her re-emergence. Holding her trusted clipboard, she wavered upon the edge of the seated circle and cleared her throat.

'You are now free to take a bathroom break, with refreshments administered from the serving hatch behind me.' She casually flicked a pointed finger over her shoulder. 'We will recommence in fifteen minutes.' With a curt smile and an about-turn, she returned to a darkened side room.

Around the main room, people stood and stretched. They turned to one another in hushed tones. Warrick, however, remained where he sat, uncertain of what to do or what to think. The doormen, or ought he say bouncers, were still there, motionless.

Finally getting up, Warrick thought he would wander over to the log fire — perhaps it would take the edge off the slight chill that he was feeling. Bustling across him, a couple that were seated further up on his left-hand side made a bolt for the front door. Scared or genuinely late for another appointment, he did not know. *Good luck there...* thought Warrick, sardonically. And as predicted, they were refused exit. Leaving them to their protests of indig-nation, he made his barefooted way across the room. The floor felt warmer than he thought it would.

Before he reached the fire, he stopped at a side table, where various merchandise, such as crystals, bracelets, and pendants, were on display. Along one edge sat a long wooden flute that was covered in strange markings, and on which feathers and beads hung from its main body. A small paper label said: Native Shamanic Flute. Behind this, propped up at the back, was a handmade drum also covered in feathers and beads, with an inset image of a native American Indian smoking a pipe. The label beneath read: Sacred Vegan Drum. Above this, Warrick lifted a few mystic necklaces containing a variety of healing stones. He was drawn to one in particular, which had the name tag: "Tiger's Eye Gemstone (For protection, power, and courage)."

Most noticeable was the divinities motif, the interconnected rings printed in black onto large white mugs.

Reaching past them, he picked up a miniature marble replica of the *Law of Ascension* pyramid, turning it in his hands. He ran his finger over the words etched into the limestone; it felt heavy. Putting it back, something brushed his hair. Hanging down from a cotton thread, a gently turned, snowy-white dreamcatcher. This was different from others that he had seen, as this one appeared angelic, as if winged and topped with a slight white halo. And woven at its centre were words he had never seen before: *Mea Deitas.* The small Latin phrase clearly meant something to those in the know — perhaps by the end of the evening, he would find out, too.

Reaching up, he pressed a small switch on a hanging battery pack, and a delicate arrangement of tiny white lights illuminated the dreamcatcher, giving it a beautiful, ethereal glow.

It would make a stunning gift for his girlfriend, he mused, turning it back off.

That was a thought; she must be wondering where he was... He couldn't wait to tell her of his experience — if he still got out alive. She loved anything spiritual, although this evening might stretch even her open-mindedness.

Sitting beneath, there were even small black earrings hanging from a stand, representing the individual ambigram elements of: Mind, Body, Soul and Space. And as a backdrop to it all was a large poster featuring a comprehensive energy flow chart surrounding the outline of a human body. Too small to read in the ambient lighting, Warrick just gave it a cursory glance, noting that it appeared as if it had come from some advanced lesson.

Joining him at the table, someone began picking up various cream-scented candles to smell. They had all been embossed with flecks of golden symbolism, reminiscent of the ones Warrick had seen outside on the billowing cream curtains and upon the shaman's skin.

Symbology also seemed to play its part here.

Reaching the log fire, Warrick turned and lifted the soles of each of his bare feet in turn, glad of the chance to warm them. Looking around the room, he spotted Raymond, alone in a far corner, appearing extraordinarily interested in the large tapestry that hung from the wall. What guts it must have taken to face up to such a twisted mental abnormality. And how some people would try to rationalise such a degraded and unnatural compulsion, he would never know. Yet the way things were going in life, he was sure that if he did try to voice his view of such things, he would be boycotted before he started. This cancel culture was really getting out of control, mainly because the average person did not want to get involved to stop such behaviour. It was funny how they could have their point of view, but you were damned if you tried to raise yours.

The joke was that they had no idea how most people felt about their absurd, overbearing view of self-importance and irrefutable righteousness.

He wondered how much of the film industry and literary circles would also be affected by this, all jumping on the latest bandwagon to show their unwavering allegiance and propitiative leanings, when maybe it was just the lack of guts to hold their own.

Joyce and Ruby were now sipping some herbal tea, blowing at the hot water between hearty guffaws and nervous giggles. The West African dun dun drummer and the androgynous tambourinist — *was it correct to refer to this person as he/him or she/her, or even by some other wokeist label,* pondered Warrick thoughtfully — were also deep in conversation, both taking nibbles from a plate of food they had been offered. Warrick was still unable to determine the person's sex — who knows, perhaps the tambourine player was presently undecided, too.

Stopping before Warrick, a pasty-looking, plain couple in their thirties had also taken a mild interest in the attractive tambourine player. Just as curious, they too looked to one another as if in question of their sex.

The man gave a subtle nod in the tambourinist's direction. 'I can't keep up with all these genders they keep creating,' he said in an upper-class voice. 'This aggressive movement seemed to come out of nowhere, and now we are all expected to grant this fad full autonomy over our sexes. They see it as justified bullying; that's what it is. You know, some of these Eastern countries look at us as if we are the crazy ones, even to allow this insanity to gain traction.'

The woman rolled her eyes in agreement. 'And can you imagine,' she tittered, 'some poor modern writer trying to fashion a novel or script with all that inclusion, attempting to keep their publisher happy? Desperately trying to add in all the various pronoun labels just to please this small group of people...' She gave a tiny chuckle. '"They/them/he/him stormed into the room, only to be confronted by she/her/hers and she/her/her's partner, who now identified as ze/they/them. They/them/he/him locked eyes with she/her/hers and frowned, unsure if this new cis friend was really who they appeared to be..."'

This time, they both gave a hushed chuckle.

'Absolutely,' the man agreed, 'and God forbid you ever get caught saying that out loud to someone with no sense of humour, they might set up some "go-fund-me" hate group. Such childish and defensive mentality, and they wonder why they receive so much backlash from the general public. It's ironic, just because we disagree with them, they feel they can label us haters, when we're not.' He shook his head. 'Oh, how some of these characters love putting labels on others, just to shut them up.'

Placing a hand on her lower back, he guided her to continue around the room.

Warrick said nothing, but a flicker of unease stirred in him. He wasn't sure where he fully stood on all the gender stuff — it was such a touchy subject these days — but the tambourine player hadn't done anything to deserve that kind of talk. Besides, they didn't even know him — or her. The couple's comments weren't just observations; they felt like barbed jabs dressed up as intellectualism. If they have been coming here long enough, they ought to know better. Maybe it was easier to scoff at something unfamiliar than to try to understand it. Still, Warrick wasn't ready to jump into the fray. Not yet. Besides, who hadn't prejudged someone at some point in their lives, without really knowing them first?

Glad to be somewhat invisible, Warrick continued to glance around the room. The couple who had tried to leave earlier were now ambling back to where they had once sat, bickering between themselves, apparently still disgruntled with their detainment. And on that thought, Warrick pondered where the evening was heading.

He, too, was locked in a room with a group of spiritual explorers, some of whom were more devoted to the shaman and his beliefs than others. The odd thing was, unless this was one giant ruse — and it was a bloody good one if it was — something did seem to be happening in the room; he had felt it, had seen it with his own eyes. He would like to see if a group of actors could ever replicate the emotions he had just witnessed, for these were raw and unyielding, gut-wrenching and visceral. This shaman truly seemed to be the real thing, and he genuinely appeared to possess extraordinary abilities. And unless they were pumping out some unseen psychedelic drug into the air, what he had experienced was one hundred per cent real. It was kosher.

He peered around the room once more, just in case his friends had finally slipped in to join the madness. But for some reason, they were still not there.

A timid-looking man, dressed entirely in beige, including a patterned beige cardigan, and with a large set of keys hanging from his belt, shuffled over with a small tray of drinks.

'Elderberry?' enquired Warrick, smiling to himself.

'Oh, how did you guess?' asked the man, now slipping off a matching beige slipper and scratching one foot behind his other leg.

Warrick shrugged. 'Just a hunch...'

After taking a small glass, the man walked on. Warrick continued to watch him. As he approached a woman standing alone, the man patted down his thinning hair and adjusted the glasses that hung from a slender chain around his neck.

A small smile curled at the side of Warrick's mouth.

The wall lights dimmed twice, indicating that everyone should start making their way back to their seated positions. It reminded Warrick of being in the anteroom of some West End theatre in London. And God forbid that someone should get up and start singing during the second half.

Downing his drink and leaving the glass, he slowly walked back, noticing that they were unquestionably a mixed bunch. To his left, a middle-aged, perhaps upper-class woman was showing her friend her new set of rosary beads, while to his right, a man with a builder's physique was demonstrating his healing hands to another man, holding them in front of the man's face. The latter had agreed that he could indeed feel quite some heat emanating from them.

Warrick paused before two suited men talking animatedly to one another, hoping they would step aside for him.

Oblivious to Warrick, however, the first man, wearing a white turtleneck T-shirt, lightly tapped at his friend's chest.

Look, I don't think it's a question of being left-wing or right-wing... I see it purely in terms of The Ascension Pyramid. Personally, I feel that people with a left-wing mentality generally sit much lower on the scale than those of a right-wing bent — but that's just my opinion. The Left tend to be more manipulative and victim-driven, while the Right is more aggressive and authoritarian... I just hope there is a saner political group out there that can sit way above them all, one that just wants to get the job done without blackmail, bribes and lies and all the other shenanigans that pass for being a politician these days... I think the best we can do is scrap all of these governments as they are just too corrupt to continue. Either they were set up to covertly manipulate and control the masses in the first place, or they have all been infiltrated by secret societies.

'We need to move ourselves into a new realm of governance instead... where the people actually get to see what is going on and we all get to benefit as a whole — and not just those they deem are worthy.'

Finally deciding to push past with an apology, Warrick wandered on, hoping for something a little less controversial to overhear. But he was stopped again, as two more men, also in heavy conversation, inadvertently blocked his passage.

'What do you mean "why are we fighting the system?"' said a young, bearded man, displaying a modest amount of chest hair.

Warrick recognised him from earlier.

'You've heard what some of the people in here think of what's going on out there...' he said to his friend, before pointing towards an outside wall.

The other man, small and withdrawn and more sensible in appearance, with thinning blond hair, shook his head noncommittally.

Warrick, unsure whether to apologise or shuffle off, tried not to groan. He found himself standing awkwardly close to them. And now had no choice but to wait until the conversation had petered out. However, his body language must have betrayed his discomfort.

'Well, let me remind you what we are up against,' continued the bearded man. 'It's not just the bloody corporations — the world has been hijacked! You think this is by accident? You think our leaders are just stupid or weak? No, this is planned. They've sold out to global interests. The real war is against sanity itself.'

The smaller man blinked, trying to find his voice, but the bearded man pressed on.

'So, how do you weaken a society and make it more subservient?' he continued. 'First, you take down the men. You demoralise them from a young age — tell them they're toxic or unneeded. You emasculate them with drugs and chemicals, fill their heads with shame, destroy the family unit... and then wonder why society's broken.

'Women turn on them because you've encouraged it — taught them to believe any man who dares speak up is a threat. You teach that masculinity is dangerous and force non-male and non-female stereotypes. And if they reject the idea, you call them "internalised misogynists" or attack them with this defensive "mansplaining" nonsense. It's everywhere. Look around you, man!'

Warrick tried to look away without being obvious. He felt his energy waning. He should have known by now that this was not the sort of group that took things lying down. His mind was simmering at its limit with an almost overload of concepts, conspiracies, and spiritual possibilities.

And still the man ploughed on. 'They're forcing this gender confusion on kids — right down to cartoons and school uniforms. But question it, and you're labelled hateful. Society frowns on winning, rejects truth, reverses gender roles, injects trans-athletes into female sports, and tells us that pride in our own heritage is "white supremacy", while calling everyone else brave for doing the same. And we all know about this other bullshit lie that "diversity is our strength". My wife — who is black, by the way — agrees they're decimating everyone's cultural heritage and diluting each country's sovereign state. I find it all quite sickening...'

Suddenly, both men looked briefly up at Warrick, as if wondering what he wanted. Warrick was unsure whether to apologise and shuffle off awkwardly or try to contribute to the conversation.

Saving him from the dilemma, the bearded man gripped his shoulder, accepting him into the discussion.

'It's a nightmare, isn't it?' the man said to him.

'Yeah… erm…' Warrick began, but unrelenting, the man dove straight back into his message.

'And wait until this transabled movement gains more traction — you know, where some of these people are literally blinding themselves or lopping off parts of their body because they think they should've been born disabled. I mean… *really*? Who is funding this madness? Why would you even try to normalise it? They need help, not validation!'

Warrick tried not to groan. True or not, all this unrelenting "unconventional view of the world" was becoming tiring, even for him.

'And don't get me started on the medical lies — hiding treatments, pushing endless fear porn. You really think this is about health? No. It's about control, enforcing their will with Digital IDs — as if they are trying to help us. It's about dividing us into manageable herds. Meanwhile, the media twists every story, edits interviews to vilify the good and glorify the corrupt. They turn criminals into victims and heroes into threats. It's all back to front and upside down. Surely you can see it?'

He drew breath — not even waiting for an answer — only to speak faster. Warrick shifted uncomfortably, trying to pretend he was fully listening.

'And now the censorship! If someone tells the truth, they're cancelled or silenced. Their bank accounts frozen, jobs lost, reputations destroyed. Not because they lied, but because they dared say what you're not allowed to. It's thought policing. It's digital authoritarianism. And people lap it up because it's branded as progress. Yet the sheep and the lemmings, bless them, trundle on in absolute blind oblivion.'

'But why?' said the small man, struggling with it all. 'You make it sound like the whole world is working against you. It's too much — it's unreal!'

'Ahh, but is it?'

'And who is doing all this, anyway?' He looked to Warrick as if for backup.

'The "who" are the elites behind all governments — the invisible psychos who want a One World Government. Otherwise known as a shadow government.'

'Oh come on... why? Why would these "invisible sociopaths" do this?'

'Jeez... where have you been?' He dramatically bit his own fist. 'I just don't get most people. They accept the way life is — without questioning anything...'

Once again, the smaller man seemed about to speak, but the bearded man had gathered too much emotional traction to be stopped. Warrick let out a silent sigh, hearing himself plead that the man bring the subject to a rapid close.

'They've dumbed everyone down with entertainment, poisoned our food and air, turned us against each other over race and class — and behind the scenes, they mock us. There's footage of satanic drag queens in government-funded shows dancing for children. But nobody does anything. Guys, I'm telling you, they trick people into thinking guilt, victimhood, and compliance are virtues — and those who question anything are shamed or exiled. They prey on our kindness. They twist it until it becomes self-destruction.'

The smaller man gave a weak laugh. 'Come on... that's a bit—'

But the bearded man cut him off.

'You think that's where it ends? No. Look up who controls the charities.

Follow the money through the non-profits. You've always got to follow the money. Child trafficking isn't a dark fantasy — it's a protected industry. That's why whistleblowers vanish, why investigations hit dead ends. You think it's random that powerful people all seem to gather at the same creepy art installations and weird spiritual events? The symbolism is everywhere — they're telling you who they are. And nobody believes it, because it's so insane!'

'To be honest, this all sounds insane. Isn't it just... just evolution?' the smaller man said, timidly.

The bearded man raised his eyebrows. He even looked at Warrick, shaking his head.

'No, it's not evolution. It's by design. It's all out of a psychological warfare playbook — crafted by elites so fearful of people stronger than them, they have no choice but to strip them down to control them. Then they can rest easy, reassured their supposed "enemy" lies submissive.'

The smaller man exhaled heavily, rubbing the back of his head. 'Still seems a bit much, don't you think?'

The bearded man laughed. 'Is it? Is it though? Look around, fellas — take a good look. Just because you don't have delusional or narcissistic aspirations doesn't mean others don't. A narcissist can be one person, or a group of people, hell — even a planet-wide dictatorship. All beautifully hidden, so people defend their psychotic narrative without realising it.'

He playfully grabbed both Warrick and the small man by the shoulders.

'They just sneaked in through the back door of "human rights" to manipulate and control the populations of the world — under the guise of equality and aid. This was done to prevent anyone from suspecting foul play. Ingenious. Insidious.

'The modern-day Trojan Horse. The agenda was so extensive, so spread out over time, nobody could predict what was happening until it was too late. If anyone sits at the bottom of this ascension pyramid, then they do.'

The small man and Warrick shared a fleeting, non-verbal understanding.

'You want proof?' the bearded man continued. 'Just look at the world today: it's in chaos.'

Warrick frowned. He wasn't sure whether to laugh or take it seriously. Part of him wanted to join in, but he feared the man would never stop. If he were honest, he had had enough and now just wanted to sit back down.

'And the worst part?' the bearded man said, leaning in. 'They convince people that speaking out is the problem — not the evil, but the exposure of it. So decent people shut up. They keep quiet for peace. For their jobs. For their families. But silence doesn't protect us — it enables them.' He shook his head.

There was a pause as the man stared at them both, as if willing them to see everything he had just downloaded. But the smaller man said nothing, clearly lost for words. And Warrick was still slowly trying to digest all he had said. He felt as if someone had tilted back his head and poured in the entire Encyclopaedia Britannica for the evening. He doubted he would remember a fraction of it.

'So yes,' added the man, with finality in his voice, 'that is what we're up against — and that is why some of us fight. And this is why I'm here. To become saner, more equipped, and ready to help awaken our fellow man with the aid of The Divinities.'

Warrick gave a half-committal response and quickly extricated himself as the small man continued to question the other.

Did these people ever switch off? It was bad enough listening to the heavy dialogue during the rest of the evening.

Straight ahead of Warrick, a stocky woman with a long black shawl was explaining to a painfully thin older woman with a light blue tint in her hair that all she had to do was disagree with the material world around her. She then pointed to a painting on the far wall and explained that all the woman had to do was either tilt the painting to one side, or lift it off the wall altogether, using mental energy. The woman, in turn, had strained so hard that her face had turned red, and she began to feel dizzy. The large woman had gone on to explain that that was not quite what she had meant, and that she needed to review her course materials before retrying.

Just before taking up his seated position once more, Warrick overheard the attractive young woman he had seen in the garden earlier, sipping on her elixir, lower her voice to a whisper. She was part of a close-knit group of three: herself, a slick-looking Italian man in his late twenties wearing an office suit, and a red-haired woman whose appearance suggested she had borrowed someone else's clothes. And if anything were to make a person, including Warrick, eavesdrop on a conversation, it would be someone suddenly whispering.

'Well,' began the attractive woman, 'I, for one, have no time for all this black shamanism that some want to bring back into vogue. If they cannot see that only white shamanism is the true source of enlightenment, then they're not worth having around. I'm sure they only say it for dramatic effect.'

'No, no,' corrected the scruffy woman with red hair, 'I only said my friend was attracted to things like that, as she said they sounded exciting. I doubt she'd actually do anything about it — a bit like her satanism phase.

'It was all the mystery around Aleister Crowley and his mystical Tarot Cards that hooked her. But I think she's now into Qigong or tai chi.'

'Oh, I thought she was into that Constellation Therapy? No, wait... I meant... that erm... Canadian Gateway Experience?'

'Yes, she's tried them all, I think, but can't seem to make up her mind. Besides, I don't think the opinions of these warped and paid-for celebrities help either. The thing is, each time she does find something that works for her, she then listens to some anti-believer on the web or TV and panics, running with their bad experience rather than her own reality. She's just not stable, and the ironic thing is, she's had everything she needs around her all the time. It's odd, she can't seem to see it — like a blind spot. She just doesn't stick to one thing long enough... In my opinion, she's either running from something she can't confront, or looking in the wrong place for something that might not exist. Who knows, perhaps she finds excuses to justify her behaviour.'

The attractive woman scoffed. 'Makes sense, otherwise I don't know why she flits from one belief to another so quickly — she's too flighty. She's obviously still looking for her right path. Why don't you bring her here — perhaps she'll settle? The shaman would fully understand her personal crusade. He'd know all about the Baha'i teachings she also briefly followed, and her search for Bodhi or quest for Zen and all the other random stuff she has picked up.'

'You'd think she would come, but she says the timing is not right, so go figure... But, probably because of her legal background, I think she is worried that unless they have a solid codified technology or set of professional techniques to follow, which can also correct itself or its effects upon a person — you know, if things were to go wrong — then she is leaving herself open to gross mental instability or spiritual malfeasance.' The woman sighed, picking at her cardigan in disappointment. 'Maybe a good, solid and trustworthy partner is what she really needs...

'She could do with a nice man — but even then, when she does, she doesn't seem to appreciate them until they are gone. Her insecurities, I suppose... Keeps finding daft reasons to pick them apart.'

'What do you mean?' questioned the other woman.

'She gets too worried about what other people think all the time — a terrible weakness. Maybe she just lacks vision and isn't thankful for what she's got each time. You know, lacks gratitude or something. And she's met some lovely men...'

The young Italian man nodded in agreement. 'Been there, done that...' he sighed. 'Worrying about what other people think of her choices is definitely a deadly trait. I lost a beautiful girlfriend in the same way. She just wasn't stable in herself; too wrapped up in her own head and own personal survival to see what was right in front of her. Selfish, really... I would've given her the world if she'd let me. But...' He broke off, sharing a forlorn smile.

'I think she misunderstood me. When she was going through a real rough patch, I tried to take on more of our chores, the small and the invisible things. Even something as simple as having tea ready when she got home at night. Maybe she mistook that care for control, when all I wanted was to give her a little extra peace and calm.'

He paused, smiling inwardly.

'To her, it might have looked like I was "taking over", but I was only ever trying to love her in the only way I knew how. I don't think she ever really noticed how much of my life I set aside for her, how much I gave up, just to keep her steady. She never saw what it cost me — or maybe she didn't want to...

'I made the mistake of trying to fix all her problems — so she probably thought I wasn't listening to her — when she just wanted to vent... but the truth is, I was. So, despite her upsets, her anger, and her ups and downs at the time, all I was actually doing was trying to stop her from falling completely.'

He slowly shook his head. 'At the end of the day, I was carrying her — she just couldn't see it.

'There I was, acting as part of a team, but she... she was acting solo, unaware of my protection. She missed it — completely.'

The man let out a steadying breath, taking a moment to keep his emotions in check.

'I think that's the saddest part, that she never really understood how much she meant to me. I just wanted to see her happy.'

He looked up with a watery smile.

'Oh... you poor dear,' cooed the scruffy woman, before squeezing the man's arm.

'And in the end, well... she had to play silly games and unnecessarily test my loyalty. Then she took it too far and ruined everything. Even she was spinning from the regret of her own actions in the end. Seems my extra love and devotion were all for nothing.' The man sighed again. 'Silly girl... left me gutted like a fish.'

The two women shared a look of deep sympathy. And Warrick, too, felt his loss as he quietly listened to the weight of a man who had loved with everything he had, and still lost.

'Anyway,' the man continued, as if to conclude, 'I think she was always looking for something better, which, to be fair, is not always a bad thing. But still...'

For a moment, nobody spoke. Even Warrick, despite eavesdropping, wanted to interject and further console the man over his lingering loss. Such unnecessary pain.

The scruffy woman nodded with understanding. 'Well, my friend also seems to think the grass is always greener elsewhere — you know the story... Not sure she'll ever learn.'

'Hmmm,' agreed the attractive woman with a nod, 'regret is such a powerful disabler. The poor thing sounds a bit lost...'

'Sadly...' added the scruffy woman. 'Although, I personally think my friend gets too influenced by the brainwashing nonsense on these social networking apps about how toxic men are or what the ideal man is supposed to be like. She is forever scrolling on her phone, checking out people's random content, feeling she's missing out. And I'm telling you, I've told her, like, a thousand times, not to take advice from her critical girlfriends, who, I might add, couldn't hold onto a good man to save their lives. But, she knows best... and would rather chop off her own arm than admit she was wrong. And then she wonders why her life is so messed up... So stupid... and all self-created.' She tutted, both frustrated and upset by it all.

'I feel for her, I really do,' she added. 'She's actually quite a sweetheart and really deserves to be happy. But it's like she can't seem to have what is right in front of her. Self-destruct, I suppose...'

'Or,' pondered the man, his attention back on the present, 'she is harbouring a guilty secret or two, and feels that confessing up here would only make matters worse — falsely thinking that her crimes would be used against her — when they would never be, they would actually release her from her guilt and free her from her past. She would even be forgiven so that she could leave her baggage behind once and for all. And as we know, a guilty conscience is a powerful catalyst for running from your troubles and your mistakes. If someone suddenly cuts and runs, it's always a red flag to me. And I am also sure it's what happens when they listen to the wrong people, so they can give themselves an excuse not to face up to their past... If she is anything like my ex, she only hears what she wants to hear — especially if it makes her right. But I am sure deep down, your friend knows what she needs to do...'

'Agreed, said the attractive woman. 'If this is the reason she flits from one system to the next, or one man to the next, then perhaps the shaman could pull these dark secrets from her. This would give her the solace she is looking for — if she only knew it!'

The scruffy woman rested a hand on the other woman's arm to interject. 'So, it could be a confront thing all along?' she added, thoughtfully. 'Mind you, if she considers them that bad, she'd probably have trouble admitting to them in front of a room full of people — we've seen how the resistance of that can be dramatised.' She nodded in the direction of the pregnant woman they had all seen earlier. 'So maybe she just needs to realise that this is a safe space to unburden herself. That she no longer needs to keep running from her past... And that withholding herself is not survival or even clever; she is just stopping herself from a clear conscience and is dragging out the inevitable.' She looked blankly out in front for a moment, thinking of the friend in question.

'It might even change her life,' the scruffy woman continued, 'stop her from finding excuses to redirect blame on others. And the sad thing is, if she never finally confronts the demons she is dodging, she might never be truly happy.

It would explain all the inconsistencies in her life: the loss of good men, unstable career paths, and her various spiritual quests for answers. I love her to pieces, but what do you do...? I pray for her, I really do. Such a shame... such a waste...'

Warrick gave himself a mental shake; rightly or wrongly, they had made some interesting points there. And what on earth were all these other beliefs? Just how much more was going on in the world?

Once the Italian guy began to speak again, sounding more to Warrick like he was trying to impress the attractive woman, Warrick decided to move on.

Still intrigued by the recent conversations, Warrick finally sat himself back down. His mind felt overloaded. It was as if he had downloaded more raw facts about life that evening than the last nineteen years combined — and the night was still not over.

But the burning question remained. What had the shaman in store for him? Like those that had gone before him, would he be exposed, enlightened and exonerated, or something else entirely? How many secrets did he, Warrick, have that he had buried out of sight, that the shaman may want to launder for all and sundry to see? Perhaps it would be this recurring incident that had happened at school, that seemed determined to spoil everything, to nullify any presence that he felt he had. Why couldn't it be something nice that he could convey to the shaman instead? Why must it be something potentially humiliating?

Warrick felt his hands start to sweat. No, he had to be strong. If that pregnant woman could redirect the shaman's unflinching gaze, then perhaps he, too, had a chance.

That's a point, Warrick said to himself, where were those two — ah, there they were, they were now talking to the woman with the clipboard. So, they were still there, then.

They hadn't tried to climb out some rear window — well, not yet at any rate.

The lights around the room dimmed and brightened for the last time, and the remaining people made their way back to their seated positions.

Warrick took a deep breath — the final straight, he told himself. This was it. What new mind-bending technique was he to witness this time?

~ CHAPTER SEVENTEEN ~

Is or is not?

As if gliding back into the room on a magic carpet, the shaman reappeared.

He slowly turned on the spot, reorienting himself with his devotees and catching the eye of each one in turn.

Warrick shuddered as their eyes briefly met. Whether it was the thrill of the unknown or the fear of his upcoming disclosure, he couldn't say.

The shaman rubbed his hands together as he prepared for the second and final round.

'The answer,' he began, 'to the earlier question is, for all intents and purposes, ideally for another time. Whether it is or is not true is known. But let us not put the cart before the proverbial horse.'

Warrick frowned. What was the last question again?

But the shaman pressed on.

'Let us keep it simple — keep it about your spiritual path. Some utterances have suggested that our system is akin to the Yogi school of thought in Hinduism, in that one must follow, to some degree or another, a system of physical and mental exercise.

'There may be some truth to this. But to the best of my knowledge, our system is unique — it has not been found anywhere else. Nevertheless, it is the same as in any field of study: you must apply yourself along a focused path of truth — of reasoning. Something which you must tread.

One cannot simply be told about it. One must experience it for themselves.'

Before he could continue, a hand shot up directly in front of him. He paused, considered the smiling woman, and gave a single nod for her to speak.

'Erm... with regard to my last question — about aliens — I just wanted to know if you could elaborate a little here? There are all these sightings and crop circles and stuff, so... I was just wondering, are these aliens also spirits? Just with a different body type? Only... they're not trapped down here like the rest of us, right?'

It was the same calm, female voice from earlier — the one with the soft West Country accent. Conservatively dressed and composed, she sat with a kind of serene clarity, as if her very aura were swept clean.

Good question, thought Warrick, now slowly coming to terms with the idea that the cosmos might be much bigger than he'd been led to believe.

The shaman took his time before responding.

'It is true that much goes on amongst the stars — whether it be Expeditionary Rescue Missions or the various Invader Forces. They still pursue their own current path, their own life trajectory. After all, they are playing a completely different game from us. And who is to say... that it is not we who are the aliens?'

The woman pulled a "that's a good point" face and nodded to a friend who clearly shared her thoughts.

Warrick sat a little straighter, amused at this constant insight into the universe at large.

The shaman was smiling now. 'As intriguing as these diversions are, let's save them for another time,' he said, drawing a slow breath. 'And before anyone asks — at this time and place, we are not getting into: The Galactic Alliance, The Galactic Federation of Worlds, The Interplanetary Corporate Conglomerate, The Earth Liberation Project or even visitors from Arcturus...'

He slowly turned full circle to make sure that everyone was keeping up. 'Nor,' he continued, 'are we going to entertain any interpersonal interactions with the various alien races such as The Tall Greys, the Venusians, the Blue Avians, the Pleiadians or any other benevolent entity, including characters such as the mysterious Valiant Thor.'

When several people around the circle nodded or made knowing remarks, the shaman acknowledged them with a subtle nod of his own.

'But — ' the woman began again, her hand half-raised.

'I understand,' he said, cutting across gently. 'However, to dive off on such quantum tangents — to discuss these off-world planetary reset concepts, such as Project Odin — rather distracts from our evening.'

The shaman nodded slowly to the woman, to gain understanding. She, in turn, finally grasped that the subject, although not ignored, was to be discussed another time.

He refocused. 'Let us return to your original question. Suffice it to say: a body, in any form — alien or otherwise — still requires a being at the helm, so to speak. Let's keep our attention on what matters: your ascension out of the cyclic entrapment within the human race — or should I say... from human bodies.'

Warrick blinked. Couldn't he, just for five minutes, say what he meant in layman's terms? Would that be so hard?

And so... did that mean these extraterrestrial entities were real or not? He kind of answered without answering — like a politician. And who on Earth were all these other galactic bodies and corporations? What did they have to do with the spirit? Or was he merely hinting that there were more things in heaven and earth than we dared imagine — things governing our fate from above?

Warrick exhaled sharply, puffing with frustration at the relentless inflow of new concepts.

From somewhere on Warrick's left, a woman scoffed loudly enough for the shaman to turn ever so slowly to look down upon her.

Like many others, Warrick leaned around to see who had been so rude. A plump and pasty-faced young woman, with a self-satisfied smirk upon her face, sat slumped with her arms tightly crossed in front of her. Unabashed by her exposed layers of rolling flesh, she merely leaned back as the shaman approached. She did not even attempt to cover her protruding stomach as her clothes rode further up her body.

Getting a better look at her, Warrick thought she had rather a pale and waxy complexion, with various facial studs and piercings through her lower lip, right eyebrow and nose. She tucked her unkempt and mousy-brown hair behind her ears before pulling up her sleeves. Beside her, originally next in line to be addressed by the shaman, a more timid, younger woman buried her head in her hands.

The shaman turned to the plump woman. 'You wish to say something, my dear?'

The plump woman crossed her arms, tutting pointedly. Beside her, the same timid woman looked up at the shaman for help.

'Is she a friend of yours?' asked the shaman, turning to the timid woman.

'Erm, hello...? Did you just presume my pronoun?' interrupted the plump woman.

The shaman, taken aback, took a moment before replying.

'Your self-proclaimed what?'

'Duh, it's called a pronoun. And you just presumed mine.'
A few people, including Warrick, groaned.

'And your point is?'

A smug grin grew across the woman's face as she looked out to address the room at large. 'Yes,' she began, in a self-approving tone, 'I've been itching for him to get to me. Can you not see how oppressive that is?' She lifted both hands to gesture her disapproval. 'Will these people ever learn?' she said to the ceiling, before turning back to the circle. '— That he would arrogantly assume my identity.' She slowly over-accentuated the revolving of her index fingers to point to herself.

The shaman raised his eyebrows. 'You mean, like you have just done with me?'

She smiled back at the shaman in a way that suggested that she thought she had him on the back foot. 'I just want some respect.'

'No, you just want some appeasement. But, perhaps if you'd politely requested that I address you differently, we may have engaged more amicably.'

'Wow, how defensive are you?' she rallied.

The shaman tilted his head, seeming to find her rather curious, utterly unaffected by her confrontation. 'And yet, you still felt the need to try and humiliate me in front of a room full of people, with the injustice you feel?'

'I knew you'd react like this. This is why I came. I said to my sister that you were some old fraud.' She turned to the younger, timid woman on her left, who had been inadvertently bypassed. 'And voila!... What did I tell you!' She threw up both hands again as a gesture of glaring proof.

The sister looked mortified as she peered up at the shaman. 'I am so sorry, I didn't know she was going to react like this. I... I thought if she saw what you could do, then you might be able to... to help her... or something.' She turned to her angry sister. 'You are embarrassing me! Why couldn't you just listen and keep your opinions to yourself?'

'Help me? *Help me?* replied the sister, indignantly. 'I'm not the one who needs help. From what I can see, he is the one who needs help.' She turned back to the room at large. 'Listen, none of you need any help, you are all as nature intended — quirks n' all!' she shouted.

Around the room, people scoffed and groaned in disapproval.

'Then, why are you here?' cried Joyce from across the room.

Others, too, nodded and jeered in agreement.

The shaman lifted a hand to assert calm.

The woman stood up, wrenching off the mousy-brown wig that she had been wearing, exposing a brilliant head of bright blue hair. 'Thought I'd save you the bother of commanding me,' she spat at the shaman.

One of the bouncers who had been standing by the rear French doors made his way over to stand behind the woman.

'You can call off your dogs — I'm entitled to my say. I paid enough to do so, didn't I?' She placed her hands defiantly upon her hips and glared back at the shaman.

Beside her, her sister closed her eyes with dread.

Here we go again, thought Warrick — did these people never learn? Here was another person who did not seem to have witnessed any of the incredible things that had happened over the last few hours. She was too busy preparing for her turn to make a mockery of the shaman and his system of belief. This was clearly the only reason she had turned up. It would be fairer to say that she had purposely ignored all that had gone on before her, so she could vent her building wrath of blame and accusation, quick to point out how she had been victimised.

Warrick mentally shook his head. Here was another one with a giant chip on their shoulder.

'Tell me,' began the shaman, 'what problem are you trying to resolve?'

'Me? Problem? Resolve? Oh, I see what you are doing. Well... it won't work on me! Save it for all these other suckers.' She nodded her head knowingly. 'What a racket this is!'

'For God's sake, Kate, why are you doing this? hissed the younger sister through gritted teeth.

'To show you that there is no... no spiritual journey. It's all just theatre. Just some money-making scheme. Flesh and blood, that's all you need to worry about. I don't care what was discussed earlier; anything to do with the spirit is just horse shit, and I cannot sit here and listen to any more of it.' She paused, crouching down to her sister and grabbing both her hands. 'I am only doing this to protect you.' But when her sister looked dubious, the angry woman stood back up to continue. 'There was even some professor somewhere in Israel who recently said that with modern electronics, they could prove there was no such thing as a spirit or a soul. He said that this lingering concept of a God and this soul ideology was now over.' She gave a small burst of laughter, enjoying the adverse effect she was creating. 'And by putting a microchip inside a person's brain and hooking them up to the web — The Internet of Things or Internet of Bodies, I think he said it was called — they can now control a person's thoughts, feelings and actions. So, there is no need for a god, as this Internet of Bodies or Things is now the closest a person can get to a real one. So, you know, perhaps we really need to just "follow the science" like they keep telling us...'

The sister groaned. 'But science has nothing to do with the spirit! One deals in the physical and the other in the ethereal realms.' She looked up at the shaman beseechingly.

Outside, rain had started to hammer against the windows again, its intensity greatly enhanced by the building wind.

The shaman, however, was still standing where he was, but appeared distracted. Then Warrick thought he knew why that was; vague images had now begun to emerge about Kate.

Kate waved a dismissive hand before her. 'And you can stop all that, glassy-eyed, nonsense.'

'I see... I see...' said the shaman, although seeming to address his observations rather than Kate's comment.

'Look,' said Kate, 'I've kinda said my piece, so you know...'

Peace or piece? thought Warrick. Either way, was that her idea of peace?

'Besides,' Kate carried on, 'I think you've over-cooked this now — don't you?' Wagging an authoritative finger in the air when the shaman did not answer, she continued. 'Yeah, well, you can skip the "big brother talk" and trying to convince me otherwise about religious matters. Or were you going to give me the "but I'm spiritual but not religious" spiel instead?'

But when the shaman continued to ignore her, Kate turned back to the circle at large. 'Hell, perhaps this movement is designed to undermine the church, to spread disinformation with these spiritual conspiracy theories as he sees fit. Did you ever think of that? Or maybe you don't, because you are all too far gone to see. Oh, the irony of it...' she guffawed loudly. 'I am starting to think that this Economic Forum ideology that most people are just "useless eaters" is probably right after all! Viva woke, and the awakening to the real truth!'

'Then leave, if you don't like it!' bellowed a man from across the circle.

'So why are you here?' demanded another voice, which was echoed by various others, just as frustrated.

'Yeah!' jeered another.

And Warrick understood this building protectiveness. And as the catcalls began to escalate, Warrick looked back at the shaman to see how he would react. But for some reason, he appeared to be letting the resentment build. It seemed most unlike him to allow such tensions to heighten, but then again, he seemed to have a reason for everything.

Reaching fever pitch, the shaman finally scanned about the circle with an acknowledging nod, before raising his hands for calm.

'Is this the reaction you wanted to create?' asked the shaman, turning about the room with his arms open.

Kate smirked.

Then, seeming to find what he was looking for, the shaman refocused his attention on Kate. 'Let's first address a few of your more colourful comments. We are not interested in anti-religious movements, antidisestablishmentarianism sympathies, suspected reptilian oligarchs or the various other conspiracy theories — whether true or false, fact or fiction — that are banded about the world in reckless gay abandon — case in point: The Protocols of the Elders of Zion — the apparent desire for Jewish globalisation. And I would not think twice about letting my reiterations misguide you into anything untoward. I only want to share my wisdom, so that one does not get lost in the embroilment with earthly pursuits that do nothing to free man from such distractions. I understand the curiosity factor, but let's leave it to those who have nothing better to do.'

Kate raised her hands to her waist with the air of a stroppy teenager. She appeared to leer up at him in some lazy rolling stance.

'But this is your own made-up ideology, isn't it? Based on what — some lame epiphany?'

'Perhaps, if you had done some research or read my early books on empirical evidence, you would know the answer to that.'

'Aren't shamans supposed to "conveniently" have some invisible spiritual guide on hand, to nip back and forth from the various spirit realms to give them secret inside info at the drop of a hat? Or are you going to pop off to the spirit world while we wait for your return?'

The shaman gave a cursory look about the circle, as if wanting to make sure his ardent listeners were all as amused as he was, at this constant attempt to undermine the evening.

The shaman nodded ponderously. 'Let's not speculate on whether I converse with spirit guides, advanced ethereal entities or even Starseeds and the like, to bring forth the wisdom of the ages. My path is my own, but we journey together, where love and divinity will be our chaperone.' The shaman closed his eyes, becoming still at these words.

Bringing his hands together in prayer, he lowered his head reverently.

Warrick fidgeted. Unaware he was whispering loud enough to himself to be heard, Warrick repeated the word Starseed in such a questioning manner that the man to his left leant towards him, lowering his voice.

'They are the divine ones that walk amongst us.' He then nodded as if this was generally understood. But with Warrick's look of confusion, the man continued, placing both hands over his heart.

'These are normally spirits of such purity, of such divine power that they can inhabit a human form at will. However, some may have been temporarily tainted by the ills of man. They are sprinkled around the Earth, guiding and enlightening all that they meet. Although some are dormant and have forgotten who they truly are, why they are here and where they came from. Yet their psychic abilities remain intact, lying hidden, just below the surface. However, on the whole, they are special intellectual beings who do not always reveal their true selves. Such people always leave a mark on you, whether you choose to stay connected — spiritually, I mean — or not.'

Warrick nodded sagely. 'So how do you know if you are... are a dormant Starseed?'

The man returned Warrick a warm smile, placing a tentative hand on his arm. 'You feel that you do not belong, have never really fit in, or have ever wanted to. It's as if everyone else around you is in some deep-seated social agreement — conditioning, some might say — that you were never party to.' He gave a final nod, as if that clarified the matter, before leaning back to face the shaman.

Warrick's eyes glazed over; this was now bordering on the fanatical. Had he been wandering around in such a blinkered state that this side of life had never even occurred to him? Or was it that he had been so thoroughly sheltered from this otherworldly spiritual side of life by the determined conservatism of the middle classes that it had never even been acknowledged as an acceptable existence? Or, in reality, was this just some hyperbole of delusional desire by the feebleminded in some vain and desperate attempt at an alternative reality? If so, welcome to the ethereal world of the fluffy-minded. Otherwise, if any of this was true, then just how much had been held back from the society at large, and was it now too late to re-educate them?

Kate was now rolling back her sleeves. 'So, what is your secret, then? Are you a mind-reader?' she scoffed. 'I need cast-iron proof, you see.' She smacked the back of her right hand into her left. 'And can you provide it?' she asked in exaggerated disbelief.

'About your past, I should say so,' replied the shaman. 'Not a pretty sight, but...' He inclined his head ever so slightly.

Warrick grinned to himself, before catching someone else's eye across the circle, both now thinking the same thing — that she was about to get her well-deserved comeuppance.

Kate shook her head at the ceiling, in an over-acted effort to show her disbelief.

'Please, Kate!' hissed the sister.

Finding her words, Kate went on. 'Okay, for argument's sake, I'll play your little game, but if I find out that you have just been digging around in my past like some Mickey-Mouse fortune-teller, then I will go to every press outlet and have you exposed for the fraud that I know that you are!' She pointed aggressively at him.

There was another pause, as the shaman did not respond straight away. He just held his position, watching her as if she were some animated curio.

'So be it,' said the shaman.

And Warrick was sure he detected some slight flicker of innate pleasure as it flittered across the shaman's face, whilst he turned momentarily to gain agreement with the watching crowd.

'Let's see now,' he began. 'Like many on a similar quest, you have a strong desire to correct the wrongs of others — even at any past point in history, seeking justice at every turn — seeing it as a worthy pursuit, at any cost, despite any repercussions, and curiously, even fighting for causes that are not your own.'

Kate shrugged to indicate that she was not impressed.

'For example, protesting fully naked with your breasts painted in the rainbow colours of the LGBTQ+ community at a rally down in Brighton.'

At this comment, Warrick, as well as a few others, leaned further forward to see if this image or at least a ghostly imitation of it, was now being paraded before her.

The smugness on Kate's face vanished, and she turned accusingly to her sister. But her sister merely shook her head defensively.

'Who is Jamie, may I ask?' probed the shaman.

'That's private!' snapped Kate.

'Not — to — me...' replied the shaman slowly.

Kate began shifting uncomfortably, visibly gritting her teeth.

The shaman continued. 'Well, if she is as brazen as you are, and it seems that she is...' he swiped at the invisible images that only he and a few others could see, 'then the burn marks that you both endured on your bodies, after gluing yourselves to those fuel tankers — during one of your many protests — may take some time to heal. Perhaps you should rub some more Aloe Vera on her when you get back home tonight.'

Kate's eyes slowly closed. Unmoving, she continued to grind her teeth together.

Warrick smirked to himself; she only had herself to blame.

'Bastard!' she hissed in a dangerous tone, as she looked back at the shaman. Then her eyes flickered briefly towards her sister.

'She already knows,' said the shaman, offhand, '— she has for a while. And the good thing is, she does not care, and she does not judge.' Kate, however, remained motionless.

'Well, I think that is proof enough for the time being,' said the shaman rather jovially. 'Now, let's — if you are still happy to cooperate — address this rather conflicting business of there being no such thing as a spirit.'

A shiver ran up Warrick's spine as he hoped the shaman would do something else out of the ordinary. But as Kate continued to stare ahead, determined, it seemed, not to show her emotions, Warrick wondered if she would try to throw a spanner in the works.

Then, to Warrick's surprise, Kate stepped back out of the circle and began to pace back and forth. Behind her, the ever-weary bouncer unfolded his large arms.

Warrick could feel the tension amongst everyone present. Here was another angry activist-type, blaming the world for all its wrongdoings, lashing out at anyone with an opinion that even remotely contradicted their own. And why was it that all those who frequented the lower echelons of the ascension pyramid never twigged that these were the negative attributes that they freely dramatised? It must, therefore, stand to reason that the lower you fell, the lower your awareness of such contradictory survival actions you enacted…

As Kate paced, she began having a silent dialogue with herself. She appeared to be asking herself questions, pausing to consider her answers before continuing to pace. Unnaturally patient, the shaman watched on, his arms resting upon his lower back.

After this seemed to go on for longer than necessary, her sister interjected. 'Kate… Kate, if you don't want to do it then… then just come and sit down.' Kate, however, ignored her. 'Kate… for God's sake, everyone's watching!'

'Then let them watch!' Kate spat.

The sister looked back at the shaman for guidance. But the shaman only had eyes for Kate.

After another minute of pacing, Kate finally stopped and stepped purposefully back into the circle.

'Ladies and gentlemen...' began the shaman. But once again,

Kate interrupted, tutting loudly and exaggeratedly wincing to accentuate her perceived grievance. But the shaman ignored her. 'Ladies and gentlemen,' he repeated, 'before we begin this next consignment of instructions, I would like to —'

'Wait, wait, wait!' said Kate, interrupting with both her hands raised. 'You can't just move ahead without my agreement. Your continued assumption that I am now in agreement with you is just astounding. I have not agreed to anything yet. Have you not considered that I might be damaged by whatever you are attempting to do? We might all be offended by your... your bombastic demonstrations, and my sister might actually be secretly upset by what's going on here, but is too scared to say anything? Have you given this any thought at all? No, probably not...' she added sardonically.

'But I'm not!' interjected the sister, looking from the shaman to her sister.

Kate waved her sister down.

The shaman steepled his hands together, tapping them briefly against his bottom lip. 'You use the word "all" as if you speak for everyone, when you do not. Is that not also an assumption?' Kate's head bobbed slightly as she considered this rebuttal. 'I would imagine that it is all a matter of perspective, Kate.

What upsets you may not upset your sister, and what upsets her may not upset you. But you will find that nothing actually happens to you if you feel offended, other than the fact that you decide to what degree that you want to be offended. You can choose to be selfish and dramatise everything like a spoilt teenager, or acknowledge the fact that someone else has the right to disagree with you and be able to voice their, albeit contradictory, opinion. Fair, is it not?'

Kate's dramatic eye roll was now indicative of her current rigid mindset.

'Look,' she said, with barely hidden exasperation, 'it is you who seems to have some problem with the human body — going to such lengths to dismiss it.'

The shaman shook his head. 'Nothing wrong with having a physical, biological, carbon-based engine to run around in. It helps you to enter the game of life down here on Earth. And whether it runs its natural life cycle or is extended with Med-Bed technology is for the user to decide. The things they can do now with advanced healing technologies at a subatomic level are astounding. I advise that you check it out, if you wish to prolong your body's longevity, that is.'

Kate narrowed her eyes.

The shaman laughed, although more to himself. 'An interesting state, is it not, that if you wish to travel some distance, you then have to situate your physical body — your organic engine — inside a mechanical engine, such as a car. And suppose you wish to travel even greater distances. In that case, this mechanical engine may even be further placed inside an even bigger mechanical engine, such as a cargo train or an aeroplane. One "machine" operating independently inside another. Analogous, to some degree, perhaps, to the soul being situated within the body.

Quite amusing... ad infinitum...'

In condescending defiance, Kate folded her arms. Resentment was now twisting at her features. 'If you say so. So, are you only going to help "those" you think are worthy of ascension?'

Warrick stared at her in disbelief. After all that had gone on in the room that night, where had she been? On a silent protest — refusing to acknowledge anything that was happening? She really did seem like a disillusioned and lost soul, unknowingly grazing at the bottom section of the ascension pyramid. Not only did she act like some online troll, but now that Warrick thought about it, she even looked like one.

Then he caught himself; it was an unnecessary critical thought. He could justify it all he liked, but he doubted he would hear the shaman say something like that. Perhaps this was one of those small moments where he could start applying what he'd been taught.

'The Divinities are for all,' the shaman went on, 'and not, as some might postulate, excluded from either the vulgar or the gentry — they are for all levels of society. They are even for the middle classes, who are the hardest to enlighten from their comfort zones. The ascension to a better life, to a truer life, is for all to travel, at their own behest.'

Kate puffed audibly. She looked from her sister to various onlookers around the circle. 'Okay,' she said finally, shaking her head despite herself, 'what have I got to lose?'

'Then let's see.' The shaman took a step back, twiddling his thumbs, thinking something over, occasionally looking back at Kate's aura. Finally, he seemed content with something and turned to face her. 'Now, I am going to give you a series of instructions. I do not want you to query them or think about their implications. I simply want you to carry out the actions the instant the orders are given. Don't worry if you cannot comply the first few times. Is this understood?'

When Kate opened her mouth to comment, the shaman leant forward with a look that reaffirmed his unreserved compliance. Despite some inner conflict, as she bit her lip ring, she nodded.

Warrick was convinced that she was now regretting her decision, just in case she was proved wrong.

Once again, the room held its collective breath.

The shaman crossed one outstretched hand over the other, before indicating that she should do the same. Stepping towards her, the shaman linked his hands with hers, so that they created the figure of eight.

The woman to Warrick's right took in a sharp breath, 'The infinity loop,' she said to herself.

'Now,' began the shaman, in his deep, authoritative voice, 'we begin.' He took in a few, long, deep breaths. 'I want you to command that your body remains still, whilst you, as a spirit, back out of your body.' Kate's eyes widened. 'Just let go of the body and slowly slide backwards.'

'You want me to do what?'

'Remember what we agreed?' Confused, Kate nodded.

From her facial expressions, it looked to Warrick as if she was constipated. After a moment of internal straining, she stopped.

'Did you do it?' asked the shaman.

'No! How can I, if I am a body?'

'Again!' he boomed, 'I want you to command that your body remains still, whilst you, as a spirit, back out of your body.'

Kate began squirming where she stood. Once more, she seemed to be straining with much effort. After a moment, she stopped.

'Did you do it?' asked the shaman.

'Not sure,' she said slowly, now smiling to herself as if she had one over on the shaman.

'Kate...' said the shaman sternly.

Realising that arguing was futile, she gave in with a frustrated sigh. 'Okay, okay... just give me a second.' She shook her shoulders. 'Now, Kate, listen to the precision of the instruction. I want you to command that your body remains still, whilst you, as a spirit, back out of your body.'

Warrick watched on in rigid fascination, also aware that he, too, was attempting this, although at a subconscious level.

'Did you do it?' asked the shaman.

'I... well... no... of course not!' she replied smugly.

'Understood. Now, for the next instruction: I want you to command that your body remains still, whilst you, as a spirit, move from side to side inside your head.'

For a moment, Kate became boss-eyed before rocking from side to side.

'Kate, I want you to command that your body remains still, whilst you, as a spirit, move from side to side inside your head.' Again, Kate began to rock from side to side.

'I feel dizzy,' she said, now closing her eyes.

'Understood. Next instruction: I want you to command that your body remains still, whilst you, as a spirit, move back and forth inside your head.'

Kate slowed to a stop before slowly beginning to rock back and forth.

Opposite Warrick, on the other side of the circle, he caught at least two different people also swaying where they sat, similarly attempting the shamanic instruction.

'I feel weird,' said Kate after a moment.

'Understood. Once again, I want you to command that your body remains still, whilst you, as a spirit, move back and forth inside your head.'

Kate appeared to be doing as she was told.

'Thank you, Kate. Now, here comes a variation; I want you to command that your body remains still, whilst you, as a spirit, move both back and forth and side-to-side inside your head.'

Kate paused, thinking this over, before appearing to gently move in various directions.

'Again,' said the shaman, his attention highly focused, 'I want you to command that your body remains still, whilst you, as a spirit, move both back and forth and side-to-side inside your head.'

As far as Warrick was concerned, it was as if the shaman was trying determinedly to dislodge an iron bar from a concrete slab.

Abruptly, Kate's body stopped moving.

'How long do you want me to do this? said Kate. 'I mean, I can do it, but I must look pretty stupid.'

'Understood,' repeated the shaman. 'Are you doing it?'
'Well... my body is,' she said.

'Are you sure?'

Still unmoving, Kate opened her eyes.

'What the...? But... I am still moving... I don't understand...'
'What exactly is moving?' asked the shaman.

'My... no... hang on a minute.' She looked down at her arms, still locked in place with the shaman, and then at the room around her. 'What have you done to me?' The shaman did not answer. 'I feel different, like I have been melted out from a block of ice or something. It's soooo weird. I'm not sure I like it. I prefer things to stay as they are... Put me back!'

The shaman looked around at Kate's aura, seeming to decide on something. 'Understood,' he said again. 'Okay, let's try this again; I want you to command that your body remains still, whilst you, as a spirit, back out of your body.'

The effect was instantaneous. Both shock and awe lit up Kate's face in equal measure. And around the room, there seemed to be a perceptible, collective withdrawal of breath.

Warrick blinked — how was this even possible? Unnecessarily, he leaned forward and squinted. And, as the reality hit him, Warrick's jaw dropped as he witnessed the slightest ghosting of Kate as she backed slowly out of her head, only to float but a few feet behind her body. It was the most mind-boggling thing he had ever seen. So here it was, undeniable proof that there really was a spirit, the individual themselves, residing within a human body.

Warrick ran a self-check of the unprecedented event before him; so, the spirit itself, slightly spherical in appearance, had slowly slid out from behind Kate's head, surrounded by a kind of ghostly, corporeal facsimile that appeared to approximate her actual body. He shook his head; this must be what people really ought to refer to as one's spiritual body, as opposed to some resurrected duplicate.

As Kate's spirit form opened her mouth, her actual body followed suit, clearly as synchronised as a puppet with its puppeteer. 'I... I feel like myself,' Kate began, looking around the room as if she had only just arrived. 'It's weird... I mean, I actually feel like myself for the first time in... in... oh I don't know... it feels like forever.' She breathed a great sigh of relief. 'But... if I feel like myself now, who have I been pretending to be all this time whilst... whilst inside my... my...?' She looked back at her body, with more intrigue than concern.

'And the funny thing is, I've been trying to find myself for so long... and yet... I was just buried inside all along...' she smiled to herself. 'It's strange,' she went on, 'it's like I have been wearing various overcoats of "different mes" all this time. Like…like carrying other people's personality over my own…'

The shaman nodded sagely.

Multiple questions began to emerge inside Warrick's own head: How could this be? Why was this so? Was everyone like this? Was this by design? Or was it some cosmic design fault — a flaw in the human psyche? Or… or… His mind seized up. An incomprehensible phenomenon had just burst into being before his very eyes.

As Warrick stared about the circle, looking to share in this once-in-a-lifetime rarity, it was clear that only a very few had also witnessed the complete clarity of this bewildering occurrence. So why him — why Warrick? He never could before — could he? Had the shaman awakened some innate ability that he never knew existed?

Unable to stop them, tears trickled down Kate's physical face as she smiled, despite herself. For she had now glimpsed the truth of who she really was. She could deny it no longer. Here was a subject that she could now never dismiss nor refute. The mental burdens that had hardened her features and weighed heavily upon her frame seemed to have lifted. A brighter and softer person now peered out from beneath a rapidly clearing persona. And incredulously, she even appeared to look younger. Here was the real Kate, here was the sweet, untarnished and unburdened Kate. No mental baggage to distort her face and feelings, no blinkered and fixated views of the world and no hate with which to lash out at her distorted perception of life's great canvas.

And like many others around the circle, Warrick, too, continued to look on astounded.

'Truth beyond doubt,' began the shaman, turning to the room at large. 'Either it is or it is not.'

~ CHAPTER EIGHTEEN ~

The Spectral Realm

Kate, unaccustomed to floating unaided outside of her body, was gently ushered back to her seated position. As far as Warrick could tell, she remained in a state of giddy euphoria for some time, slowly getting used to her heightened existence. She had sat back down, carrying a similar vacant look of some bemused inebriate. The shaman had pointed out, alas, that the bulk of her new condition was not permanent. He explained that as she slowly slid back into her body, some of the existing ailments and mental issues would creep back in to vex her. He'd gone on to say that, for a more permanent state of being, a far more comprehensive application of his techniques needed to be employed. But for now, he had done what he had done to create an everlasting impression upon her. And Warrick was in no doubt that this would have done the trick.

The weather outside continued to lash against the windows, occasionally pulling Warrick's attention back from the night's event — a true feat, considering the phantasmagorical happenings that had presented themselves.

The shaman, as always, pressed on to address the people around the circle, Kate's sister being one of them. For these excited souls, the shaman had conversed rather jovially, answering more questions about the universe than Warrick thought necessary for this particular evening. But he seemed happy to do so. His grip on a multitude of subjects was astounding, leaving Warrick to wonder where on earth he had found the time to study so much.

Yet it was the shaman's distinct distraction at something unseen, connected to one black woman, that seemed to change the shaman's mood instantly.

It was not fear that rooted him, but tangible wariness. Suddenly, his eyes were darting about the room looking for something that Warrick could not see. He moved about the circle as if searching out some trespassing shadow. He squinted and crouched, whilst his eyes were alert with caution.

The action was so unlike him that a ripple of uncertainty began to build, as people tried to follow his haphazard attention.

'The mirrors!' he announced, as if in accusation. 'Cover the mirrors if you will.'

He pointed to four different locations, where staff instantly obeyed. As before, they shuffled out of the rear room, making their way behind the jostling circle. Black cloths were then thrown over gilded mirrors and those embedded into the elaborate upper sections of the surrounding wood panelling.

'Distractions!' said the shaman to the room at large. 'Pick your battles — know when to fight and when to ignore. In the world of shade, that most cannot see, entities roam. Sometimes they are just lost and forlorn, whereas others are deliberate in their ambulation.'

Warrick chuckled to himself; the shaman was as cryptic as ever. It appeared that they had now moved on, into the ever-ambiguous and spectral realms of the unseen — the world of ghosts and phantoms, apparitions and wraiths.

Warrick thought about past stories that people would share, where they had seen ghosts moving about old buildings and along draughty corridors or even floating over the cots of the newly born — a frightful thought for any new parent.

That said, Warrick did have his own story, wherein he had witnessed a maid walking through a kitchen one morning as he sat at a friend's breakfast table. The friend had had her back to him as he drank his tea, before a thin and nearly transparent spirit of a young serving woman had wandered out from the middle of a wall, only to make its way around the table with a tray, until disappearing into the larder. Upon telling his friend, she simply laughed and said that she had seen the maid dozens of times; her spirit, or memory of her, was stuck in some perpetual routine and had probably been doing so for hundreds of years. She'd also added that it was not a real wall, but rather a bricked-up rear servants' staircase, dating back to when the converted house used to be fully staffed. The vivid memory had never left him.

'Is there something in here with us?' asked the woman to Warrick's right. She scanned about the room, clearly seeing nothing.

'That, my dear, is the question,' replied the shaman. 'Is it a something or a someone that appears to be watching us from beyond the veil?'

The shaman paused, looking about the room, causing everyone else to follow suit.

'So, what of this land between worlds,' said the shaman, more as a statement rather than as a question, 'where some argue its existence is more of a mental or emotional concept rather than that of a factual reality.'

Warrick inwardly groaned.

'But, yes,' he went on, 'there is one here that has been watching us in utmost fascination. There were others, initially attracted by the mirrors perhaps, but — for now at least — there is just the one.'

People were now looking this way and that, eager to see any ghostly form. Now and then, someone would point out a wavering shadow, only to be disappointed that it was just that.

'I... I have a question — if you don't mind,' asked an elderly Jewish woman, her hand rising into the air. The shaman turned to face her. With a friendly face, the rather squat woman, with cropped ringlets of grey and white hair, adjusted her seated position. 'Listen darling,' she continued, pushing her large glasses securely against her nose, 'this subject of ghosts confuses me, and I don't want to lose track of what you're saying. I take it that Kate finally moved out of her body, which is nice, but how is that different from a ghost?' The shaman considered this before inclining his head slightly. But the woman continued before he could answer. 'And how can a person really define these areas with no real proof of their existence? I mean, not being rude or anything, but I cannot actually see what's going on at this level, and religious texts and ancient scrolls that I have read are also no real proof of anything actually connected to this spiritual phenomenon. Or anything godly come to that... some are just a bunch of words written down by some old monks and such like, many moons ago.' She nodded and gestured to those nearest to her as if for confirmation. 'And,' she raised her hand again to indicate some addition to her questioning, 'some of these mediums and psychics can be a bit hit and miss — if you know what I mean.' She gave a little chuckle. 'So... no one really has any scientific proof — do they?'

When the shaman did not answer immediately, she added. 'Or... or do they?'

'Well, a few things do come to mind,' said the shaman. 'There have been various scientific studies completed over the years — one or two in particular. One was around 1906 in Massachusetts, and another, many years later, in New York — both in the United States. However, this has also been verified in other countries, such as here in the UK, where they claimed to have measured the human soul as it left its mortal shell. Microscopic measurement, it was claimed, indicated the event happening at the moment of death. I believe that one such measurement was 21 grams, no less — a most fascinating study. However, I personally believe that it was not the soul or spirit that they were weighing, but that of his mental masses, instead, a kind of condensed electrical energy.

'An understandable error, but a mistake nonetheless, for the soul and the mind are not the same thing; they are completely separate entities, despite their interconnected association. It is this "mind", this generally intangible network of concise memories, that carries the varying weight of mental burden, and not the soul itself. Extricating one from the other has been one of my most ardent activities.'

'But don't we carry our memories in our cells?' asked the woman.

'No,' said the shaman, there are nowhere near enough cells in the body to store the ever-growing expansion of spiritual lifetimes and their unfathomable 3D memories. Remember, you are not your body.

'Your body has its own separate cellular memory, which only facilitates its genetic evolution. Otherwise, at a protoplasmic level, you would also remember your parents' memories as well — and can you? No, you cannot.'

Once again, Warrick wanted to put the shaman on hold. That last bit alone was an interesting point. But what was he now saying? Thinking back to the Divinities, and of its composite parts of: Mind, Body, Soul and Space, the shaman was saying that he was actually freeing the soul from any burdening of a troubled mind, thus lessening or removing the mental "mass" that was weighing too heavily upon the soul. This, in turn, could be seen to press itself upon the human body in its various guises.

This made sense to Warrick, as there were people he had met in their early twenties who looked as if they were carrying all of the woes of the world on their shoulders. It was all starting to make more sense now.

'But remember,' continued the shaman, now addressing the circle, 'knowledge is power. And clarity is the key here. The road of the humanities, as well as the various philosophies and other ologies, can only help your search, so long as you do not travel the path too wide and in too many directions. Do not mix different belief systems, or you run the risk of one system conflicting or undoing the work of another. So, choose your path and stay focused and true.

'As I have already stated, there is more than one way off this mortal coil. There are even those who speak of a spiritual technology that can accelerate the way out — a laser-precise way to pinpoint those chains that hold one back. And if you wish to choose this different path over my own, then you are free to do so. I harbour no prejudice.'

Warrick's ears pricked up a little further. So, there were others who had also managed to find a way out of this life-and-death continuum. Just how did they even know that there was something to get out of? Also, that suggests they had a way to rid a person of their mental demons — this was good to know.

'Choose your route to freedom,' continued the shaman, 'never wavering and never looking back. And that goes for good, solid, trustworthy friends, too. Ideally, choose those clever and inspiring types that one can learn from.'

The shaman nodded to the Jewish woman, and she nodded back. Then, turning to the rest of the circle, the shaman continued.

'And let it be said, that ignorance is no defence. Was it not the good German priest, Bonhoeffer — Dietrich Bonhoeffer — who stated that *stupid people were often more of a threat to the world than evil people, that stupid people could not reason and were therefore a greater liability to that degree?'* The shaman laughed. 'And I think that even Aristotle observed that: *"A fool contributes nothing worth hearing and takes offence at everything."'* The shaman nodded at those nearest to him. 'And we certainly know that they exist in the world, as some are particularly vocal at this point in time.' A few people laughed. 'Think now: have you ever tried to point out their wrongdoings or the immoralities of theirs or others' actions, only for it to fall on deaf ears? Another good lesson here, for they can easily fall into the mindset of the mob by blindly following the masses or any "self-appointed" authority. A good test is this: can they self-correct?'

The shaman paused, looking about the circle as if throwing out the rhetorical question.

'Can they, with the aid of newly acquired data, alter their direction or their thinking? If not, then let them be, for they are on their own blind path to a limited existence. Just take a snapshot of their position upon the ascension pyramid, and this will give some insight into their plight. And some, you will even notice, will mechanically exhibit all the social responses akin to one of Pavlov's dogs —' the shaman interrupted himself, '— forgive me. Pavlov was a Russian psychologist who conducted social experiments, wherein every time he rang a bell, his dogs would automatically salivate in anticipation of food. And thus, we often see the same thing here. A figurative bell is rung and the stupid, with no or limited analytical capabilities, automatically react, just like any machine with limited computational power.'

A man opposite Warrick was nodding so enthusiastically that both he and the shaman nodded at one another.

Warrick thought back to a few instances down at his local pub. Yep, there were definitely some stupid people down there on a Friday night.

The Shaman turned back to the Jewish woman. 'Here's another point of reference for you — especially for those drawn to more mystical and esoteric teachings. I'm speaking of _The Book of Creation_, also known as the _Sepher Yetzirah._ It's an ancient Jewish text, believed to be from either the 6th or the 13th century, depending on which scholar you ask. It explores how God brought all things into being — a powerful reminder that reliable data is the foundation of sound understanding. But to really grasp its depth, you have to go beyond the surface. You have to explore the language itself.'

He paused again, then added with a knowing look, 'If you want to tie yourself in intellectual knots, then by all means, carry out a deep dive into the Gematria — the 2nd-century system of 32 mystical number-letter codes. But be cautious. It's easy to lose your way chasing meaning down endless blind alleys. In many ancient alphabets, each letter corresponds to a specific numerical value. But why does that matter? Why am I bringing this up?'

Why indeed? thought Warrick wearily, rubbing his temple.

'Because,' the shaman continued, 'some who have studied Gematria with care believe they've uncovered something profound — evidence that God, or some supreme intelligence, has woven an intricate, deliberate design into existence itself. Some even suggest this pattern extends into our DNA.

'They hypothesised that the atomic weights of elements in the periodic table could be matched to the number codes in these ancient texts — and that this alignment led to a direct translation: *"God Eternal Within the Body."* Think about that. If true, it's extraordinary. It suggests that life — down to the molecular level — might be part of an intelligent design. So it begs the question: Is everything around us part of a plan?

'Are we truly, undeniably, children of God? Or — more radically — is this proof that we're living in an artificial, intelligently designed matrix?'

Warrick looked about the circle, to see if others were struggling with this as much as he was. And judging by their dazed expression, some were.

The shaman paused, thought for a moment, then continued walking ponderously around in a circle. 'Just ask the aged philosopher Aristotle, with his *Prime Mover Unmoved postulations,* in which he considered the first cause of all motion in the universe to be created by God or some divine thought.'

The shaman smiled. 'Herein, one begins to see that others, too, have found some hidden correlation with which to hitch our mortal wagons to the stars.'

The shaman turned back to the Jewish woman. She nodded back to him, although somewhat questioningly, as if considering this new information.

'And, for the more scientific amongst you,' the shaman continued, now scanning the rest of the circle, 'has anyone here heard of DARPA?'

Two hands soared into the air, and both men smiled in acknowledgement at one another across the circle.

'Defence Research Projects Agency, or DARPA, is an advanced US military group that studies, as one of its fields of interest, AI — artificial intelligence. I believe it has an advanced avatar programme, in which they have refined a mind transfer technology, meaning, they can relocate "consciousness" (as they consider it) by downloading it into a computer.'

There were a few gasps around the circle, followed by some hushed exchanges.

One of the two men who had put their hand up earlier did so again. 'And not just a desktop PC either,' he said, knowingly. 'I heard they have been putting them into human clones and stuff too, and that they have been working on these "living skin" over computer-driven mechanical exoskeletons for donkey's years, using advanced gyroscopic electronics to stabilise a human-like form for creating future super-soldiers. I think that it may have been British Aerospace, in liaison with British Intelligence, that were doing that back in the day.'

'Yes!' agreed the other man, who now also had his hand up. 'That, and these robotoid and cybernetic bodies they have been building — synthetics — basically, synthetic clones: Human 2.0!' He grinned broadly. 'And think what happens when you upload a quantum AI into a body like that. Terminator, here we come...' Both men nodded at one another.

'And,' continued the first man, 'what the general public won't be able to get their heads around is that they have been doing this sort of thing for decades.

'I think the first cloning was done in the thirties or something. The joke about Dolly the sheep being cloned in 1996 was a decoy to prevent the public from thinking that cloning humans was even possible. Or just showing us these clunking modern robots so that we would never suspect that they can now create ones that look and act exactly like us now. Keeping the "normies" in the dark, as usual!'

'Then they need to check out "clonaid.com" on the web, for a reality check!' added the other man. 'It still blows my mind that you can even pay to have your dead pet or child cloned — for real! All they need is some DNA, and they could literally build an army of clones, with enough people's DNA.' Both laughed in agreement.

More whispers skittered about the circle at this, and Warrick was not surprised. Where had he been? Why he had not heard about all this other stuff, he did not know. Was this merely another instance of more censorship, keeping information from the general public on a need-to-know basis only?

The shaman smiled, nodding at both men as if already knowing this insightful information.

'Quite so,' he added. 'And as you have said, there are other rumours, using various hi-spec technologies, to be able to forcibly relocate a soul from one body to another — even if the latter is a laboratory-grown clone of the original. Handy if the original is too ill or damaged to function any more. An interesting concept if you have the money to keep a spare body in a deep freeze or a perpetual sleeping state until required — in full or in part.' The shaman laughed. 'Oh, how some people are so emphatic about living forever in the same shell. But let's not digress...' he added cheerfully.

Personally, despite the shaman offering the Jewish woman scientific and scholarly research to back up the existence of God and the spirit, Warrick thought the woman had probably bitten off more than she could chew in asking the questions in the first place. And Kate, too, come to that

— if she had come back down to earth now — should also have the scientific information that she was so demanding of.

Nevertheless, Warrick's mind continued to buffer the deep complexities of the shaman's current thesis. If Warrick understood correctly, here was another, albeit wordy, relationship between Man and his body, science and the ever-mysterious, deep-rooted connection to God Almighty. Warrick was sure that there must be a more succinct way of conveying this, but still, the shaman probably just wanted to acknowledge that there was yet more proof. However, different from his own, this realm of possibilities existed. It was like sitting in an advanced class for hard-core theologians and atomic physicists, where both science and spirituality had a more complex interplay than was generally first thought.

After some more general murmurings amongst the circle, the shaman gave a sturdy clap to get everyone to refocus. He dismissed another momentary distraction from beyond the circle, before putting his attention back on his ardent followers.

'Do not forget why we are all here. Do not become too focused on a single form of self-improvement, as both the application of action and dedication to studying materials are necessary for a stable path forward. Glibness and arrogance are not your friends.' He waved a warning finger.

'Not wanting to play devil's advocate, but just because something was written many moons ago, does not necessarily mean that it is the actual word of God. As blasphemous as some will naturally take that opinion to be, as it flies in the teeth of the stable pillars of wisdom to which they cling, it should be said that you still have to find your own truth.

'People generally assume that because something is written, it must be true. However, ancient transcripts that have been interpreted and then reinterpreted over and over again, sometimes tend to become both diluted in meaning and wrongly replicated to the point where infuriating contradictions and misunderstandings occur.

'Don't be told what your truth is; go seek it out for yourself. The television, the newspapers and the governments generally tell you what your truth ought to be, but it would be a lazy and foolish man who would simply acquiesce and not question.'

He gave a decisive nod before turning back to the black woman he had recently approached.

'You,' he commanded, in his familiar deep tone, 'stand up!'

The woman lumbered to her feet, straightening out her clothes. Smartly dressed in jeans and a flowery blouse, neatly complemented by a shimmering shawl, she rubbed her hands excitedly. Jewellery sparkled from her clusters of bracelets and rings.

'It's Selene, isn't it? Let me first congratulate you,' began the shaman, with a bow. 'I see that you are a proud mother of three and have created a wonderful family environment.' The woman smiled as the shaman continued to look about her aura. 'Yet, despite this, you are relentlessly burdened by an ongoing secret... that you have shared with only one other. Is this true?'

Selene's smile faltered. 'Yes... yes it is.' Tears instantly filled her eyes, and she closed them in dread.

Beside her, a hand reached up to offer a tissue. A second black woman frowned as if wondering why she had never been party to this secret. Warrick was undecided whether they were friends or sisters.

The woman dabbed at her eyes, careful not to spoil her make-up.

The shaman lowered his voice. 'This entity — it takes the form of a young man, I believe.'

'Yes,' said the woman, sniffing.

'I see. How long has he been bothering you?'

Selene took a calming breath. 'Since I was around fourteen or... or fifteen.'

'And can you see him in the room right now?'

As Selene scanned the room, fresh tears filled her eyes as she nodded.

Heads around the circle began swivelling left and right, as eyes darted around for a glimpse of this mysterious ghost.

The shaman turned back to the circle. 'Entities such as these go by many names and can appear in many forms. Some mythical and some...well, it depends on your background, I suppose.'

Warrick stared about the room, unable to see anything. But, on second thoughts, was there something or some presence in the far top, right-hand corner of the room, looking down upon them all like some malevolent church gargoyle...?

The shaman continued. 'Some entities — or beings — that covertly engage with, or at least try to engage with humans, whether sleeping or resting, tend to abuse their victim without their awareness. They will taunt them or smother them, depending on their intention at the time. The demonic female form is known as a succubus, and the demonic male form is the incubus. But, regardless of their names, or their preferred form, their behaviour is, nevertheless, insidious.'

Selene remained silent, occasionally fanning herself to control her distress. Once or twice, Warrick caught her giving a reassuring smile back down at the woman by her side.

The shaman raised a hand to Selene to indicate that he would be back with her shortly.

'They do not always try to seduce their victim, but may very well just try to intimidate or control them. Spurned lovers, vengeful enemies, or the lost and lonely can be targeted, and be the reasons that they continue to pursue a person, whether the person knows it or not.'

He turned to Selene. 'Is this not so, my dear?'

Selene nodded, pulling her shawl further around her shoulders.

'So, tell me your story,' said the shaman, forming a steeple with his fingers and tapping them against his lips.

Fascinated, Warrick shuffled himself closer to see the woman better, noticing that others around the circle were doing the same.

Selene cleared her throat and took another nervous breath. 'I'll keep it as brief as I can. It started when I was at home. Everyone was asleep upstairs and I'd gone downstairs for a glass of water — or milk — I forget which. And I suddenly felt I was being watched.' Selene reached around to the back of her neck and steadied her voice. 'I remember my body locking up, as this... this strange coldness filled the room — it was as if this entity or being or whatever you want to call it, just arrived in my space. I couldn't see it, but I could feel it floating there. I remember the hairs on the back of my neck and along my arms standing on edge.' She reached out with her hands as if reliving the moment. 'It was a funny sensation, like I knew the person... but there was just something off — you know? I wasn't scared at first, as it was like someone from a distant memory returning to me.' She looked up at the shaman and gave a gentle smile. He, in turn, nodded his understanding.

'Anyway, over the next few years, it returned more and more. It seemed to become increasingly irritated or frustrated each time. And I, in turn, would take it out on my family and friends... but how could I explain myself? No one would believe me. Sometimes I could just feel it watching me, getting closer each time.' Selene rubbed at her arms and cleared her throat. 'At around sixteen or seventeen, that's when it properly started.'

She took a deep breath. 'I remember waking up and seeing it for the first time. It wasn't very clear, more of a mass of twisted anger, really, but I remember not being able to move. I had never been so frightened. I couldn't even cry out — I was physically scared stiff.' Selene's breathing began to labour. 'It was glaring directly at me, with this demonic stare... it seemed so angry... just so angry — like it really, really hated me. I could sense an intense evil directed right at me. I remember tears just flowing down my face, and I wasn't even able to wipe them away.' Selene paused, taking a few deep breaths. She looked back up at the shaman, giving him a glassy-eyed smile. The shaman gently nodded.

After dabbing at her eyes again, Selene apologised to the room before continuing. 'On one occasion, I woke up in my bed with the feeling that it was trying to get inside me. I know... it sounds crazy, right?' She shook her head as if not believing her own memories. 'And no, it wasn't a dream or some teenage fantasy; it was an external sensation, like I was being spiritually touched or caressed. I could even feel it when it finally entered me.' More tears ran down her face. 'Yes, it turned me on, but it was also wrong — so, so wrong. It was a sly and dirty thing.' Selene shook her head, but still seemed lost in the reverie. 'Only by getting up and throwing cold water on my face or making myself food and drink in the kitchen, did the sensation go away — but I think he was always there in the shadows — watching me.' Selene took a steadying breath and smiled down at the woman next to her, who rubbed at her leg supportively.

'Another time — again on my own — I was in the dining room, and wham! It came at me with such force that I was almost jettisoned out of my body. It's hard to explain, but it was like I was being dragged out of my body by it. It took every ounce of strength I had to cling to my body.

'I remember being so cold and feeling myself slipping out — I was so scared that day! Anyway, I got myself to the hallway mirror and I kept repeating my name, address and the time and date, so that I wouldn't forget it. I think that saved me from completely leaving my body at the time. Anyway, the thing hung around for ages that night, and I barely got any sleep. I was so scared that if I went off to sleep, it would be able to drag me out when I was not in control.' Selene gave a large sigh. 'So, as you can see, I was now petrified of it. And I couldn't trust it, as I never knew what it would do next.' She paused, rerunning the memories. Unexpectedly, she gave a small laugh. 'The only other person to see it was my boyfriend at the time. He walked into my bedroom on one occasion, only to see it floating just above me. He could see that I'd been crying and that I looked completely drained. He shouted at it to leave before forcing it out of the house. The entity was just as surprised as I was. My boyfriend did the same thing on two other occasions when we were in bed. Once, he woke up and found it floating over me, trying to intimidate me as usual. And another time, he woke up with a jolt, with it floating over him, just staring with its usual rage and hatred.

And again, my boyfriend just marched it out, shouting at it. Tyrone never seemed to be affected like me — it was odd. He wouldn't talk about it, particularly, just kind of accepted it for what it was. He said he could occasionally see these things but generally took no notice.' Selene sighed. 'God, I miss that man — so strong, so stable...' She grinned at the memory. 'Anyway, for the next few years, while my boyfriend was around, this entity seemed to leave me alone. And I thought it had finally gone forever.' Selene gave a hollow laugh. 'Then one day, just after Tyrone proposed to me, I got the news that he had died under "unusual" circumstances.'

There was a collective gasp around the circle that almost threw Selene off course. 'But I knew... I just knew it was that evil demonic bastard... that it had killed my Tyrone. It was its revenge for him protecting me — I just know it. I have never cried so much in my life... I don't think I'll ever get over losing him...' Selene was now staring into space, lost in the tragic memory.

The shaman remained motionless, allowing Selene to take her time. Around the room, nobody else dared move or make a sound.

Selene's harrowing story riveted everyone.

'The police said it was sabotage,' continued Selene. 'Aha — wasn't that the truth!' She jabbed a finger into the air, pointing, as if to lay the blame at the entity. 'Because nearly every nut and bolt had been loosened on his *motorbike* — *like* that can happen — the bike practically fell to pieces as he rode up that motorway. I've still got the newspaper clippings... he didn't stand a chance.' She continued to stare into space. 'There were no suspects, as everyone loved him. I loved him... I still do. He was my whole world — my saviour, my hero, my everything.'

She turned to look around the circle and pointed a long, painted fingernail into the space.

'And women, listen-up, as this bit's for you: if you find a really good man, one that looks after you and protects you and can hold his own — 'cos that is just as important — then for the love of Jesus, look after him!' Selene crossed herself. 'I see so many of y'all just bitching and complaining and just stamping on your man. Don't do that — you protect his name and never badmouth him! You ignore negative comments from your "besties", for those ain't your friends. Real friends don't do that! And let him be a man — don't take that from him.

'A home ain't a home' without a good man — and I don't care what these kids are told today! If he is loyal and keeps trying to improve himself, then you've got to join him on that journey — listen, you've got to remember you are a *team* — and it'll make you stronger.' She paused, thinking, waving her finger in the air again. 'Listen, you grow together or you grow apart. And let me tell you, when he's gone, he's gone, and you might never meet another like him. So come off your phones when he is with you and be with him — show him that he is more important than whoever is on the other end. Stop with the secrets.' She paused again, shaking her head. 'You know who you are… I see you in the restaurants, giving more importance to some "text" than to him.

'I bet you do that in bed too… It's an invisible wedge… and… and it'll weaken your bond. Don't do it, don't drive him away, 'cos when a good man is gone — proper gone — he ain't never coming back.' Selene smiled despite herself, as she held back more tears. She gave another steadying breath, looking around at the others in the circle. 'Sorry… I just… I just don't want you to lose that one real chance of happiness that I once had…'

Selene stared down at the floor, still pained by the injustice of the loss. After a moment, Selene gathered her thoughts and returned to the memory. 'But the one thing I'll always wonder, is if my Tyrone actually did come back — you know, as a spirit — and got to see his son — that he never got to meet…?'

Despite the ongoing storm outside, the room was, as one, in total abject silence. Here and there, a few women were dabbing at their own eyes. And Warrick was not ashamed to admit that he almost felt the welling of his own tears at this wicked tale of loss and injustice.

What a resilient woman she was!

Selene looked up to the ceiling, raising her arms in the air, as if questioning God for her predicament. 'I can't prove it-any of what I just said — of course I can't. But I know — in here...' She patted over her heart. 'This demonic entity has never been as cruel or threatening since, but he has constantly returned. You know... sometimes I spot him lurking or sulking in corners or watching me when I am on my own. He follows me everywhere. But most of the time I can just feel him.' She gave another great sigh. 'I don't think he will ever leave me — but I must live in hope, mustn't I!'

Selene finished off with a strained smile at the shaman.

'Thank you, Selene,' he replied and inclined his head once more.

'Ladies and gentlemen,' said the shaman, readdressing the room as he turned about the circle, 'mustering up such determination and strength is something we can all learn from.'

Warrick arched his back to stretch it and then changed his seated position. How some of them sat like this for so long was not natural, he decided. His bum was now so numb that he was getting pins and needles down both legs. Getting comfortable, he rested his arms behind him.

As if reading the shaman's mind, one of the rear helpers reappeared with a three-legged stool. Selene took the seat and sat down, facing the shaman. The shaman, in turn, took a step closer and placed his hands behind his back.

'Okay, Selene, now concentrate — tell me where he is.'

Selene took a nervous breath and rubbed her hands together. After a moment, she began to scour the wooden-panelled room for the demonic entity that had plagued her since she was a teenager.

'He's just moved near the fireplace,' she said, pointing. 'And he seems agitated.'

'Uh-huh,' acknowledged the shaman. He turned his head to see for himself.

Everyone in the circle also turned to see if they could spot the entity. One or two indicated to the people nearest to them where they had seen it. Both pleased and surprised, Warrick, too, narrowed his eyes to see this oddly malformed entity bobbing about next to the fire. Like the maid he had seen a few years prior, it was practically translucent. It was not a complete manifestation, as it was predominantly just the top half that was visible. It was a strange projection of its original body form, appearing to be composed of an undulating energy mass. It was like it was made up of an angry cluster of writhing electric eels. And it was now looking back around the room, in stark amazement, clearly never having seen so many people stare back in its direction.

After nodding to a rear staff member, another three-legged stool was brought over to the shaman. He moved it adjacent to Selene and sat down.

'Now, Selene, I would like you to call the entity over so that you can address it directly.'

'You want me to... to what?' she stammered. 'No, I... I can't do that. There must be another way?' she said, placing a hand to her heaving chest.

'If you do not confront him, this will never end. Do you understand me?' Selene shook her head. 'I will be here to guide you.'

Selene froze, words failing her. She began shaking her head, looking down at the woman sitting next to her. The woman, in turn, rested a supportive hand upon Selene's knee.

'Get his attention, Selene,' pressed the shaman, 'and do it now!'

Despite a clear internal struggle, Selene looked over to the fireplace and stared directly at the entity. 'Well?' she began in a nervous tone, 'what are you waiting for? You want to talk, so let's talk.'

There was a pause before the confused and suspicious entity suddenly flew over and stopped abruptly, directly in front of Selene's face, intrigue and mischief emanating from its undulating form.

Affronted, Selene jolted backwards, taking in a sharp breath.

~ CHAPTER NINETEEN ~

Samsara

The shaman scratched at his chin — another conundrum for him to unravel. To Warrick, he was like the ultimate problem solver, with the mind of an engineering fault-finder combined with a master chess player. How on earth was he going to outmanoeuvre this devilish trickster?

'Do you recognise him?' began the shaman.

'Do I... What? What do you mean?' gasped Selene.

'I mean what I said,' replied the shaman.

'No — how can I possibly recognise him?' she retorted.

'I see,' said the shaman.

Turning to the entity, the shaman addressed it as if it had been originally invited into the room.

'Excuse me,' he began, and the entity turned to face him. 'What is it that you want to resolve?'

As the shaman was only ten or so people away from Warrick now, Warrick was close enough to see the entire scene unfold. When the woman to Warrick's right whispered, asking him if he could see what was happening, and Warrick replied that he could, he received a flow of admiration.

The entity surveyed the shaman, undecided if he was a friend or foe.

'Let me help, if I may,' continued the shaman, and he began his usual perusal around the entity's space.

Unprepared for this, the entity drew back defensively, resting against the ceiling.

'It's okay,' reassured the shaman, 'I will help you to resolve this ongoing situation. I will help you with this incomplete communication — if that is what you wish?'

Warrick's eyes kept darting from the shaman to the entity and Selene in tense fascination. A strange thrill was beginning to build within him, and he felt himself itching for the entity to now sit before the shaman. It was now his turn to be scrutinised.

The man to Warrick's left gently nudged him. 'Any idea what's going on?' he murmured. 'I can't see anything. This guy,' he indicated to his left, 'says he can see a black shadow moving about the room, and when it passed him earlier, he could feel a cold draught.'

But before Warrick could answer, the man had leaned back towards the guy to his left and returned to a whispered conversation.

And like a few others, he was now pointing to the ceiling.

Warrick stared up at the entity, wondering what it must be thinking. Was it still as apprehensive and angry as it appeared? And just how many other entities were hanging around, not knowing what to do with themselves once their body had died?

After a while, during which the entity glided back and forth about the room, it finally came to rest before the shaman.

'Thank you,' said the shaman. 'Just hold fast and I will... ah, yes... I see...' he continued, carrying out his usual inspection.

Beside him, Selene shuffled in her seat, watching on with a somewhat blurred understanding.

As with everyone else in the room who had undergone an intense inspection, vague images now appeared about the entity. Warrick was reminded that this was still just a spirit with memories, albeit without the attachment of its body. And this was the case in point here, wherein it proved that memories were stored outside of the body, and that the brain was more likely to be a "bio-electrical switchboard" for the functioning of the body.

It was when the shaman brought forth one particular memory that the entity almost solidified in the air. Utterly surprised that the memory had been unearthed, the entity began to waver. Warrick was wondering if it was about to bolt from the scene. The shaman, however, continued to perform some unusual hand gestures, attempting to force the memory to play, but he seemed unable to do so.

Oddly, Selene looked away, either unable to see this memory byte or subconsciously ashamed at what it would reveal.

Yet, despite whatever he tried, the memory would neither budge nor play. Turning back to Selene, the shaman asked her to refocus her attention on the entity.

'Okay, Selene,' started the shaman, 'this... this is one for the record books.'

Warrick almost wanted to laugh out loud. This one was? This entire evening was like some psychedelic trip into a Mary Poppins chalk painting.

Selene looked at him, confused.

The shaman gave a reassuring nod. 'This may need some extra time, perhaps out of the scope of this evening's limited time frame. However, we shall see. So, let's see what we can do. It will require taking one step at a time. So, open your mind to all possibilities and eventualities, and we may shoehorn this case wide open. Okay?' Selene nodded with uncertainty. 'Firstly, it appears that this entity is harbouring a connection you have had in the past — a relationship maybe.'

Selene baulked at the idea. 'What do you mean: "a relationship?" I have never laid eyes on this evil and twisted thing in my life!' She pointed up at it accusingly.

Indignant, the entity began to bob up and down. In turn, the shaman raised his hands to promote calm between them.

'In the past...' repeated the shaman, ' — another lifetime perhaps — I am not sure how many back. But he has been looking for you for some time. We need to determine what went wrong and then develop an altruistic approach to extraction. In other words, you are to give up your own distant memory — if it is pertinent — for us to review.'

Selene threw her hands up in disbelief. 'What? I mean... what? What does that even mean?'

'It means that, whatever happened between you both in the past, is so highly charged and occluded that any joint memories that you had together have created an impasse so intractable that you are both making it very difficult to unravel the occurrence. For this to work for both of you, to achieve some kind of resolution and move forward, I need you both to allow love and light into your personal space and allow it to permeate your native auras. Please do not fight me or the memory. Truth will prevail, if we allow it.'

Selene shook her head, fresh tears forming in her eyes. 'But I don't remember any past lives — I don't even believe in any.'

The shaman gave her a kind smile. 'As a proposition, what if you were to complete this life, and find that there was no "ethereal white light", no one waiting for you, no heavenly Zion or Garden of Eden that awaited you, or that there was not even a Heaven or a Hell? What if you found yourself floating around — like our visitor here — without a body?'

He gestured towards the floating entity.

Confused and somewhat overwhelmed, Selene shook her head, raising her hands for him to slow down.

'What would you do? Would you hang around in a bored and agitated state for perpetuity? Or would you pick up a new body and start the game of life afresh? Bearing in mind that unless you agree to forget the life you have just departed, you would carry all of your baggage into the next one...' He gave her a gentle smile. 'Most, I would wager, would gladly want to forget — forget the regrets, the losses, the mistakes, the embarrassments, the... well, the list goes on...'

Selene blinked, trying to comprehend what he was saying.

Then she half-laughed and half-spluttered. 'Oh... is that all...?' The shaman smiled again.

'It is just life after death — *samsara*, as it is known in Hinduism. But let's keep it simple for now and not get into things such as your memory being forcibly wiped clean by those outside one's earthly pursuits — these highly complex concepts merely muddy the waters.'

Warrick shook his head, thinking, what?

Selene sniffed, dabbing at her eyes. 'Well, I wouldn't want to remember any past life — this life has been painful enough already.'

'Ahh...' cooed the shaman. 'Could this not be our entry point into some lost truth?'

Selene frowned. 'Hang on... just hang on a second. Let me...' She playfully tapped the sides of her head. 'Let me just get my head around that for a moment. So, you are saying that if I have decided to forget my last life —'

'Or any other for that matter,' interjected the shaman.

'Erm, yeah... then any situation I may have had with this entity could be trapped inside a forgotten lifetime — a forgotten memory?'

'Exactly,' said the shaman, simply.

Selene laughed. 'Whoah... now that... now that's a big ask!'

She looked back at her cousin, and they shared a bemused laugh.

The entity that had been patiently watching was now beginning to move about in a state of fascination. And its transparent form was starting to fade in and out.

'So then,' said the shaman, eagerly, 'are you ready and willing to see where this goes?'

Warrick felt goosebumps appear on his arms. What a ride this was going to be — a deep dive into her past lives!

But Selene suddenly became withdrawn. She pulled the shawl she had around her shoulders tightly about herself.

'You know,' she began, her voice now timid, 'I... I don't think I can. In fact... no... I am not willing to. I... no, I don't want to. It's going to be more than I can take. This life is still raw for me. It would be like pouring salt onto an open wound.' She looked squarely up at the shaman. 'I'm sorry, the answer is... the answer is no.'

The shaman nodded slowly, once again deliberating on his next move.

The entity, however, was not amused. It swelled and vibrated in equal measure. Then, with a burst of absolute rage, its vague, translucent form turned into a swirling black mass before disappearing completely. At the same time, all of the lights extinguished, and the many floor candelabras blew out in a rush of icy air, plunging the room into semi-darkness. Following this, the windows, as earlier, swung violently back open, allowing the storm outside to blast inside the room. Many people jumped in fright, followed by gasps and cries of surprise.

Once again, the staff members ran to secure the windows, battling the wind and rain. But despite being forcibly shut, the atmosphere was tangibly different. Steady streams of candle smoke still drifted into the air. It felt electrically charged now, as if the room had been pressurised. Something was wrong — something was very wrong.

Warrick rubbed at his neck as the temperature in the room began to plummet. A cold chill now swirled about the room, as if trailing an invisible force. The wooden beams overhead began to creak and groan as if straining from an unseen, heavy weight. Warrick got the distinct impression that the room itself was struggling to contain the enraged entity, or perhaps, it was the entity that was struggling to contain its uncontrollable rage. As soon as Warrick began to see his breath before him, he realised just how dangerous the evening had become.

Around the circle, staff rapidly moved about to relight the candles. Another staff member, holding up an elegant peacock feather, began wafting a burning wrap of sage and cedar around the entirety of the circle, which Warrick was informed was called a smudge stick.

Selene instantly burst into tears. 'I'm sorry,' she said to the shaman, 'I can't... I just can't!'

Then, with a thunderous roar, the fireplace flared up, its yellow flames licking out into the room, causing those nearest to throw themselves to one side. The wave of heat that followed caused everyone to turn away or cover their faces.

Selene cowered, her hands reaching up to her neck and chest as she took in anxious breaths.

The shaman stood sharply up, concern appearing upon his face for the first time. He scoured the room, but he too seemed unable to locate where the entity had gone.

Selene reached down to huddle with her cousin, and others, too, began to sidle towards one another. Once more, all eyes were on the shaman. An odd silence seemed to fall over the room as if all the air had been sucked from it.

Everyone was looking about in fearful apprehension, squinting into corners and checking over their shoulders. Something was definitely not right, as the twisted malevolence began to thicken the very air that Warrick was trying to breathe.

'Show yourself!' commanded the shaman. But nothing happened. 'Stand before me and confront me!'

A high-pitched sound began to resonate within the room, which caused everyone, including the shaman, to cover their ears. A moment later, Selene was scooped up onto her feet and thrown across the room as if by some giant invisible hand. She skidded across the parquet flooring until coming to an abrupt stop. Curled up like a rag doll, she remained motionless. Everyone else in the room froze. Even the bouncers stayed where they were, although primed for action.

'Enough!' bellowed the shaman.

But the air in the room remained cold and oppressive.

A Crow to Eat

The shaman tentatively walked towards Selene, remaining vigilant. A second later, Selene was dragged back by some invisible force along the entire length of the circle, before stopping abruptly once more. The people nearest looked terrified, all but one old lady, who crawled forward from her crossed-legged position to reach out to Selene. To pay for her interference, however, the entity reformed into a black human silhouette and hauled the old woman back by her hair. The woman screeched, reaching up to her hair as it was pulled skywards. Others in the circle darted to her aid. After a small struggle, the woman was released, falling back into their arms.

To Warrick's surprise, the woman recomposed herself, tying back her hair and pulling up her sleeves. And after beating off the unnecessary fussing of her colleagues, she readied herself for a second round. This old woman was not going down without a fight.

Nobody seemed to have the faintest idea what to do. People were looking from one to the other, fear, confusion and apprehension etched upon their faces. Although two of the bouncers stepped towards the edge of the circle, they too paused, as if waiting for some sign from the shaman.

But the shaman was nimbly making his way over to the dun dun drummer and his associate, before whispering something that Warrick could not hear. Moments later, the drummer had withdrawn a handheld drum with rows of coloured beads hanging down, and the younger, androgynous-looking musician picked up a long wooden flute, similar to the one that Warrick had seen on the table.

After quietly conversing with the shaman, they began to play.

As the shaman returned to Selene, a haunting melody flowed from the wooden flute, which was further enhanced by gentle rhythmic drumming.

The shaman crouched beside Selene. She remained perfectly still, her eyes firmly closed, but the spirit, floating above them, appeared to bob back and forth in apprehensive agitation.

The shaman stood back up, his mind appearing to race. He then turned rapidly on the spot, one arm extended, his index finger pointing at everyone as he went past. 'Solidify the circle,' he cried, 'link arms or hold hands. Stay connected — unite the circle.'

Everyone followed the command, some even crossing over their left and right arms to do so.

The shaman then began undulating his hand through the air like a theatrical conductor. And those directly in front slowly began to hum. The humming expanded contagiously around the circle, until the whole room was resonating and swaying in unison with a solid rhythmic melody.

Warrick marvelled at the power their combined resonating voices seemed to produce. Could this unified response to the shaman's exhortations finally help neutralise this seemingly demented and violent entity?

The person wafting the burning sage and cedar began a second lap. And at the back of the room, more logs were thrown onto the crackling fire as the flames rose and fell in the chimney's backdraft, while the wind outside picked up once again.

Feeling uneasy, Warrick prepared himself for another onslaught of shamanic chanting, desperately hoping they would keep their dancing to a minimum.

But this time it was only the shaman who danced. Treading lightly around Selene a few times, he began to sing. Slipping into a world of his own, he slowly paced and occasionally jumped about inside the circle. He flung and gestured his arms as if summoning or conjuring up some unseen force. At one point, it seemed like he was chanting around an imaginary fire pit in some hypnotic trance. In harmony with the group, his voice rose and fell from a reasonably high pitch in a nasal quality to a low vibrational resonance.

Warrick watched on in fascination.

After a minute of solo dancing, the shaman crouched low, thrusting his arms into the air, as if channelling more positive energy into the room. Then, from an unseen pocket, he lifted what looked like prayer beads, kissed them, and offered them up to an invisible source.

Once he had stopped singing, he slowly rose again from the floor. Appearing re-energised and almost excited, he looked around the room, perhaps even beyond the circle boundary.

Warrick could not see or feel anything in addition, but he was not sure he really would. His senses were practically teetering at their very limit as it was.

The shaman gestured to both the musicians and the circle to lower the volume to background level. And reapproaching the centre of the room, he addressed the area above the fireplace.

'I can see and feel your anger, your resentment at Selene's denial,' he said directly.

The entity watched on, its incorporeal manifestation reforming into its original, albeit very angry, image.

'Work with me, and I will help you — will help you both,' the shaman continued. 'But you need to let the barriers fall; allow me to access what happened so that I can guide Selene to remember. The memory is buried deep and needs to be coaxed forth. She is scared, so we need to proceed together with tolerance and care.'

Pondering this, the entity visibly calmed, its appearance becoming more solid and relaxed, indicating to those who could see it.

Reaching down to Selene, the shaman cupped her face in his hands, and she opened her eyes.

'How are you, my dear?' he asked.

'Is he gone?' she asked meekly.

'Alas, not yet. It is going to take all three of us to pull this off.' Selene closed her eyes in dread.

'This will not end until you confront this past event. Some things in your past will never be resolved until you look them squarely in the eye and see them for what they are — no matter the momentary pain it causes. For if you resist the truth, the lie will stay with you forevermore. Time is not always the great healer if it contains an untruth. Unshackled shame, pain and regret can follow you for an eternity. Let's cut them loose whilst we have this unique opportunity before us.'

Feeling resigned to the situation, Selene slowly nodded, fresh tears falling down her face.

'Okay, I give in!' she sobbed.

'No!' exclaimed the shaman, 'You are not giving in, but giving up in memory only.'

Helping her to her feet, Selene sat back upon the stool. She wiped again at her eyes before making herself comfortable.

'I am ready,' she said nervously.

As far as Warrick was concerned, she looked anything but ready.

'And so we begin,' said the shaman, sitting down beside her.

The shaman then waved over towards the watching entity, who drifted down once again.

'As hard as this may seem right now, I need you both to relax, to loosen the walls of defence you have constructed about you. Let go of the fight, the blame, the denial and the hate, and be willing to let me protect you whilst you do so.'

Flustered, Selene looked back down at the woman next to her. 'This is my cousin, Desiree,' she said with a smile. And the shaman inclined his head in acknowledgement. Desiree squeezed her cousin's hand in support.

'Good,' said the shaman, 'now close your eyes and begin the process of letting go, letting all your barriers slowly melt away.' Selene did as she was told. 'And you,' said the shaman, turning back to the unsuspecting entity, 'can do the same.'

The shaman proceeded to lift both hands, each reaching out into the vaguely visible memories that had begun to swim before both Selene and the entity.

So now he was performing some kind of hybrid parallel group divinities technique, thought Warrick. He was spiritually addressing both the living and the dead through the same process simultaneously. Who else in the world could carry out such a feat? And this was, once again, more proof that a person carried his mind with him as a separate cluster of memories, in some spiritual containment and not within a group of cell membranes. How many scientists would surely repudiate this alternative concept, as it would completely compromise their limited materialistic beliefs?

As the main lights slowly returned to their dimmed state, Warrick was able to see more clearly what was happening. It appeared as if the shaman was trying to extract the same memory that they both shared.

For the entity, its earlier memory re-emerged rather quickly, but for Selene, only a swirl of grey nothingness kept emerging.

'Selene,' began the shaman, 'using the current image of the entity, try to find any long-since-passed memories, as insignificant as they may seem, and tell me what you see?'

But Selene kept coming up with nothing. Over and over, the shaman tried, using different questioning methods, but nothing seemed to emerge for her.

'Okay, Selene, for now I shall address the entity, and so all you need to do is listen.' Selene nodded. 'Although you may not see or hear the entities memory being played too clearly, the theory is, that I hope it will approximate your memory to such a degree, in terms of sight, sound, frequency and emotional content, that it ought to jar the memory into rising from your occluded past and into the present to be viewed.'

The shaman rubbed at his hands, giving Warrick the impression that he was making this up as he went along. Probably because he had such a thorough grasp of the spiritual realm, it gave him the confidence to recall such a random, deep-seated memory.

The shaman returned his attention to the entity. 'I need you to remain where you are, and allow me to access the memory.'

The entity was expressionless, its ethereal form still floating just above the floor. Taking this as a yes, the shaman proceeded.

Firstly, he indicated to both the musicians and those still humming around the circle to cease. The only sounds now being heard were the crackling of the fireplace and the now muted storm outside. Reaching up to the frozen memory, he attempted to enlarge it before finally managing to unlock it.

For those who could see the faint footage, it was more like looking at a vintage film reel than taking a sneak peek into someone's actual past life.

The entity now appeared as a handsome young man, checking his appearance in a gilded mirror. He was neatening his dark hair and twisting the ends of his thin moustache. He had the air and looks to rival the devilish mystique of Oscar Wilde's character Dorian Gray.

Apprehensively, he checked himself before addressing his Edwardian attire. Cut from expensive cloth, his perfectly tailored morning suit ensured that he was impeccably dressed. He clamped his walking cane beneath one arm and proceeded to lift an engagement ring for review. He took a calming breath and prepared to repeat his well-rehearsed lines.

But a knock at the door caused him to look up, seeing through the mirror. As it opened, he hastened to place the ring back into his pocket. A young maid, dressed in her customary black and white uniform, entered before stopping to curtsey.

'Miss Audrey De Vere, sir,' she said. And stepping aside, she allowed the visitor to walk in.

'Thank you, Rose,' said the man. Then, addressing the visitor, he asked, 'Some refreshments, perhaps? Or maybe some freshly brewed Chinese tea? I'll wager it could have bested the East India Company's finest consignment.'

With perfect poise, the pretty young woman smiled, despite herself. Elegantly styled in a pearly-white ruffled tea-gown, she took another step inside the room. She was the perfect picture of virtue.

And yet, although pleased to be there, something seemed to be troubling her.

'Yes, that would be most generous, thank you, my Lord.' Then she too curtseyed.

'Right away, sir,' concluded the maid, and she walked out, closing the door with a muffled bang.

The man turned his back towards the fire, just as it crackled loudly. Somewhere outside, a dog barked.

As if waking from a slumber, Selene took in a sharp breath, placing one hand to her chest.

The shaman paused the entity's memory and turned to face Selene. In the space just before her face, where there had been just a swirl of grey mist, a tiny spark of imagery had now started to emerge.

Mesmerised, Warrick forced himself to perceive as much detail as he possibly could. He was so tempted to slowly inch himself around the circle so that he could have a front-row seat.

The shaman refocused his attention on Selene and began to coax the memory forward. After some considerable concentration, the shaman released a steadying breath of his own. He then carefully activated Selene's long-forgotten memory.

The memory opened to depict a woman following a maid through an elaborate entrance hall, decorated with hanging chandeliers and lustrous furniture. She nervously plucked at her embroidered sleeves with a white-gloved hand before taking a calming grip upon her matching parasol.

Stopping at a large door, the maid knocked before entering. She curtseyed before speaking.

'Miss Audrey De Vere, sir,' she announced. And stepping aside, she allowed the woman to walk into the room.

The parlour was of a similar grand design, featuring beautiful furniture, lustrous rugs, and long, hanging curtains.

'Thank you, Rose,' said a handsome man standing before an open fire. He continued to address her, gazing at her reflection in a large, gilded mirror that hung over the mantelpiece.

'Some refreshments, perhaps? Or maybe some freshly brewed Chinese tea? I'll wager it could have bested the East India Company's finest consignment.'

'Yes, that would be most generous, thank you, my Lord.' Then she too curtseyed.

'Right away, sir,' concluded the maid beside her, and she walked out, closing the door with a muffled bang.

The man turned, his back toward the fire, just as it crackled loudly. Somewhere outside, a dog barked.

The shaman paused the playback.

Warrick was speechless. He had now seen two memories of the same scene — past life memories at that — seen through the eyes of two different people.

'Now Selene,' began the shaman gently, 'how are you holding up?'

'Kind of lost for words,' she croaked. 'I just watched one of my past memories in my mind, that I never in a million years would have believed that I'd had. And the funny thing is, I actually do remember that scene now. And yet, at the same time, I don't want to remember — it's odd.' Then she laughed. 'Just how long ago was that, anyway? I've gotta see me squeeze into one of those dresses in this body. And I was white — actually white. I ain't never gonna get over that, I can tell you!' she laughed again.

The shaman smiled. 'Yes, we've all been a lot of different people in a lot of different bodies over the centuries. We have fought on opposite sides of the same war, prayed to different deities and changed sexes over and over again. Perhaps that is why some people have such mixed emotions — food for thought. And during each lifetime, we were adamant that only we were right at the time. It appears that the joke has been on us all along. I tell you, we've been stuck in one hell of a game!'

Warrick baulked at the implications of this comment.

'Okay, Selene,' continued the shaman, 'this is it. Now that I have your memory ready, we are going to run with it while we can. I must warn you that it could contain anything — good, bad, or indifferent... in fact, anything. It may contain a lot of sadness, a lot of grief, it may even contain shock and disbelief. But this is why we are here, at this moment, to confront it and resolve it. Once we begin, we must see it through to the end — regardless of the content.' He rested a hand on her shoulder. After taking a deep breath, she smiled and gave him a nod of approval.

The entity was now completely still, its silhouette more definable, more human, and more akin to the person in the memory. He was just as focused on Selene as the shaman. Warrick gave an involuntary shudder.

As soon as the memory began to play, Selene reached out to the shaman for stability. The scene picked up where it had left off, and she was now approaching the man.

'Please, call me Alastair, I think we have known each other long enough now.'

'As you wish... Alastair.'

'Look, as you know, I am not one for... for beating about the bush... so...'

Then, without another word, he had knelt on one knee and had raised a ring between his right forefinger and thumb.

Taken aback, she, in turn, gasped, clutching at her chest. 'Oh... oh my... you... I...' She shook her head. 'If I had known... I just... my Lord — Alistair, please get up. Please get up. I'm so sorry, I... I regret to inform you that I am already betrothed, sir.'

Clearly confused, Alistair stared up at her before getting slowly to his feet.

He thrust the ring back into his pocket and turned to glare into the log fire.

'Forgive me, but I thought we had reached an understanding? At our last meeting... the last dance we attended, I thought I'd made my affections quite clear.'

'Yes, you did, sir, but... but you also said that you had urgent business to attend amongst the colonies — imminently — and would be away for many a year. So, I presumed that you only had intentions upon your return, if any at all. What is a young woman to do with such contradictory loquaciousness? And further, to be quite frank, I was not at liberty to wait that long.'

'Well, you presumed wrong, Miss De Vere,' he snapped, his anger rising. 'Can you not call this engagement off? And who is this other suitor? Do I know of him?'

'Sir, I beseech you to lower your tone. It is not I that am in the wrong here, for I did not know of your feelings or intentions.'

'You knew!' he said with a sly smile. 'Don't play the innocent with me.' He agitatedly toyed with his cane, waving it in the air. 'Such candour... such nonchalance... How could I have been so blind? I was even preparing to overlook any dowry inadequacies.' He shook his head, staring back into the fire. 'And there I was making future plans — plans for you as the mother of my children. Well, I curse the day you try to have them with another...' He gave an angry grunt of a laugh. 'Already deflowered, no doubt, by this other... Just be honest with me!'

'How dare you, sir!'

Seconds later, he was upon her, his hands around her throat. 'You have made a fool out of me,' he hissed. 'Why would you do this? Why allow me to escort you to so many social events, waltzing you about at the dances?

I was enamoured with you as I proudly presented you as my potential consort. And why let me take you for so many turns about the grounds, if not to take advantage of my good nature? Was it the money you sought?'

'Sir, you are hurting me — I cannot breathe!'

'Yet you allowed me to do all this, giving me false hope, when all this time your heart lay with another. 'Tis a cruel joke to play on one who truly cared for you, Miss De Vere.'

Alistair shook her so hard that her vision began to blur.

'Sir!' she garbled. 'It was not my intention, truly.'

'Liar!' he spat venomously, before tightening his hands around her throat.

Violently coughing, she clawed at her throat, desperate for air.

But he tightened his grip still further, applying the pressure remorselessly before casting her limp body to the floor.

As she lay on her side, she stared unmoving at the fire, whilst the flames drifted in and out of focus. Out of sight, she heard him march out of the room, only to slam the door behind him. Still unable to breathe correctly from the tightness of her dress, darkness finally overcame her as the vision drew to a close.

The memory had come to an end.

Simultaneously, back in the room with the shaman, Selene was breathing heavily, one hand at her own throat and the other clasped by her cousin. The entity had not moved as promised, but he did appear agitated. Warrick wondered if it was shame and regret that now possessed him, that pinned him to this half-life?

'Open your eyes, Selene,' said the shaman. 'Now, whilst this memory is still fresh in your mind —'

'He killed me?' she interrupted. 'I was going to be married...

I remember now... and he killed me.' She looked directly up at the entity. 'You killed me, you actually murdered me!' She held her head to stop it spinning. 'Then why do you still haunt me after what you did?' The entity lowered his head. 'Is it because you want to apologise?'

But the entity bristled at this comment, causing both the candles and the lights to flicker briefly. People around the circle continued to sit, unable to comprehend the unfolding of this latest saga, seemingly too great to take in.

'Then what do you want?' cried Selene. 'You have haunted me for so long, and now you have destroyed my current life. Just tell me what more you want from me and then... leave — me — alone!'

The entity began to swell with anger, embroiled in his swirl of contradictory emotions; he held his ground. But something still unsettled him as he bobbed and fidgeted in the air.

'Selene,' said the shaman, softly but firmly, 'I want you to scan your mind back over the memory, and see if there are any possible questions that he had not received an answer to?'

'Me? But I'm in the right here — he killed me! Why should I still go digging around?'

'Selene, it is all in the past, but for him, it is still very much like the present. He has not moved on from it. He is still hung up on that incident. I am sure that reviewing what he has done to you will help to unburden him of his crime, but the fact remains that some untruths still persist. Tell me, what else do you remember about that memory? Try looking a little earlier.'

Selene sighed in protest before closing her eyes. 'Well, it's a bit vague in places and I am not actually sure if I am making this up, but here goes.'

Her head jerked from side to side, as if she were replaying more of the memory in her mind's eye. 'Well, yes, I did go to see Alistair. And I think I did love him.' She frowned at her own words. 'Erm, yeah, I think I really did. So then... why did I...' As she pondered this, she twisted the engagement ring she had never taken off. Then her hand moved to her womb. Taking in a gasp, she spoke slowly, her eyes kept screwed tight. 'He was right, I was lying about something. I... I was pregnant — I was with child at the time, and I needed to marry quickly. The other man, who was a good man, was also the father.' She paused, still trying to make sense of the memory. 'It looks like I loved you both,' she said, looking up at the entity, 'but I actually loved you more.' The entity seemed to swell even more, bobbing and swaying like a balloon caught in the wind. 'But it was true when I said that I thought you were not intending to marry me for over a year. I was completely heartbroken, as I thought you were just being polite — a way to let me go. So, I finally had to agree to marry the other man.'

Selene took a moment and steadied her voice. 'Alistair, I am so, so sorry I lied. I broke your heart, I can see that now.

'But you broke mine first, even if you didn't know it. But I did love you, I honestly did… It appears that we have just had a massive misunderstanding. Times back then were were difficult for women — really difficult. I did not want to be an outcast or left on the shelf… my insecurities would never have allowed it.' She gave a great sigh as the truth was finally released.

Alistair became quite still. His recreated image of the man he once was became so vivid that even a few more people whispered to one another that they could see his outline.

'I have forgiven you, Alistair, so I hope you can find it in yourself to forgive me now. I never meant to hurt you.'

For a moment, Alistair just seemed to stare back at Selene, before finally giving in to a slow and forlorn nod. Overcome, Selene's hands flew to her mouth as she choked back a few tears. Alistair then turned to the shaman, also giving him a small nod. In return, the shaman inclined his own head.

And, with his questions finally answered, the mysteries that had plagued him for decades were resolved. Alistair visibly diminished to the size of a small, glassy orb before disappearing out through the locked French doors.

Immediately, the lights became brighter and the atmosphere in the room changed. The palpable lack of air and distinct drop in temperature had been resolved. Warrick felt as if someone had opened all the windows and let a fresh breeze cleanse the room of its stuffiness.

At this, Selene finally burst into tears of relief. She threw her arms around her cousin and let years of fear and anxiety pour from her.

The shaman slowly rose and stretched — an unspoken signal that this had been his most draining interaction of the evening.

For Warrick, it was the most unique exorcism he would likely ever witness.

A spontaneous round of clapping took the shaman by surprise, though he accepted it with a graceful bow. Warrick was happy to contribute. Besides, the group's admiration seemed to act as a kind of stimulant, momentarily restoring the shaman's spent energy.

A gentle sense of realisation washed over Warrick, grounding him in the moment. It was as if someone had pulled back the proverbial curtain at the Emerald City in the Wizard of Oz, revealing that the truth — and the world itself — were far vaster than he'd ever imagined.

How narrow his life had seemed before. How many, he wondered, would go through life with such a limited view, blind to the full spectrum of existence?

Belief was a fickle thing. It could be delicate or brutal. But one thing was certain: it had to be lived to be understood — experienced, in one form or another.

'During this evening,' the Shaman continued, his voice calm and assured, 'many of us — perhaps not all, but certainly a good number — have borne witness to some fascinating truths about human behaviour, past lives, and the nature of the spirit... the spirit, of course, in its many forms.

'Before we move forward with the proceedings, allow me to offer a final reflection on one of life's more mysterious phenomena: the journey of the soul between lives.

'Religious texts, spiritual traditions, mystics, near-death experiencers, and even the self-appointed sceptics of the more aggressive keyboard-warrior variety — hidden behind their glowing screens — have all contributed to this conversation in their own way.

'And yes, those who have briefly left their bodies during surgeries or accidents often return with profound accounts, suggesting that out-of-body experiences are far more common than most realise. Regrettably, many Western philosophies and cultures have been conditioned to dismiss such accounts out of hand.

'But what's important to understand is this: the psychic no man's land we drift through between lifetimes is not always entered by choice. Preprogrammed and pre-implanted compulsions compel us to report back, before being wiped clean to return into our next corporeal existence. And the life cycle begins once again. Live die, repeat... Ad infinitum.'

Beside Warrick, the woman to his right clutched at her necklace as her mouth opened in disbelief.

Warrick gave her a gentle smile as she shook her head in amazement.

'This lack of spiritual sovereignty,' the shaman went on, 'or should I say basic knowledge, is often the result of ignorance, or internal blocks, both mental and spiritual, that cloud our ability to be fully autonomous. But why can't we override this naive and automated cycle? What is this compulsive behaviour?'

Agreed, thought Warrick, feeling frustrated, so just tell us and put us out of our misery.

'Here at The Seers College, you'll begin to dissolve those barriers. You'll begin to restore that long-forgotten spiritual agency. But understand — this journey must be walked alone.

'We've discussed many times the importance of preparation.

Preparation not just for this life, but for the transition that follows.

'And so, I say this gently, but clearly: when the time comes, and you find yourself permanently exterior to your current body, as it lies in its final resting place, resist the instinct to rush toward the light. Stay present. Let the impulse pass.

'It's understandable to yearn for reunion with those you've loved. But the difficult truth is that many of them may have already returned to Earth in new forms, living new lives. In essence, they have begun their new game afresh. That is, after all, part of the soul's apparent progression, or dare I say it, entrapment down here. A turn of phrase that will be hard for some to hear.

'Some may reject this idea. Some may feel anger or grief. And if this thought stirs something uncomfortable within you, take it as a gentle sign: perhaps you're not fully rooted in this present life.

'Knowledge invites deeper understanding — and in this realm, that rule holds fast.

'It's human to crave connection, to long for continuation. And perhaps, one day, a reunion will come — when the time and form are right. But let us not cling to the comforting illusion that our loved ones are idly suspended on some cloud, waiting for us to arrive. They, like us, have their own paths to walk.

'If every soul waited for reunion, none would return. Of course, I understand this perspective may challenge your beliefs. And that's okay. You're entitled to hold your truth, just as I am to mine. If imagining reunion brings you peace, honour that feeling.

'But know this: once you've experienced yourself fully outside the body — perceiving clearly, unclouded — you may see reality very differently.'

The shaman took a breath, seeming to deliberate his further thought upon the matter.

'Do I believe we're here to mystically learn lessons across lifetimes, with no memory or awareness of what's been learned? No, I do not. 'Do I believe instead, some are coerced and misled by forces more powerful than themselves? Yes, I do. That doesn't mean growth can't occur — but what good is learning if the wisdom is erased at each new turn of the wheel?

'Shouldn't the soul's journey be cumulative, rather than wiped clean with each reincarnation? Surely, this cycle isn't divine learning — it's a trap for the unsuspecting. More food for thought…'

Joyce, as far as Warrick could see, was wiping her eyes at this.

Besides her, another woman gave her arm a comforting rub.

'I offer you only the truth,' continued the shaman, his arms outstretched, 'as I have come to know it — not through doctrine or ancient ideologies, but through empirical experience. What you do with it is entirely yours to decide. Embrace it. Question it. Discard it. That, too, is your right.'

The shaman inclined his head and slowly turned in a full circle, his presence seeming to steady the air in the room.

Warrick sat stunned, still swirling in this latest insight into a world so unknown to so many. Was it true? Could this really be how things worked? It would surely upset many religious minds, especially those who clung, fully tethered, to biblical references and dogma like a lifeline. But for him, it made more sense than anything he'd heard before. He was lucky, he thought, to have the openness to consider new truths, to stretch the boundaries of his education. Others, he feared, would never be able to.

Perhaps this — quietly recognising the struggle in others — was the beginning of a vow yet unspoken, a mantle he was only just starting to realise, was maybe his to carry. It felt entirely right; he had the capacity and willingness to help others, so this would be a natural next step. Was this his calling after all...?

He glanced back toward the shaman. Just who was this man? How had he risen above the planet-wide amnesia that had veiled humanity for so long? This bewitchment that had vexed Man down the ages was as insidious as it was destructive. A perpetual circle of deceit and lies. Without envisioned and enlightened men and women like this, how would Mankind ever seek to escape such an invisible entrapment? The true answer: they would not. Perhaps, at last, The Seers College held the answers he now longed for.

The shaman's eyes briefly met his own.

'No matter the disguise, no matter the depth of darkness,' the shaman said gently, 'truth will always rise again — to find the light.'

~ CHAPTER TWENTY ONE ~

Social Piranha

The nearer and nearer the shaman got to Warrick, the more anxious he became. He constantly attempted to clear his mind of any and all pictures and memories, determined to bury everything out of sight. It was, after all, just a kiss...

And so, it went on, person after person, psychic reading after psychic reading. It was like nothing Warrick had ever seen or heard of before. Each stood up for their very own personal analysis and current life evaluation.

Luckily for some, it was merely a dusting of gentle advice and heartfelt guidance. In contrast, others, it seemed, were subjected to the usual intense wrath of open grilling, as more and more personal secrets were pulled from under people's very noses. Their innermost thoughts and feelings, their weaknesses and their bad habits, all laid out bare for all to see. But there they all stood, each in turn, no one forcing them, no one making them. They all came of their own accord, offering themselves up like lambs to the slaughter, one by one, all emotionally crumbling under his all-knowing gaze and powerful confrontational methods.

Yet the common theme of the night still ran true — that each and every one of them, once the shaman had addressed them, sat down outwardly lighter and inwardly unburdened.

Even the room itself provided a pleasantly languorous feeling of calm with each new completion, where relief and forgiveness united them all in their quests for both inner peace and truthful solace.

Nothing escaped this shaman. He saw everything: every thought, every feeling, every picture and every personal interaction in one's past, all in glorious 3D technicolour — sight and sound alike. It was as if he were looking at a person's memory banks, like one would view the moments captured in the many segments of a film reel.

If there was ever an evening demonstration of psychic and spiritual power, then this was it. He was truly all-seeing and all-knowing. At that moment, Warrick certainly felt that this magical man, this beacon of hope for some, deserved the awe of amazement that swam about him in the room that night.

Behind him, he heard the front door open and close, and two people walked in late. As they passed him, Warrick could see that it was the two friends who had invited him: Rumi and Sumera.

Rumi was of Indian descent, whose family were traditional Sikhs. However, his refusal to grow both his hair and beard, and his later decision to Westernise his spiritual beliefs, did not go down well. Nevertheless, he was a proud yet gentle man, now approaching his thirties, and was open-minded in terms of other paths of enlightenment. His linen trouser suit appeared tailor-made, and the unsurprising use of sandals gave him more of a Mediterranean air. His wife, Sumera, was of mixed race, part Pakistani, part Indian and part Bangladeshi. A fairly petite and pretty wife, she had a penchant for flowery dresses and hair bands. Despite being somewhat subservient to her husband, she nevertheless exercised her will over their spiritual beliefs and attendance at local meetings and soirees. At only twenty-one, she was also one of the youngest at this evening's event.

Not noticing Warrick, his two friends walked round to the far side of the circle and sat down next to Joyce. The others in the circle shuffled around to accommodate the latecomers.

Clever, Warrick mused. They had definitely been to such an evening before, considering that they had just sat down at the correct side of the circle, after the shaman had passed.

Unaffected by the latecomers, the next man stood slowly up to face the shaman.

The shaman considered him for a moment. Warrick, too, watched as a collection of smoky images began to materialise in the air. Although wispy and ill-formed, they still solidified with enough substance for him to make out the various miniature scenes ready for inspection.

Looking about the room, Warrick became convinced that only a small few could also see these personalised incarnations. Was this some new mental or spiritual skill he was beginning to develop, or had he always had such an ability that just needed coaxing?

Warrick pondered this thought. Had he experienced any such psychic phenomena before? Was he suppressing his own memories, or perhaps had he simply forgotten? Many times, he had picked up his mobile phone just before it rang, because he had a feeling a certain person was going to call — only to be surprised that it was indeed them. He'd always brushed that off as a coincidence, laughing afterwards. But was it? Others had mentioned similar occurrences, making him think it was not some special skill after all.

And now he came to think about it, what about all those moments at home when he felt like he wasn't alone in the room, when the temperature had suddenly dropped? He'd never actually seen anything, but he'd had a strong sense of someone there with him. Other things too — unexplained things — had happened around him as he was growing up. He remembered now. He must have blocked them out.

He'd messed with the Ouija board a few times—with very disappointing results. He had even tried automatic writing, where you allowed loved ones or any local spirits access to the pen you were holding so they could guide it around the page to write out any message they wanted to share, which was actually far more effective.

Even so, these last two activities had always left him wondering just who he had been communicating with. He wasn't sure whether to feel comforted or unnerved.

Then the space around him seemed to tighten, and suddenly, a strange resistance to revisiting his own memories in this area began to slide in, trying to redirect him. It was an odd sensation — one that made him feel as though he wasn't supposed to look or remember such things. Maybe his mind was doing so to protect him...

But protect him from what? Some buried psychic truth? Did everyone experience this kind of mental interference? Perhaps this was why so many people dismissed otherworldly phenomena so easily — because the mind would silently step in and erase or bury such observations.

Whether this was a safeguard or simply a malfunction of the mind, he did not know. Still, the idea intrigued him. And once again, the shaman's voice echoed inside his head: "Unless he learned to understand his mind, he could end up being a slave to it." Or something along those lines... All the same, he did not like the idea that his own mind was taking it upon itself to censor various aspects of his life. Shouldn't he at least have the final say?

It was so easy to invalidate one's own psychic experiences.

And yet, as doubtful as he was, there was still that lingering thought — or even hope — that maybe, just maybe, he might have some dormant Starseed bloodline itching to come to the surface.

A log cracked in the fire, sending a flurry of sparks spiralling upward, and Warrick blinked, reminded that all of this — no matter how strange — was happening right here, right now.

The shaman subtly moved a hand back and forth in front of the man, and Warrick could see various translucent images — presumably small memory bytes — move about before him. As each snippet of the man's recalled memory presented itself, it ran its brief course, and the shaman concentrated on the image. Whether there was any sound, Warrick could still not hear, but the shaman did look as if he was listening to something.

The man, a typical-looking middle-aged guy, neat and well-presented, gave a polite cough and straightened his grey suit. He had no tie, but the collar of his crisp, chequered shirt sat proudly above his navy-blue jumper. And like everyone else who stood before this mystical shaman, he looked embarrassed and apprehensive. He rubbed his hands against the sides of his trousers and attempted to stand a little straighter.

Eventually, the shaman dropped his attention from the man's past memories and put it back on the man himself.

'So, Frank, isn't it? Is there anything you wish to discuss with me?'

After the initial flinch at hearing his name said aloud, the man diverted his eyes from the shaman's. Unfocused, they appeared to move about the room. Under normal circumstances, one would assume that this was just normal behaviour upon being confronted. But as Warrick could now see these faint memory bytes around the man, he concluded that it was these regretful past incidents that the man was reluctantly reviewing, consciously or unconsciously.

Warrick shifted himself on the floor, alleviating the numbness forming in his legs. Warrick also wondered if these particular memories were lingering because the man had his attention fixed on them, due to some past regret or upset. Maybe this was why the shaman could see or read them, as they were at the forefront of the man's mind.

'I... I have a problem with my daughter,' he offered apologetically. 'We seem to rub each other up the wrong way all the time. We can't seem to... oh, I don't know — get along, I suppose.' He paused, pondering the following sentence.

'Do go on,' encouraged the shaman.

'She, erm, wants to be an artist.' He rolled his eyes, then spoke rapidly as if wanting to get everything out before he was interrupted.

'Not sure who put that crazy idea into her head, but nevertheless, there you have it. It's embarrassing — you know — I mean, why an artist of all things? Just what am I supposed to tell people? The shame... an artist in the family... I've tried to stop her, but will she listen to reason? No! She knows best — typical teenager.' Frank shook his head with the weight he appeared to be carrying. 'Oh God, why me? Why is it that I have to have an "artist" in the family?' Before the shaman could reply, the man went on.

'I'm sure you understand, what with all the weird stuff you have to listen to.' He swept his hand dismissively about the room of other devotees present. 'I mean, what do I have to do to convince her it's a waste of time? She's never gonna make it as an artist. They're always skint, mixing with oddities and similar dreamers — always out of touch with the real world. I've said to her, told her, that she is wasting her time, and that she will never ever make it... But will she listen? She's just... so... so defiant. And I'm sure she doesn't get it from me. I don't know why she has to be so different; she just needs to get a real job like everyone else.' Frank shook his head again, as if there was nothing he could do.

The shaman took a moment to look around at the others in the circle, almost as if trying to capture their impressions of this new selectee.

'Ahh, I see,' said the shaman, 'she has become a disappointment to you. She has created embarrassing situations, not wanting to fit into a normal way of life.'

'Yes!' said the man with a triumphant clap of his hands, 'someone at last understands my predicament.'

The shaman nodded before gazing briefly at the man's floating images.

'Tell me, said the shaman, 'what do you consider is a normal way of life? I mean, considering all that you have seen and experienced tonight.' He swept both his arms about the room.

Frank seemed confused by this comment.

'Well, most of it went over my head, to be honest. It's okay if you believe this sort of thing, I suppose. It's all a bit unreal to me. I just want my kids to be normal, especially my daughter. She could do with coming here — it's her brain, or whatever it is, that needs cleansing.' There were murmurs of disbelief and hushed pockets of tittering. Even Warrick was taken aback by the man's blindness to the evening's dramatic happenings.

The shaman paused, clearly thinking on how to handle this man's negativity.

'We think in terms of facts and reality. Wishy-washy spectral beliefs or the conjuring of some latent jinn are not what drives us nor inspires us, Frank. Results count, and one's happiness is our true purpose.' He gave the man an encouraging smile.

Frank, however, opened out his hands in a gesture of mystery, and sucked in air through his teeth, generating a sense of uncertainty.

'It's more a mental issue she has than a so-called spiritual one,' he added.

Has this pig-headed narcissist not been listening? thought Warrick.

Frank looked back at the shaman with a subtle, jeering smile that irritated Warrick. It was an odd sort of a provoking smirk.

The shaman considered Frank. 'Firstly, let's address your views of artists, shall we — of which you are entitled to, I might add.'

Frank rolled his eyes and stared up at the ceiling as if not wanting to be challenged.

'I presume that you have artwork on the walls at home?' Frank frowned. 'You watch films and TV shows, do you not?' Frank ignored him. 'You may also have seen breathtaking sculptures, monuments or even gothic buildings that defy imagination. These are all created inside the minds of great thinkers and creative artists alike. From the flourish of a painter's brush to the intricately executed design plans for religious temples, all, in varying degrees of skill, are intrinsically creative.'

Shaking his head slowly, Frank gave the distinct impression that he was both uninterested and had not been understood by the shaman.

This time, the shaman stood back, as if looking over Frank's complete aura, before pacing contemplatively up and down. Frank's eyes followed him with wary curiosity.

'Do you read, Frank?' asked the shaman, eventually.

Frank swallowed as if his mouth were dry. 'Of course,' he replied indignantly, 'I have my own library — of sorts.'

'This is good... this is good. Tell me, have you even contemplated what it takes for a writer to conjure up a story, for them to weave and build, word-by-word or even, letter-by-letter, a credible narrative? And this is not to mention their carrying out of painstaking research, therefore carefully floating upon the air the abstract world which they have delicately woven about the reader?'

Frank did not move, but Warrick could tell that he was unavoidably taking in all that the Shaman had to say.

'It can take tremendous mental mind power and literary parlour tricks to get the reader to follow the whole storyline, so that they lose themselves within a completely new reality.'

Reluctantly, Frank nodded, although still struggling with the notion that he would, at some point, have to admit that he could possibly be wrong.

'Then we have the magic of musicians and the mastery of great singers, all with the power of euphonious seduction. You have heard, have you not, of that quote by Shakespeare: *"If music be the food of love, play on?"* What a wonderful turn of phrase!' The shaman turned full circle, grinning at everyone as he passed, his hands outstretched as if sharing this delightful news.

'Some of the most accomplished actors have trod the boards of live theatre, only to make the most ardent demons weep into their hooves and the most ethereal angels tear at their wings for the injustice they observe. This is art and creative artistry at its finest.'

Frank's head dropped to his chin, and he smiled despite himself.

'Being an artist can be a finely tuned affair, Frank, as not all are blessed with such ability. But it is, nevertheless, a skill all of its own, and a very valuable one at that. Your daughter has a great gift; help her to nurture it and not bury it. It is nothing to be ashamed of — if anything, it is to be admired. So, be proud! The path of the artist is not necessarily plagued by some mysteriously whispering will-o'-the-wisp, but can be twisted by those who have failed, those who are jealous, or simply the ignorant and the corrupt. To the devil with them I say — all of them!'

A burst of unexpected clapping from around the circle even seemed to take the shaman by surprise. Warrick, in total agreement, clapped as if this, too, would help cement this truth into the blind, restive heart of this stubborn middle-aged man.

Frank winced, struggling to deny this contradiction to his stalwart beliefs. He looked about at the other people in the circle as if hating them for going against him. There was no ally here.

Once the clapping had abated, Frank confronted the shaman.

'Funny thing, your opinion... as it is your opinion. However, I see what you're saying, and you have some interesting points there. Whether it's for my daughter, well, who can really say? Is she going to be one of these great artists you speak of? I doubt it. But I guess at the end of the day, it's up to her. I can only help guide her as I know best. If she decides to pursue this artistic path, then so be it. And when it all comes to tears, at least I can say I tried.' He gave the shaman an oily smile, but the shaman did not smile back.

Smug bastard, thought Warrick, I know what he's doing. He just has to be right, doesn't he...

As Frank began to sit himself back down, the shaman shook his head. 'I don't think so, Frank.'

Straightening himself back up, Frank stared defiantly back at the shaman.

The shaman, however, simply brought his hands before him and began twiddling his thumbs together as if contemplating which desert to choose from a delightful menu.

'I see that you confide your concerns about your son and daughter to your wife,' began the shaman. The man nodded. 'But also, your son to your daughter and your daughter to your son. And as such, all now think less about the other because of this, and yet nobody is any the wiser to the source of their dislike...' the shaman added, squinting inwardly at images that only he could see.

A stillness began to surround the two men as they stood, now oddly similar, facing one another.

Then the shaman visibly reacted to something he was looking at. 'My, my... You have been busy,' he added. The man frowned. 'You have manipulated their views of each other, little by little, comment by comment... otherwise known as gaslighting.'

The man physically jerked where he stood. Simultaneously, a rush of pictures came into being about him. Some were unmoving, while others were running in small loops, similar to modern GIF images, where the image would run a few frames before repeating itself.

The man looked momentarily overwhelmed.

The shaman lifted a hand as if to calm him.

'Did you know that there are some sea snakes that deliver more toxic venom than a cobra? Their method of killing, through biting, contains a deadly mixture of neurotoxins and myotoxins.

Once bitten, the victim can do nothing to defend itself. Now, in parallel to this, some people, in an attempt to weaken what they consider an enemy or threat to their survival, also take minute bites out of their target. Not enough to create an obvious attack, but over time, a weakening effect takes place. Unaware that they are actually under attack, the target never sees it coming. They eventually succumb, and being too tired to fight back, they are unprepared for when the predator goes in for the final kill.'

Frank furrowed his brow, wondering where the shaman was going with this information.

'And,' the shaman went on, 'there is also an interesting freshwater fish, the piranha — you may have heard of it — which, for reasons best known to itself, will prey upon its own species for survival. Being an omnivore at heart — able to obtain energy from either plants or animals — and, in this case, including other freshwater life, it actually has a choice of which to focus its attention on. But its cravings are uncontrolled, and it will act accordingly, without any constraints.' He paused dramatically, taking a breath, 'Oddly enough, there are some humans that tend to mimic these two underwater predators, wherein these behavioural traits are focused upon the people about them. And these unsuspecting victims are never aware of what is happening until the last minute.'

Warrick leaned further forward, fascinated by these insights into human relationships. Here was the social piranha. Reflecting on his own family life, Warrick's older brother came to the forefront of his mind. Here was a young man who also seemed to mimic the characteristics of the sea snake and piranha. He was always making constant remarks to Warrick, nullifying all that he seemed to say and do. It was all done under the guise of "helping Warrick to be realistic about his dreams and aspirations". This way, Warrick could take his head out of the clouds and focus on "more important things". But if this was "help", then why did he always feel saddened and disillusioned afterwards? Clearly, this was not help but an effort to weaken him. Just what threat did he pose to his brother — jealousy perhaps?

If only his parents could be here now... he thought. Perhaps it would give them the insight they needed — to finally see how his brother really acted. Would the veil of truth drop for them, he wondered? Since he held no credibility in this area, maybe the shaman had the altitude necessary to help them see just how insidious his brother could be — family or not.

The thought stirred something raw and uneasy in him — a mixture of vindication and sorrow. Maybe it was the injustice that bothered him most. Still, the fact remained: he now had a clearer view of who he was really dealing with — and that truth alone was powerful enough to steady him.

Warrick returned his attention to the man being addressed. His faint images had now become a disordered mess, seeming to be playing one over the other. Some snippets had frozen, whereas various still images depicting a young girl shouting at an older woman remained motionless. If Warrick were a gambling man, his money would be on them being mother and daughter in full verbal conflict.

One by one, the rest of the moving images paused, as if in mid-cycle. It was like looking at a computer opening too many windows before freezing up. The last few to stop were of the man himself, seemingly caught passing secret communications to the woman Warrick presumed was the girl's mother.

Frank, however, just looked on as if mentally vacant.

For the first time, the shaman did not respond instantly.

He looked at the man differently, like a critic would study a piece of art, or like a mechanic would approach a complex conundrum. Then he began doing something he hadn't done before, leaving Warrick utterly astonished.

The shaman began to change his posture, slightly slouching, while his hands danced nervously between his pockets, and out before him as he intermittently interlocked his fingers. At the same time, he began loosening his facial features. Lines of woe appeared upon his forehead, and a general look of apathy began to manifest behind his sorrowful eyes.

Slowly but surely, the shaman's features altered to reveal a hangdog expression. It was as if he were mimicking the man before him in his entirety. Body movements and facial tics were also neatly duplicated, as if they were part of his own behavioural patterns. By the time the shaman had finished, they both appeared to be carrying the same amount of mental baggage.

Frank became uneasy, peering at the shaman as if he were looking at an unexpected reflection.

The shaman had somehow become a living, emotional facsimile of the man's entire existence, taking on his troubles, torments, and stresses. It was as if he were trying to look through the eyes of the man himself.

The man's mouth fell open, and as if like a delayed mirror image, the shaman followed suit.

Then, taking the lead, the shaman stood upright, closing his mouth. Quick to imitate, the man went through the same movements, with only the slightest lag. There was a pause as the shaman contemplated something. Then both men blinked at the same time — this time in unison.

They were now in sync.

~ CHAPTER TWENTY TWO ~

Incorporeal Transcendence

Warrick shook his head, more transfixed than ever at this new skill. How did he know how to do such things? Was it something anyone could learn on this spiritual path, or was it just some innate ability that the shaman alone possessed? Perhaps it was something he, too, could learn within the teachings of these Divinities?

The shaman raised a hand to the man's face, and without touching him, slowly swept it down as if commanding him to sleep.

The man visibly relaxed, his eyelids drooping.

'I see that you and your family are divided,' said the shaman, peering at the floating images.

Even Warrick nodded to himself in agreement.

Shrugging, Frank said, 'I am a simple man. I have simple needs. I guess some would say you could tell the time by me. But what's wrong with that? Nothing, I should say,' he said, answering his own question. 'But these kids — my daughter, well, they are all over the place. They make my head spin. My daughter, especially, can make me feel quite sick with all she has going on. I don't know what's wrong with her, jumping from one project to the next. I know she thinks I'm old-fashioned, but at least I'm stable. It's just not normal to be achieving so many different things — she should be satisfied with her lot in life.

She should just pick one thing and be happy, other than all this flighty behaviour.' He sighed before continuing, 'I try and get my wife to see sense too, but... well, she just thinks I am getting boring...' his voice tailed away.

Frank looked mindlessly about the circle, not taking in anything around him.

The shaman, closing his eyes, raised his hands to his temples as if heavily concentrating. 'You... you have slowly created a false impression of your children to your wife, haven't you? You have some cleaning up to do.' Again, the man frowned, clearly confused.

The shaman opened his eyes and began squinting into Frank's various memories. 'And... my, my, you have created quite the conundrum, I see. Despite loving your daughter, you don't really like her, do you? An odd, but fairly common phenomenon.'

For the first time, the man looked at the others in the circle, shame and embarrassment etched across his face.

'Well, she is making a mockery of my life,' the man replied as if this justified it.

'Is this really so?' questioned the shaman.

'Of course it is,' he retorted, anger building in his voice for the first time. 'How dare she undermine everything I have done or stand for. I brought her up the best way I could; paid for her car, things she wanted... and that bloody nose job. Me — I paid for it!' He jabbed pointedly at his chest. 'She's been spoilt — and do you know how she repays me? No? Well, let me tell you: by questioning my views on life, defying my will, and by being bloody different, just to spite me. Does my brain in — you know?'

More frozen images materialised about the man, making him appear more encumbered, more oppressed. Warrick narrowed his eyes, trying to separate them from one another, curiously trying to figure out if there was a common theme or person within them. But they were too jumbled for any sort of comprehension.

'I see,' began the shaman, 'and what about her point of view, her finding her way in the world, and her having the freedom to think for herself?'

The man gave a disgruntled jeer.

'It's not uncommon,' began the shaman thoughtfully, 'for a parent to be jealous or resentful of their offspring.'

'What!?' bellowed the man. 'Me... jealous of her? Are you mad? Let me tell you, that girl — and my son, for that matter — are prime examples of these new millennial snowflakes. Stuck on their damn phones all day, no social skills, no manners, selfish and obsessed with this internet madness. Always posting images of themselves, desperate for someone to "like" them and validate how sexy or interesting they think they are. It's all fake! Just how insecure are these kids today? They're brainwashed — all of them. Some are so moronic they can't be bothered with basic grammar. I've even seen letters with numbers in place of actual words — can you believe it? Now they think English grammar is old-fashioned and should be dropped!'

Warrick felt himself slump with another internal groan. He was even becoming slightly angry. These people really did love to moan about life, didn't they? This older generation was so out of touch; that was the real problem. Or was it...? Once again, Warrick forced himself to be objective. He could feel a defensive wall building inside him. But if he was honest, it was more of a reactive and somewhat protective survival instinct. Perhaps it was because he, too, spent wasteful amounts of time looking at nonsense on the web. His screen time on his phone apps was, to be truthful, shameful. Why he thought other people's fake lives were more interesting than his own, perhaps reflected a lack in his own life. Which, ironically, was exactly why he was now sitting there.

The man gave a bark of a laugh. 'They care more about celebrity gossip and scandal than the real world.

And they blame our generation? Ignorant morons. They can't compare with us — they never knew the freedoms we had. Now it's cancel culture everywhere. Can't say this, can't say that. Don't upset him, don't compliment her.

'They're being raised with no backbone. Self-proclaimed victims — the lot of them! Nothing's ever their fault. Responsibility is at an all-time low. The world owes them a living, and blaming others has become their favourite tool.' He shook his head. 'I heard a teacher once ask a room full of kids what they wanted to be when they grew up. Do you know what they said? "Famous." Just famous. When asked, "Famous for what?" they looked confused. No ambition to contribute to society. They want it all handed to them.

'And now we've got fifteen-year-old millionaires, these deluded "influencers," giving life advice? What? And other kids look up to them like it's normal! The insanity of it... What a mess!'

Even Warrick agreed to this, although there may have been a smidgen of jealousy there, if he really admitted it.

The man laughed in disbelief. 'And now they don't even know what sex they are! Please — it's got to be a joke. Who taught them that? Some woke government pawn sent to confuse them with ideology? And we're supposed to just roll over and agree? When the people finally snap, heads will roll — you mark my words.' He pointed at the shaman.

The shaman continued to listen, nodding slightly.

Frank paused, shaking his head. Warrick glanced at the shaman, wondering if this was the time to interject and end the tirade, but the shaman seemed to know Frank wasn't finished. And sure enough, he wasn't.

'Their idols now are sexually and morally degraded pop stars and reality TV morons — all into satanism or some weird occult stuff, no doubt.

It's a bloody shambles. Gone are the days of style and elegance, when manners and decorum mattered. Even when you try to be polite, they mistake it for flirting or want to claim for sexual harassment! It's unbelievable...'

Frank's eyes darted around unseeing as his mind tried to make sense of other confusions and injustices that had been slowly grinding him out of his mind.

'Their basic education's been manipulated,' he continued, now tightening his fists. 'And even the curricula's been hijacked by spineless puppets with political agendas. And the result? A delusional, misinformed bunch of school-leavers who think they know it all. They don't even realise they've been misled. And now they think marriage is outdated, winning hurts people's feelings, and we should throw open every border and let in anyone — criminals, degenerates — just to prove how tolerant we are! It's lunacy.

'They should be furious at the ones who run the schools, the borders, and the media — not at the parents who raised them. Glib fools. But you can't tell them that. Teens know best, right? What do we know — we've only been around three times longer! God, it winds me up!'

Frank drew a slow breath to calm himself.

A few others around the circle were also nodding their heads to one another at this last outburst.

The shaman let him vent — like releasing steam from a pressure cooker — allowing the deeper truth beneath all the anger to begin to show.

'And now,' Frank added darkly, 'they're trying to convince my own white race to feel ashamed of themselves — after all we've done for the world! Makes me sick. "White supremacy," they chant. Just do your damn research! The people creating all this racial division should be exposed and shot!

Or hanged! Bring back the guillotine — it worked for the French. It just drains the life out of you. So sad... so sad.'

His face had turned red, and both his fists were clenched again with frustration.

The shaman gently raised a hand to calm him, attempting to meet his eyes.

Realising how far he'd let himself go, Frank lowered his head.

'I'm... I'm sorry,' he muttered sheepishly.

The shaman nodded. 'I absolutely hear you. I truly do.'

'Good, I thought you might — but what can we do about them? 'Cos I, for one, have no idea. And please don't just ask me to pray — a fat lot of good that has done.'

Around the room, Warrick could see others still nodding and referring to the people beside them. It was a touchy subject, especially these days, he thought.

The shaman smiled. 'No, I think we need more than the power of prayer to fix this situation. However, as mature adults, we do have a responsibility to help shape this latest batch of offspring. Any adult knows how infuriating teenagers can be with their "I know best" attitude and cocky arrogance. Mainly because we, too, were unknowingly exactly the same, as we started to find our way in the world. Wanting to appear knowledgeable and self-sufficient is a natural progression, albeit frustrating for others, I know.' He smiled.

The man nodded, letting out a resentful sigh.

The shaman looked about at the growing images, now almost ten layers thick, that practically hid the man from view.

He tapped his index fingers against his lips, clearly thinking about his following response.

'So, one thing at a time. Let's start with your responsibilities.'

Frank placed his hands on his hips, taking up a defensive pose.

The shaman stepped to one side and appeared to select one of the images. As it moved towards him, it began to play.

Warrick squinted, trying to make out the scene. Surely if this shaman could also hear what was going on, he should, too. He concentrated hard, straining his ears.

As the memory played, Warrick could hear the man's voice, although somewhat muffled. The man himself looked about as if wondering where the voice was coming from. After a moment, he seemed to latch onto the memory and watch it from his mind's eye.

It was evening in the scene, with the backdrop of a kitchen, as a girl — his daughter — sauntered into frame. Warrick raised his eyebrows, indicating how pretty he thought she was. If he were out at a club, this was just the sort of girl he would try to chat up. She was gesturing excitedly about her night out, but Warrick could not grasp what she was saying. Behind her, a young man, whom Warrick presumed to be the brother, strolled in, although a little the worse for wear.

'Kissed two girls tonight,' the young man boasted with a cheeky grin.

His sister rolled her eyes. 'They were drunk.'

The brother feigned hurt feelings, 'So?'

The father shook his head. 'You should not let him get into such a state — I mean, look at him.'

'Me?' said the girl. 'Why's it always my fault?'

'If you paid more attention to what was going on around you, other than trying to get every man's attention, then you wouldn't be in this state every week. I mean, look at you both, what an absolute embarrassment...'

They both looked down at their clothes.

'And must you dress like the local hooker?' he added to his daughter.

Becoming upset, she looked to her mother for support.

'Yeah,' replied the brother with a smirk, pointing accusingly.

The sister pulled up her top, covering up her exposed cleavage. The father looked at his wife as if she were responsible. The sister's face turned red.

'And YOU,' added the father, turning to the son, 'you think you are special, too, don't you — God's gift?' His voice had become resentful. 'Well, let me tell you — you're not, you are the same as everyone else. You are just as ordinary as the next guy — nothing special at all. Why in heaven's name would you want to be different from everyone else, I can't even imagine. It's about time you were brought down to earth. Too cocky for your own good, that's your trouble — strutting about the place like a damn peacock. I'm surprised you can still get your head through the door.'

'Frank!' said the mother loudly, slamming her tea down so hard that it splashed onto the kitchen counter. 'Must you be so nasty? They are young — let them have their fun.'

'You're too soft on them,' the man replied. 'Now, the two of you have a shower before you get into bed, you both stink — and not just of alcohol and cigarettes.' He waved his hand dismissively.

The brother and sister looked at one another, clearly upset that their convivial evening had been brought crashing down with such unnecessary vitriol.

His wife gave him a hard stare, to which he just shrugged.

'They've got to learn, Pam. I've told you this time and time again. You let them walk all over you. I see how she upsets you,' he said finally, with a vacant smile.

The video image then stopped as abruptly as it had begun, freezing on the man's face.

Warrick shifted on the floor, irritated with the man's unabashed smugness. Unfazed, the shaman placed his hands behind his back and waited patiently.

Warrick frowned, looking from one man to the other, wondering how on earth the shaman did not feel the urge to punch this guy on the nose.

The man cleared his throat, 'I erm... I regret that particular evening. I... went too far, but I can't take it back. Besides, I was right — wasn't I?'

The shaman gave a slow and non-committal nod, with what seemed to Warrick to carry some careful deliberation.

Sweeping an outstretched hand before him, the shaman brought another video image into view.

This time, just the man and woman were in the memory byte.

They were lying in bed together, each with their respective book.

'I hate to say it, Pam, but you have to see that she is all over the place. All these highfalutin dreams are just that — dreams. She'll never be an artist; she's not the type. That's for other people.'

The woman tutted. 'Well, she is only seventeen, she's still finding out what she wants.'

'Oh, do be sensible, Pam, she's delusional — her head's in the clouds half the time. And now she wants to be an artist, for God's sake — and you know what they're all like.'

'But if that's what she likes... Mary at work says that if artistry runs in her veins, then she should follow her heart.'

'Oh, don't you start, you're as bad as she is — and what does she know? She's hardly an expert on the matter. An artist? Don't make me laugh! I wouldn't be surprised if it were drugs running through her veins.'

'Don't say that, Frank — that's a horrible thing to say.'

'What else could it be? I just hope she is not a bad influence on her brother... if he's not careful, he'll be going down the same aimless path as her. He's not the brightest of kids after all.'

The woman's tone dropped as she lowered her book. She reached over to her bedside table and took a sip of tea. She stared ahead, thinking.

'I... I guess you are right.'

'I know I am,' he said firmly, 'I always am. I don't know where we went wrong, I really don't. I mean, you know yourself, you are always arguing with her. The problem is, she doesn't respect you. So don't let her get to you.'

The woman began to well up. She sniffed as she wiped at her eyes. The man just shook his head, conveying his disappointment.

'See... look how she upsets you.'

The memory froze, indicating that it had run its course.

Warrick, as well as many others, shook their heads in mutual disgust. Narrow-minded bastard, thought Warrick. If anyone is being brainwashed, it's the mother. No wonder they keep arguing; the mother is being poisoned against them. He is truly an invisible "piranha," creating hidden dissent. And none of the family realise that this negativity is being secretly introduced, causing friction between them.

An unexpected surge of emotion rose in Warrick's throat upon thinking about the insidious, destructive disharmony being introduced into what would probably have been a loving family bond.

Once again, Warrick thought of his older brother, who delighted in stirring things up behind the scenes between people at home. He was definitely another one of these "piranhas", playing the professional victim and constantly creating upset within the family.

And he was damn good at it, too. These victim-y types of people always manage to get others to feel sorry for them, so when it comes to others picking sides, they would always defend the "apparently" suppressed victim. It made Warrick shudder to think how many people would waste years of their lives fighting with someone they loved, because they could never spot the hidden antagonist. Just how many families had been torn apart like this, he wondered?

When Warrick looked back at the man, he was staring at the floor. So, here's another person forced to confront their past behaviour, he thought.

Warrick's dislike of this man was such that he wanted to raise an arm in protest at him even being there. He did not deserve the help that was being given to him. He was a venomous and spiteful man, a man without a backbone, and with no capacity to see another person's point of view — prejudiced in favour of his own self-importance and self-assured opinion.

Just then, a thought hit Warrick. Was he now doing the very thing that he despised this man for doing? Was he now being so self-assured that he was closing his eyes to another's point of view? Far from berating himself, Warrick challenged himself to take on a different and unbiased perspective of this man, a man whom he didn't even know.

Swinging his view 180 degrees, a more liberal and liberating experience began to wash over him. For if he honestly looked at it, this man had finally gathered the courage to stand before the shaman and be publicly exposed for the deeds that he had carried out. Beneath his blasé facade, this man knew deep down how the shaman worked — how he got his results. And yet here he was, prepared to face his misguided and confrontational past and to emerge a better man.

And that took some doing. Unexpectedly, Warrick's dislike turned to admiration within a few wise shifts in his viewpoint. The man was just confused and out of touch. He needed educating, not punishing.

The shaman, however, had not finished with the man. 'Your sweeping general comments are only intended to discredit your targets — or in this case, your children. And it appears that you have successfully destroyed their credibility, and thus your wife can no longer take them seriously. And therein, you have achieved your goal — if you can call such a callous, self-serving act, a goal.'

The man placed his hands upon his hips again and began breathing heavily. His face drained of colour, leaving his skin a rather pasty white. Visible beads of sweat appeared from nowhere, and Warrick thought the man was going to be sick.

'I... I can't be wrong,' said the man, 'I just can't be wrong...' He reached blindly out as if to steady himself. 'I'm never wrong.'

'Really?' said the shaman quietly, 'who told you that?'

The man peered up at the shaman as if he were seeing him for the first time. He squinted as if his eyesight was suddenly impaired.

'Tell me,' said the shaman, 'did you or did you not carry out such actions?'

The man did not answer. He was determinedly battling with himself, seeming desperate not to acknowledge what he had been doing to inhibit others around him for so long.

He clenched and unclenched his fists, trying to make sense of his exposed behaviour. Momentarily losing his balance, he threw his arms out beside him before reaching up to hold his spinning head.

Surrounding the man was now a blur of hundreds of ghostly images, some attempting to run their repetitive loop, but only flickering and juddering.

After a moment, the man became quite still, and the shaman stepped forward, placing his hands upon the man's shoulders.

'Stay with me, Frank,' encouraged the shaman, 'do not dismiss truth, as raw as it is. And do not shut yourself down into complete denial either. Embrace your past and your misdemeanours. As clever as your deceptions have been, you have, in reality, been working off a lie, thinking that the suppression of others was key to your survival. But as you can see, it has not been.'

The man faltered as the reality of his actions finally hit home. He began to crumble inwardly as reality sank in. Moments later, he was quietly sobbing into his hands.

Once again in the room, another person had been reduced to tears. Regret and embarrassment had diminished this man into a state of disoriented despair.

'Now that you have seen the truth of your actions, you have no choice but to see the sort of person you have been — despite the outer personality you have projected.'

Placing his hands behind his back, the shaman allowed the man a moment of reflection. Frank stood there, as regret and remorse flowed from him in a swirling rush of shame.

Outside, Warrick was reminded of the wind, which was, once again, fiercely howling past the leaded windows and blowing down the chimney. The wooden beams in the room creaked, as the house itself moaned from somewhere above.

The man began to straighten up, with his head still bowed, calming himself with steady breaths. 'I never realised how bitter and jealous I had become. I've been a bastard, a nasty bastard,' he admitted. 'What on earth was I thinking?' He sniffed, shaking his head. He took a handkerchief from his pocket and blew his nose.

'If someone disagreed with me, they became my enemy. I couldn't stand them making me appear to be wrong, I suppose.' He gave another deep sigh. 'I have delighted in "putting people down"'. He punctuated the last line with his fingers. 'I mean… what sort of person does that?'

Taking a moment, the man seemed to rapidly scan the array of incomplete visual bytes that still floated about him. As a dawning recognition grew upon his face about his familial betrayals and corrupt behavioural manipulations, some of the smaller floating images began to fade away. As each evaporated upon inspection, the man became visibly lighter. When a particularly darkened image — that of him whispering something to his wife, with a self-satisfied grin upon his face — finally dissipated into nothingness, the man smiled for the first time that evening.

'I have some making good to do,' he decided.

The shaman nodded, 'Then make it so, Frank.'

Frank gave a final sigh, wiping his eyes and blowing his nose.

The shaman swayed where he stood, giving the man time to compose himself. Then, quite suddenly, the shaman stepped backwards with a shake, as if slipping out of an exoskeleton. It was like he was completely disassociating himself from the man before him, as if withdrawing from within the man's very skin. A brief phenomenon, like that of a heat haze, fluttered between them, and the man also shuddered. With immediate effect, the shaman's facial features and structural posture returned.

Warrick rested his hands against his temples in contemplative disbelief. And judging from a tiny gasp somewhere to his right, another had also witnessed this incomprehensible occurrence.

Once more, the shaman ran his fingers through his long hair before shaking out his arms and legs as if relieving a cramp.

'Do you remember what our purpose is... here... at this group?'

The man shook his head.

'I thought not. In essence, we are taking Man and helping him ascend to higher levels of spiritual awareness. We are taking him out of the darkness of ignorance and misplaced integrity, and we are firing him into the light of truth and knowledge. And to do this, one needs to be enlightened to realise that he is a spiritual being — that is to say, a soul. Contrary to belief, a human body cannot ascend, only the spiritual being itself can be elevated to plateaus of hitherto forgotten realms of consciousness.'

The man gave a non-committal nod of acknowledgement. Warrick, on the other hand, struggled to take it all in. Again, so much was said so quickly. He understood the concept of a soul, but it was the idea of elevating to higher states that perplexed him. Just where would he be elevated to? Was there an actual location, an independent spiritual plateau or universe, or was he to become one with the universe? Or, now unburdened by a troubled mind, was it that he would have more exterior control over his next reincarnation, his next game inhabiting or using another human body here on Earth?

The shaman raised his index finger as if to instruct the room at large.

'For this to occur, Liberation, Sanity and Truth all interchange, being brought about by the quest for and application of the enlightenment steps within the indoctrination of The Divinities themselves. Together, they provide the basis for what is known simply as Incorporeal Transcendence, which roughly translates as: the elevation of a being, not composed of that which is material. See thus:'

The shaman pointed to the back of the room, and after a moment, the overhead projector threw yet another rotating image onto the wooden floor. After a beat, the lights were switched off.

Once again, Warrick rose to a kneeling position and peered at the image. What looked like a pie chart slowly turned in a circle. Three equally spaced words sat within their segment.

Warrick squinted as the three separated words rotated past him. 'Liberation, Truth and Sanity,' he repeated to himself.

Others around the circle had also risen to a kneeling position and stared down at this latest image.

Warrick lip-read Frank, who was reading back the words to himself as they rotated past him. As if to reaffirm the words, the man pointed to them, trying to understand their significance.

Through the darkness, the shaman's commanding voice rang out. 'Accept and embrace such a trinity of harmony, and freedom is yours. There are various names given to the achievement of such a clear state of mind.

Once attained, it could be likened to the Buddhist concept of Nirvana or the primal energy awakening found in the revered Hindu Kundalini ascension. I choose to call this lucid state simply: Mea Deitas — the return to divine godliness, a restoration of one's original spiritual nature.'

The shaman brought his hands together as if in prayer. There was a click, and the projected illumination was extinguished.

'Mea Deitas...' Warrick repeated quietly to himself. Where had he seen that Latin phrase before? He presumed it referred to the final state one might ascend to — the ultimate plateau of mental and spiritual clarity, attained through the guidance of The Divinities, or Divinitas. I could do with some of that, he mused. Perhaps it would shift these damn headaches of mine, he added as an afterthought.

This time, the lights remained off, and Warrick sat back, crossing his legs once more.

'As I am sure you have heard it said,' began the shaman, addressing Frank directly, 'only the truth will set you free. I doubt there is a truer statement uttered.'

Frank seemed to be looking at his remaining mental images. He stared unfocused in their general direction, and as he did so, they began to fade. The light of truth had finally appeared to have made him admit to his past wrongdoings. As each memory was addressed and his actual behaviour acknowledged, the moving snippet faded away. Finally, as the last remaining image disappeared, the man visibly sighed with relief and for the first time that evening, he looked calm and contented.

The shaman smiled at the man and nodded for him to resume his seated position in the circle.

The shaman turned to face the other circle members. 'Belief and application are but a choice, and one that only you can make. But suppose one wishes to remove one's idiosyncrasies and eradicate the insanities of the mind, without resorting to mind-altering drugs and barbaric mental medical techniques. In that case, I offer you my path of enlightenment. It is not the only path, as I have said, as others have scattered breadcrumbs of their own design with which to follow diligently. It is your journey; may you travel it well and travel it true.'

The main lights slowly began to illuminate the room. But this time they did not reach their usual brilliance but were kept at a low level.

The two remaining people before Warrick forwent any heavy grilling and enjoyed a rather convivial conversation. In fact, the last person was even able to make the shaman laugh.

Then, finally, this last man sat down, gaining a few humorous claps as he did so.

Warrick felt a surge of panic knowing that he was the last one to be addressed. All eyes were now focused on him. This was it; the moment was finally upon him. There was nowhere to run and nowhere to hide. Everywhere he looked, the others were staring at him. And whether Warrick wanted to or not, his body just could not and would not move.

The shaman turned to Warrick, and their eyes connected fully for the first time. Warrick's whole body felt shaken to the core, and his heart was thundering away inside him.

A state of rising nausea seemed to be inhibiting his ability to think straight, let alone build up the mental blocks that he hoped would protect him from being psychologically scrutinised.

If the shaman was to expose this kiss, to elicit his premeditated contribution to kissing his high school crush, then he sincerely hoped that the teacher in question would never be named out loud. He, for one, would never utter or admit to its occurrence. As exciting as it had been at the time, the illegal embrace, if now made public, may well cost her more than her current job. As such, he would never do this — she could be assured of this.

No, thought Warrick, he must be strong; he must hold his position both physically and mentally. He must erect mental screens to hide or block any access. He had to protect his memories at any cost. No matter what came out of this shaman's mouth, no matter how personal, no matter how humiliating or regretful, he must not buckle. With all his might, Warrick focused his mind and, clenching his fists, he prepared himself for the worst.

~ CHAPTER TWENTY THREE ~

The chosen One

The shaman smiled a knowing smile, and Warrick's innards twisted even more. But within seconds, it was as if, with one lazy brush of his hand, every mental barrier and protection that Warrick had mustered was swept away with ease. The shaman was in.

A cool breeze rippled through him — both inside and outside — making him shiver. And without knowing why, his eyes began to close.

As if time itself had slowed, Warrick suddenly sensed the shaman drift through the draughty corridors of his mind. It was like being haunted by a curious spirit. Unexpectedly, he found himself trailing behind the shaman — spectators wandering the labyrinthine networks of his own organised thoughts.

It reminded Warrick of being inside a colossal library — only, instead of books and shelves, the space took the form of a never-ending lattice of trunks and branching pathways sprawling in all directions. Held together by gossamer-like strands of light, millions upon millions of images lay condensed across various nodes.

Oddly, some regions — including their clustered video memories — appeared isolated from the rest. A darker, more foreboding aura surrounded them, accompanied by faint wisps of swirling, angry clouds. In contrast, when he looked upward, other sections of the mind seemed to float more freely among the higher echelons, bathed in soothing light, with a distinctly creative and aesthetic feel.

Either he was looking at the many segments of one distinct, all-seeing mind, or the integration of different types of mind. A fascinating experience...

As they passed, some of these images stirred to life and began to play. They aligned themselves automatically, allowing him to watch them either as brief, bite-sized memories or as continuous streams of living footage.

But the most astonishing part was that each vibrant scene carried not only colour and sound, but the full spectrum of human perception. Scents, bodily sensations, and waves of emotion unfurled like delicate flowers as each video segment ran its course.

It was surprising to Warrick that he could re-experience all these past memories and perceptions in present time — and yet some appeared as if they had lain dormant for centuries.

So here it was: his very own collection of stored memories. Lifetime after lifetime of experience, all carefully filed and organised. Other beads of thin light seemed to act as a method to cross-reference everything with everything else — his personal, portable, and ever-expanding computer storage system.

One memory that began to play caught his attention. He was strolling through a very bizarre forest, one he had never recalled seeing in this lifetime. Like a fairytale dreamscape, the ethereal images showed him treading barefoot along a bracken-laden path, where clusters of purple flowers hung down from tall trees, bearing large bunches of unusual fruit. Twinkling, glowing fireflies danced freely upon the air as he continued through a shallow stream and approached a beautiful stone building that looked more like an ancient palace. Dozens of ornate lanterns gently swung from unseen branches, illuminating the forest floor and casting an enchanting yellow glow.

Warrick re-experienced the cool night air ruffling his long blonde hair, the even colder water splashing about his feet. Exotic forest smells filled his nostrils, and he even recalled the salivating anticipation of biting into one of the low-hanging fruits. He could barely deny the sensation of being naked from the waist up, so that his well-formed breasts, which sat exposed to the elements, did not disturb him. He was becoming totally immersed in a time long since lived. Warrick smiled inwardly — so he even had a past life as a carefree teenage girl. Eighteen, at a guess. It was like wandering through a living storybook.

How wonderful it would be if one could just kick back and venture into one's memories for the day.

But then another, more pre-emptive sensation stirred within him. The memory was no longer euphoric, ethereal, or surreal — this was alertness. This was fight or flight. This was raw and instinctive. Danger was close by — very close. But where...?

Warrick could feel the hairs on his current body rise from the heightened awareness, but his focus remained inside the memory. It felt so real — like he was actually there now, living and breathing amongst the forest nightlife.

Then it all became clear, as two of the yellow firefly lights blinked in unison before him, for they were never fireflies — they were the predatory focus of a ferocious nocturnal killer.

With his pulse quickening, Warrick continued to watch as the scene unfolded. Before he knew it, the creature had pounced so quickly that Warrick felt himself jolt from the shock. Just as the huge claws lunged towards him and the multi-layered teeth bore down, the gentle guiding hand of the shaman steered him back out of the memory and into neutral pathways of his mind.

Warrick gave a great sigh. No wonder he had locked that memory away.

Nevertheless, it was true — his mind recorded everything. Just how far back did it actually go? This would be the real adventure.

But a wave of uncertainty began to wash upon the shores of his new confidence, as disillusionment crept in.

Warrick wanted to give himself a mental shake, but deep inside his own mind was the last place he wanted to do it. As much as he desired this to be real, he couldn't help but wonder if he was actually just hallucinating. Were there chemicals in the smudge sticks — or perhaps in the scented candles — whose smoke still drifted lazily into the air? Perhaps they were all on some mass psychedelic trip.

Or was this like some experimental CIA, MK Ultra, Manchurian Candidate-style mind control exercise? And on that thought, were these modern-day manipulations merely echoing past-life control-based ideologies — repackaged versions of an old enemy of the soul? Okay, he was going too deep now, to the point where he even had to stop himself.

So many more questions filled Warrick's head. Just where did he start?

But at the end of the day, the shaman had still plunged into the furthest depths of Warrick's psyche — whether he liked it or not. He was in his personal space, and he had penetrated his very mind.

Disappointed with himself for not having greater mental muscle, Warrick felt that the shaman now had complete access to everything. Nothing was secret anymore.

Warrick was simply no match for this level of power; his protective mental mechanisms had failed him.

Warrick floated momentarily on the cusp of despair.

But was it despair...? No, it was not, it couldn't be. It was something far deeper. More feral, in fact.

He must learn to embrace this new awareness. And yet, despite the shaman having such access, he no longer felt so vulnerable. In fact, he actually felt the beginnings of something much greater. He was not quite there yet, but all the same, some building resurgence of knowingness — of who he really was, where he had come from, and where, if he chose, he would travel — had started to stir.

Warrick slowly opened his eyes and tried to force himself to relax.

With his palms open, the shaman slowly raised his hands.

Practically stupefied with fear, Warrick struggled to breathe. He tried to swallow but couldn't, and despite the intense dryness of his mouth, that familiar sensation of moisture began to tingle in his throat. He felt the inevitability of nausea upon him.

'And finally,' announced the shaman slowly with surprising pride, 'stand...up — Warrick Airaldo.'

Warrick paused in his slow and reluctant rise to meet him. How does he know my name? No one knew I was coming, and I wasn't even on the list. He looked about him at the others in the circle. Maybe someone else knew? But it didn't matter anymore, his time had run out; he was now the last one to stand, the remaining member of the circle left to speak—to confess all. He could feel them burning with curiosity. He looked back at the awaiting shaman and slowly continued to stand.

Finishing the broken sentence, the shaman continued, '...our chosen one.' The words seemed to hit Warrick like a freight train.

An instant gasp rang out amongst the other members in the circle.

This was then quickly followed by the sound of hushed excitement and jubilation that rapidly filled the room.

But something internal collapsed in Warrick, and momentarily, he felt his mind fall backwards beyond the floor beneath him. It was like he was drifting deeper and deeper into the centre of the Earth — falling further and further away from everyone.

The shaman straightened up, further lifting both hands in presentation. Warrick, however, felt miles away now; his only connection with the present was a thin thread of consciousness, his direct and only link with the outside world — via the smiling shaman.

Then, with a snap of the shaman's fingers, Warrick was back. 'A fine name,' he said proudly, 'it means "a ruler or some great warrior guide" — how apt, but I am sure you already knew that?'

He seemed momentarily enamoured by Warrick's very presence — honoured in fact. But Warrick just gazed back with a glassy stare.

'Ladies and gentlemen,' the shaman continued, 'once in a while someone walks into our midst, a somebody that displays a wealth of potentiality on so many levels that the masses can dismiss him as simply somebody unreal and out of reach. And I am sure that in some cases, this can cause people to resent and even reject him, believing his demeanour, thoughts, and beliefs to be merely signs of his delusional feelings of grandeur. This is an unfortunate, but perhaps a natural defensive attitude on their part, due to their feelings of inadequacy and limited abilities compared to his. He appears to them as somewhat of a social anomaly.'

Warrick's mind was sent spinning — there was just so much said with so few words. Couldn't he, for once, use some normal, run-of-the-mill words in a sentence?

Warrick was still trying to take in and make sense of the first part before the shaman turned back to him and continued.

'Yet here you still stand, invisibly battered and bruised, despite your many negative and sometimes aggressive encounters with so many that cannot and will not ever understand even so much as your very essence. May I take this moment to marvel at your persistence for one so young?' And the shaman bowed in front of Warrick.

Warrick forced a smile. He wasn't sure whether to feel embarrassed, humiliated or elated. For whoever this shaman was talking about, he was sure it wasn't him. He was being made to feel akin to some bare-footed deity, though he felt more awkward and actually rather stupid. He was only a late teenager after all — a boy to many, and barely a man of the world to most.

The shaman continued to smile at Warrick, his eyes sparkling. 'I am one of a few guardians of truth and hold a key so valuable that only when one is ready can they reach out for it. Sometimes even a blind man can see those things that others cannot.' His stare was resolute and focused. He meant every word, and Warrick could feel it. 'You, too, possess those qualities that allow you to become one of these guardians, for you are a leader of men—of many men. And if you look way, way, back in time, you will see that you have led before.'

Warrick swayed transfixed. The eye contact was as direct a connection as a laser beam. For a tiny instant, he felt as one with the shaman, and the shaman's vision became his. It was hypnotic.

But a tiny mocking voice at the back of Warrick's mind — as faint as a distant echo — seemed to chuckle. It was his father's voice, as if he had just listened to the shaman's rhetoric, 'YOU...?' It chided, 'a leader of men? Do me a favour! You can't even get out of bed in the mornings...'

Although part of him wanted to nervously laugh at this, for there was some truth to it, it was soon extinguished by the shaman's persistent glare. In fact, the shaman even seemed aware of this emerging mockery as his following statement addressed it.

'You must ignore them — the voices — these echoes of past oppression, for they will never understand your gift, for a gift it is. Although I suspect that you have always known that — deep down.' He smiled down at Warrick like a proud leader. 'And, if you are ready, your new life can begin.'

Warrick, somewhat immobile, found himself at a mental crossroads. He wavered on the spot, still tethered to this mystical powerhouse. He tried to evaluate the concept of a new life, a new future away from everything he knew — a future of spiritual enlightenment and newfound mental powers. But something was holding him, adhering him to the physical world about him — even if by his very fingertips.

Beginning to rebel, Warrick tried to break the bond, to at least break eye contact, but the shaman was not quite done. The dreamlike trance surrounding them held him in some kind of limbo, an almost paralysing state where he felt dangerously suggestible. Despite this, the shaman had still somehow activated a dormant power within Warrick that he did not know he possessed. He just needed to work out how to control it.

'And factor in,' continued the shaman, 'the fact that you can disagree with these blatant lies of a media-policed social ideology, that others will not, and cannot, and which does not go as unnoticed as you may think. These people about you, the doomsayers, the naysayers and those that cling on to the social pillars for dear life, they need you — more than you know. Believe!'

Warrick still did not move but listened on intently now, barely wanting to lose eye contact.

The shaman continued excitedly, seemingly still holding back on some inner thrill. 'Let me educate you for a moment, if I may.' The Shaman's hand reached out, like so many times before, as if to instruct. 'I want you to look inwards, but only fleetingly, and see what I see, for you radiate a beauty from the inside out. Some will never see it — but those aware enough will be blinded by it.'

Warrick tried to absorb every word. He clung on to each and every concept like a lifeline.

'The more ownership you take of those things around you, the more powerful you will become. This is one of the fundamental ingredients to a great secret.' And the shaman looked up to the heavens and opened out his arms in adoration.

Warrick, too, looked up and about himself, but was more aware of the amazing silence and calmness that now surrounded him. He gazed in question at the people who were looking upon him with intense significance, and he felt a sudden resurgence of some long-lost impulse to pick up the reins of leadership and guide them into the future, wherever that may lead.

Then the shaman spoke from the heart. 'You only look within to remove those things that don't belong.'

He stared deep into Warrick's eyes, urging him to find his inner strength and innate power as a being, and to join him in his quest for spiritual freedom, walking among the other leaders who had been chosen before him — teaching and guiding newcomers and veterans alike in their search for truth and leadership.

'Although for centuries man has been seeking the divinity that is God, had he had more faith and inner self-confidence in himself, then all he had to do was look no further than that of a simple reflection.' The Shaman paused, thinking about what he could add to this insight. 'This is not a slight on theism — the belief in the existence of one or more deities — no, but in the realisation of your own true power, that you are, in fact, your own truth, for you are your own source.'

The shaman gave another gentle and knowing smile, and then Warrick understood.

For the nearest he would ever get to God would be simply looking in the mirror. For he was a god; everyone was, to one degree or another. Every single person was a god, a creator or supreme architect of their own world and that of the outer world all about them. But some were, in truth, more naturally powerful than others, but were still reduced in their powers over the aeons of time and space, nevertheless. Withdrawn and restrained by their own doing, their powers were greatly diluted from the might of their own hand. Amazing, and now here was someone who offered a way of undoing it all, an actual way out — back to basics, back to their native state. Warrick's eyes sparkled back at the shaman.

'So, to you, my friend, I offer my hand, and may you walk with me out of the darkness and into the light. I will train you and guide you at my side, so you may learn to teach and instruct also. Then you, too, can help and guide others out of the abyss of lies and unhappiness into the incredible vistas of truth and real happiness.

'For you are Thoth incarnate, messenger of the sun god Ra, and a god in your own right. One who can change, to embrace wisdom and to enforce justice. Once you have confronted and cleaned up your past adolescent misdemeanours, the future is bright… oh so, so bright.

'But may I end on two points of personal interest?' Warrick nodded and the shaman continued, firstly in a brief poetic fashion, 'A writer you will be, a great one with the quill and parchment that I can see.'

Warrick dared not move an inch, just acknowledging with the very slightest of smiles.

'And secondly, you need support; I believe sandalwood is your natural companion.'

Warrick frowned, bemused.

'Do you have any to hand?' continued the shaman.

'Erm, no I don't,' Warrick answered, shaking his head — completely thrown by the strange question.

What on earth did that have to do with his ascension into the spirit world? It was such a non-sequitur thing to suddenly come out with that he felt completely thrown from his moment of suspension.

'Oh well, we must remedy that now, mustn't we?'

Warrick smiled again, wondering just how bizarre the evening would become. But for some reason, this rapid rise, like a soaring bubble of light, of utter belief and stabilising serenity, was beginning to burst. The suspicion that actual magic existed, that he had started to believe was possible, was waning before his eyes.

Turning on the spot as he spoke, the shaman asked out loud with his deep booming voice if anyone had any sandalwood on their person.

What are the odds of that happening? thought Warrick, speculating about what would make a tiny piece of scented wood help him? This sudden, and for him, odd diversion was continuing to pull him out of a surreal and magical ascension.

'I've got some,' called a voice from the other side of the circle.

The shaman clapped enthusiastically.

Incredulously, Warrick stared as a big, friendly-looking woman in her sixties rummaged through her heavily tasselled suede bag, before producing a small, light-brown-coloured stick. She held it up with pride, and the members of the circle all made noises of excited awe.

'Ah, bravo, my dear, bravo, pass it on, pass it on,' encouraged the shaman.

He waved the small stick of wood clockwise around the circle. As it was passed from person to person, they seemed to treat it as a sacred object, each one gently holding it up and peering at it with a mysterious expression.

Warrick stared blankly at the insignificant-looking piece of wood as it made its way towards him. The last person to his right held onto it a little longer than the others before passing it up to Warrick. She seemed to have now both Warrick and the small piece of wood in mesmerised wonder.

But the effect was lost on Warrick, and suddenly, the euphoric utopia of shamanic divinity and self-causation had now, regrettably, practically lost its spell. Warrick, however, took the piece of sandalwood and paused for a moment, wondering what to do with it. Everyone appeared to be staring at him, eagerly waiting for his next move. So, despite feeling rather ridiculous, Warrick lifted the small wooden stick into the air and held it up like a magical talisman.

Everyone gasped and cooed in eager excitement. Warrick forced a smile at his newfound admirers. He felt more like a young trainee wizard with a newly acquired wand than someone who had just been somewhat spiritually "knighted". For all he knew, he could just as well have been initiated into some black magic circle.

'May this union complete you,' said the shaman gratifyingly, and he bowed once again towards him.

Warrick, too, bowed — also dropping the arm that had been holding the piece of wood. This was his first and probably last chance to be personally addressed by a barefooted messiah, and he wanted to honour the moment with a complete and final acknowledgement.

The shaman stood upright and turned to face the rest of the circle. 'So, one and all, the evening has concluded, and may I wish you a harmonious and sinless few months until such time that we shall all meet again, in Arizona.' He opened his arms again, welcomingly. 'I am and always shall be your most humble servant,' and he bowed once again. Then everyone in the circle briefly lowered their heads.

After first nodding to the two musicians at the far end of the room, the shaman spun around and seemed to drift effortlessly back out of the room. The evening, Warrick naively presumed, appeared to have come to a close.

~ CHAPTER TWENTY FOUR ~

Guiding Light

It was finally over. Warrick blinked a few times as if an enchantment spell was lifting. Slowly around him, people began standing — some stretching and some clustering together. Warrick slipped his socks and shoes back on and looked about him.

Amused, Warrick watched the small, rotund musician sling his drums over his shoulder and amble across the broken circle with the ease of someone clocking off for the day. The man seemed more like a tradesman wrapping up a shift than a sacred performer, which, somehow, made the whole event feel even more real.

In tow was the asexual individual who looked toward Warrick and smiled. Warrick smiled back politely and unintentionally held a mild curiosity in his gaze.

'Excuse me,' said a female voice, distracting Warrick, and his attention broke away. 'I've always wanted to meet a chosen one, may I... may I hug you... you know, for luck?'

'You want to what?' Warrick asked, startled.

Before she answered, the strange woman with pronounced facial hair had thrown her arms around him and was hugging him rather tightly. Then, one by one, he could feel other people reaching out to him. Some put their hands against him, while others, it seemed, just wanted to be close to him.

'Ooh, I can feel his aura,' announced one woman to her friend as she pressed herself against him, and Warrick had to stifle a burst of laughter.

More hands reached out, touching and caressing his body. One woman cooed in relief, whereas another promptly burst into tears of joy.

'I have waited so long to meet a chosen one,' said a sturdy-looking woman. 'I had practically given up hope.' Warrick smiled gently back at the woman.

To one side, Warrick heard his friend, Sumera, boasting to an older man that he, Warrick, was their friend and it was they who had had the foresight to invite him along. She called it divine sight — a gift of the divinities themselves. She went on to validate the nearness of truth and, as such, the power of utter belief.

'I have a question,' said a man's voice, distracting Warrick.

'Me too,' said another.

It was becoming a blaze of faces, voices and waving hands. As Warrick looked about him, even more people were gathering to get close to him, all wanting to be touched by the chosen one. He stood there trying to take it all in; he'd never felt so wanted. And peculiarly, he also felt a strange sense of responsibility growing within him. Warrick began to see how prophets and religious leaders could be so quickly deified. Everyone there appeared to be looking upon him now as a newly appointed healer of men, another pillar of spiritual strength, and another guide to take them on into the light.

This was it, Warrick thought, it was beginning — he was slowly establishing followers of his own, but he was not sure that he felt ready.

Sidling up beside Warrick, a crippled man tentatively approached. Warrick, however, did not remember him constricted, and his movements jerky and unrefined. It appeared like the man had a form of motor neurone disease, a disorder that affects the voluntary control of the muscles, in which the person is no longer able to direct the motions of their body accurately. But was it? Or was it an internal conflict of nerve centres, fighting for contradictory control of the organism?

The moment Warrick questioned himself as to what specifically could be wrong with this poor man, and how one would go about fixing him, something incomprehensible happened.

A form of lightheaded detachment took place, and Warrick got the impression of sliding sideways out of his own body, only to emerge within the actual corporal body of this crippled man.

Inexplicably, this tangible, yet ethereal experience, had now given him the irrefutable proof that he himself needed: that he was indeed, in essence, a spiritual entity. It was not a physical sensation, but unquestionably an incorporeal one, where Warrick now found himself actually within the very essence of the man's biological and mental anatomy. It was like being inside a great organic, electronic structure, where the nervous system's synapses crackled about him and electrical signals flashed past him from brain to muscle and back again. Warrick looked about at the man's apparent muscular complexity. And without knowing why, he had an idea of what was really going on. The problem was not merely a physical one or a cellular malfunction, but a mental one. There was no doubt that such neurodegenerative conditions existed, but this... this particular situation appeared to have an independent source of control.

As such, treating this particular body's symptoms, as if derived from an organic or cellular disease, when they were not, would never result in improvement. All that drugs would do in this case would be to dampen the physiological aspects of the malady to a minimum. Yet the root cause would never, therefore, be addressed. Yes, the body carried out the erratic muscle motions, but under what or whose direction?

Warrick picked up the man's mental intention to raise his right arm, and after the following command from his brain, his arm began to rise. But a microsecond later, a second subconscious counter-intention was also sent to the brain, and the brain, simply acting as a control centre, then sent out the conflicting counter-command to lower the arm. Sensing this, the man's intention once more sent a signal to the brain to command that the arm be raised. But again, a secondary subconscious counter-intention directed the brain to lower it. On and on this went, intention and counter-intention, both directing the brain, and the brain trying desperately to comply. To simplify things, the muscles, when directed to react, were then each given a secondary cancellation. The result was a jerky and uncontrolled body.

But who or what was directing the body in this uncontrolled fashion?

Warrick then realised what was happening to this poor man. A mental error or rogue computation from his subconscious mind was causing a conflicting impulse to interfere with the man's muscular control system within his body. The body itself was not at fault; it was exactly carrying out the commands given to it by a faulty or compulsive part of the mind — the very aberrations that the shaman was trying to negate.

Warrick was reminded of something the shaman had said to one of the men earlier in the evening: "that the mind was a very complex machine — and if you never learn to understand it, you will forever be a slave to it." And here was a prime example.

Doctors and physicians could spend hours on various drugs and evaluations of what was wrong with this body or organic machine, but on this occasion, these were merely symptoms of the primal cause. A rogue computation was at fault, counteracting every physical action that was originally being directed by the man's mind. Fascinating! And Warrick was led on to ponder just how many other body parts could also be affected in such a way? This could open the door to numerous opportunities and discoveries in both mental and physical health, leading him to wonder why it had not been investigated further. Well, not unless it already had, but had been suppressed by the usual greed and immorality of vested interests...

All the same, perhaps this could be an additional branch of research that could be undertaken by parapsychology researchers, or a group with advanced spiritual and mental technology, or indeed, Remote Viewers — those gifted individuals who can apparently perceive remote locations from a completely different area. After all, the CIA and other governmental bodies around the world had pumped enough money into such mysterious research developments in the past.

A sudden claustrophobic sensation swam around Warrick, and he felt a tremendous urge to eject himself from this peculiar location and relocate himself back inside his own body — his own organic, carbon-based machine. The last thing he wanted was to get trapped inside someone else's body — injured, malfunctioning, or otherwise.

With a hard judder, he found that he was back in control of his own body. Feeling oddly back at home, he completed a general scan of his extremities: fingers, toes, arms and legs.

But the sensation of the other man's mental "machinery" still seemed to coat him like a layer of slime.

chapter Twenty Four

It made him feel unclean. But what on earth had just happened?

As Warrick looked up at him, the man had ceased all conflicting body motions, and his movements had become calm. Utterly astonished by what had just taken place, the man stared down at his limbs and checked them. Perplexed, he stared at Warrick, even disgusted at what Warrick had just done, even on a spiritual level, by merging or entering his mind and body uninvited — never mind poking about at its inner workings. He even seemed angry that he had had no say in the matter.

Despite this unintentional violation, Warrick still felt somewhat ashamed of himself. The shaman had opened an ability that he did not know he possessed and, evidently, did not know how to control. His new abilities were clearly growing. This may be why one needed to study and learn how to harness the power of The Divinities.

But minutes later, the man, who had appeared to have been healed, reverted to his previous state of muscle malfunction. But if anything was to be learned from this psychic experience, it was that something could be done to address the physical with the aid of the spiritual.

An authoritative tone broke through the hubbub. 'Excuse me, excuse me,' said a familiar voice.

Suddenly, walking into view through the crowd of people was the short woman whom he recognised as being his earlier host. At her side stood the two huge doormen whom he remembered seeing at the entrance doors. She stopped directly in front of Warrick and also bowed briefly. Around her, the people watched and waited, their anticipation palpable.

'May I congratulate you — an honour for both you and me, and everyone here, it seems,' she said, as she gave him a warm smile.

Warrick returned the smile.

'Walk with me a moment, I have something to show you,' she went on, and she put her arm in his.

As he walked with her at his side, the crowd parted, letting them through, and then closed again behind him, reminding Warrick of the story of Moses parting the waters of the Red Sea.

'Here, sit down,' she said, pulling a leather-backed chair from under a table where it had been recently placed.

He sat down and ran his hand over the cream silk cloth that covered it, noticing again the faint repetitive mixture of pictographically woven elemental images he had seen before. There was even an Egyptian eye — that of Horus, that he'd not seen earlier. The others that he had come across that evening were sprawled out haphazardly; the secular Peace symbol, the Omega, the Chinese Yin & Yang, the symbol for Heterosexuality, the Hindu Adi Shakti (that represented a cosmic energy force which moves through the entire universe), the Hermes God messenger icon, and the Egyptian Life symbol, which on reflection probably referred to the After Life. In essence, it was a giant symbolic map of knowledge.

Then, finally, there were the independent elements that made up The Divinities themselves.

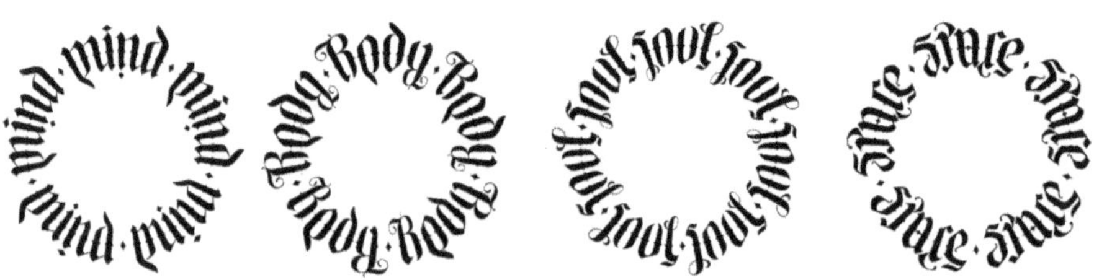

'Mind, Body, Soul and Space,' he murmured, imagining them all rotating in a clockwise direction.

'Curious, aren't they? The pinnacle of a tremendous science of knowledge, naturally umbrellaed within the revered field of epistemology. The wisdom of the ancients! Archaic knowledge which, when refined, culminated in giving us a comprehensive body of workable applications,' she whispered.

'It's quite mind-boggling, actually... almost overwhelming,' Warrick replied quietly.

'Yes, I guess it is. Although, as I am sure you can appreciate, when taking into consideration the ascension pyramid, not all can grasp the exactitude of such a vast body of data. For the lower one has descended in life, the less their ability to differentiate, especially when deciphering one datum from another. Unfortunately, these people — the ignorant, the stupid, the masses — tend to lump information together as if it contained no differences, thereby limiting their observational powers. The more you can differentiate, the saner you are.'

'Agreed,' Warrick said, nodding. This concept rang true with him.

She took a moment to mull something over, while giving Warrick a searching, almost inquisitive look. 'As an interjection, tell me, did you ever come across that famous quote from Alvin Toffler's book Future Shock?' Warrick shook his head. 'It is rather curious... *The illiterate of the 21st century will not be those that cannot read or write, but those that cannot learn, unlearn and relearn.*' She raised her eyebrows pointedly.

'A scary thought,' agreed Warrick.

'Isn't it...' the tiny woman pressed. 'So, once you implement the simple step of willingness before you decide to confront the dizzying heights that the ascension pyramid can provide, your path up to a greater existence will be laid out before you.' She smiled sweetly.

Warrick puffed. The possibilities seemed endless. A nervous thrill ran the length of his spine.

'And you are about to learn about the Divinities and what they represent in their entirety. All you have to do is sign this little waiver.' From behind her back, she produced a piece of paper.

Warrick raised his eyebrows inquisitively.

'I've got to... to sign something?' he frowned.

Then, changing his focus, a faint walnut-coloured form in elegant, shiny black, handwritten calligraphic script was placed before him. It was a delicate piece of paper that looked more like papyrus parchment and bore a rustic, classical, and old-fashioned appearance. Around its edges sat the familiar mystical signs and symbols in their black and gold leaf. Its heading was the longest Warrick had ever seen.

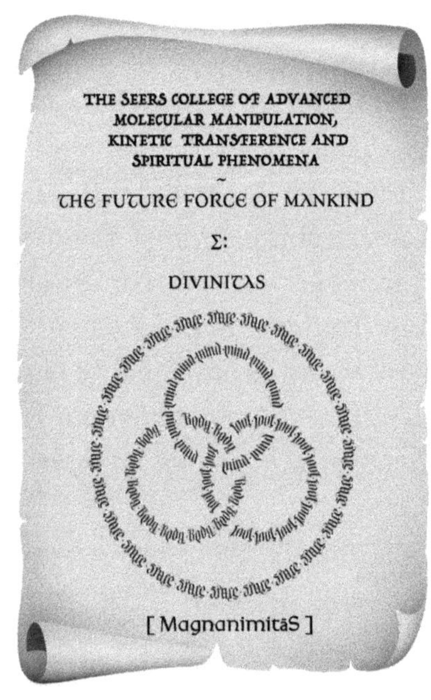

Once more that evening, he was subjected to the mystical alignment of interconnected ambigrams.

Warrick rested a finger on another unfamiliar symbol.

'It's used in its mathematical sense,' said the host, guessing his question. 'It's called a sigma, and it means "the sum of." So in our case here, it denotes that our college is the sum of the elements that together form the collective whole in our teachings and our beliefs: in essence, The Divinities.'

Warrick closed his eyes for a moment, replaying what she had just said. Why must these people speak in riddles? Did no one speak normally around here?

'And lastly,' she went on, tapping a finger at the bottom of the page, 'here we have *MagnanimitāS*, which is taken from the Latin — who previously borrowed it from the Greek — and we have encapsulated it here to represent the greatness of one's mind with the elevation of one's soul. Our own interpretation...'

Warrick blinked a few times, as if this would clear his mind of the growing overload of symbolic references and meanings.

Although his mind was, in part, a little weary from such an exhausting evening of in-depth enlightenment, it was all actually, albeit slowly, beginning to make sense. All the same, and despite sounding like some fantastic, futuristic spiritual retreat — where he would secretly learn to harness the power of his mind — it suddenly felt as if he were being asked to sign his life away for a very, very long time.

He sighed with concern; the penultimate scenario was upon him now. Ought he to sign? It all appeared so inviting and so tremendously exciting, and yet there was just something he couldn't quite put his finger on.

She placed a hand upon his shoulder. 'You are more powerful than you can possibly imagine,' she said, 'particularly so, it seems.' Warrick let out a heavy breath.

'Don't be afraid, young man, for it is all waiting for you. Your fears, apprehensions, areas of introversion and each and every doubt about any area of your life can all be dispelled by using the basic laws of The Divinities. You will be shown the way, shown and guided to overcome the negativities of your mind. And once you have attained a mental equilibrium, then you, too, can help and guide others. You have a tremendous gift, Warrick — use it wisely.'

She was now peering into him with such intensity that it was making him a little self-conscious. Behind her, there were now four doormen acting as bouncers, asserting their presence as the excited group pressed in further to witness him apply his signature.

Distracted by his heart thumping away like the earlier chanting drum-beat, Warrick cursorily scanned both the front and rear of the pages until he got to the bottom.

It sounded so enticing, so... so unbelievable. Surely it was everyone's goal to have complete power over their mind, to command their environment and to bend it to one's will. He looked back at the main title: *The Seers College of Advanced Molecular Manipulation, Kinetic Transference and Spiritual Phenomena.* Wasn't that to move or transfer energy from one form to another, or perhaps, in this case, to move things — pictures and memories, and maybe even objects — with the power of your mind? A tiny electric surge ran through his veins.

If he signed now, the induction would be complete, and his life, as he knew it, would change forever. He desperately wanted change — but... but was this really it?

Only a few hours ago, he was an "open-minded" cynic, questioning everything, but always open to different points of view and in learning new truths, but now...

The group's anxiety pressed in around him, their nervous tension continuing to build. However, something still did not sit right with him. He could not think straight. His recently quietened mind was now abuzz with conflicting impulses and indecisions. His head was swimming, and his stomach was churning. He had always been looking for something, something spiritual of sorts, perhaps, but as close as this unorthodox and fascinating group was, he was still balancing precariously on the proverbial knife-edge. He just needed a convincing nudge — one way or the other — or he feared his fragile belief in the group's unorthodox spiritual magic would vanish altogether.

'Now,' she went on, her voice sounding more businesslike, 'your training and accommodation for the first two years that you will be with us in Arizona will be £20,000. A cheque will be quite sufficient.'

There was a tangible pause as Warrick felt himself catch his breath. It was as if someone had dragged a needle across a vinyl record, creating a violent and dramatic end to something wonderful.

Warrick's eyes widened. How much? Twenty grand? Not wanting to show his utter shock at this sudden announcement, especially with everyone in the room watching his every move, he decided to suppress his initial reaction to scream out loud. He had never even entertained the idea of having to pay for the privilege of such an education. And now he thought about it, he hadn't even agreed that this was to be his new vocation in life anyway. Where on earth did she expect a nineteen-year-old to suddenly pull out £20,000 from?

He sat up slowly with the feeling of being punched in the stomach. His brain appeared to have slipped gears and wouldn't re-engage. Did she honestly think he was going to just present a waiting cheque book from his back pocket?

He kept his gaze on the table and forced himself to stay calm. 'I see...' was all he could manage. But after nobody else spoke again for an uncomfortable period, he pressed on. 'I'm afraid that I am not in the position to pay you that right at this moment.'

He was not willing to let on whether he had the necessary funds or not.

The tiny woman laughed incredulously, and that alone started Warrick's stomach churning.

For the first time, he looked at her properly — not through the haze of wonder or confusion, but with clear, unblinking eyes. There was something in her face he hadn't noticed before: a soft darkness, perhaps, or the shark-like glitter of a person used to getting her way.

'Is that so?' she said coolly, and Warrick noted the slightest annoyance in her voice. 'Well, you don't think that you are just going to... walk out of here without signing up... do you?' And her laugh, although more of a titter, rang out in nervous disbelief. It was a false and mechanical laugh.

Was that a threat?

Behind him, the bouncers resumed their positions, and the group closed in, their excitement now tantamount to suppressed euphoria. And once more that evening, Warrick felt his knees buckle.

~ CHAPTER TWENTY FIVE ~

Rank

Warrick stared back at the little woman. What had she just said He wanted to believe that he had misheard her, but with her questioning gaze upon him, he knew that he hadn't.

Warrick felt suddenly sick. There were untold layers to this movement.

What would they do if he refused to sign? Force him? As he looked up, he could see that he was now entirely surrounded by curious onlookers. He could sense their apprehension, and it only added to his confusion. What had just happened? The evening's social atmosphere had changed gears when he wasn't looking. He felt both annoyed and betrayed. The sudden feeling to make a mad run for it and escape out into the night began coursing through his veins, but that was impossible; there were just too many of them surrounding him.

And what of the people? Were they all just gullible sheep, lost and disillusioned? Or were they a collection of the stupid that roamed society, that the shaman had pointed out? Or perhaps they did need him... Some of them definitely needed someone.

Warrick closed his eyes. What was he to do? The whole evening's build-up of mystical wonder and potential mind power had suddenly come crashing down around him.

Surely this was not all fake? Surely this entire bizarre night's event was not put on for the sole purpose of gaining £20,000?

Warrick felt at a complete loss. Had he really been so gullible as to buy into such a farce? But it couldn't be, it just couldn't. He knew what he saw, what he had experienced, how the people there had changed for the better. He had witnessed incredible feats firsthand, the very spiritual enlightenment they had spoken of. And the shaman, too, had been authentic — all of it had — he'd swear it. Yet here he was, trapped like some dumb animal.

He looked back at the tiny woman. He had to stay calm. He must not react or do anything that might put himself in further trouble. He had to act like he was unfazed by this abrupt expectation of theirs.

He moistened his lips. 'What if I am not ready? What if I want to come back in ten years?' he said finally.

'You won't find us by the usual methods alone; you need to be invited in. We are self-funded and self-regulated, and we exist because we can.'

His head was spinning.

Why did she have to spoil everything? Why could it not have been all that he had been looking for?

Warrick gave an awkward sort of half-smile and clasped his hands together on the table. For a brief moment, he stared back at two of the Egyptian 'all-seeing' eye symbols that were placed at random angles upon the silk cloth. He created a crease in the fabric, bringing them closer together, and in an instant, they looked as one.

And right now, they just seemed to be watching him.

Warrick knew little of Egyptian symbology — if anything at all — but what he did remember was that these were the eyes of Horus, the sky god. And this "eye" was a symbol of protection, of health and royal power, and not that of the "All-Seeing Eye" associated with current satanistic trends and blanket occult associations. He wished he now had such power, so that he could ascend to a place where he could command over the masses and dictate his will upon his loyal subjects.

It was an impossible situation. But it came down to this: was he a Chosen One or not? Was he destined for much, greater things — or not? It was now looking very unlikely, but... the contradictions were enough to make his head explode. Had the Shaman's intense gaze — that piercing sense of being seen — been just another illusion, crafted only to flatter and extract?

He ran through it all again. Had everything he'd sensed, witnessed, and experienced truly been real? Warrick tried to break the night into parts, to analyse each stage, but his thoughts were becoming a blur. Chosen or not, he had to act.

Somehow, he needed to outmanoeuvre these people in conversation if he were ever going to get out unscathed and with his credibility still intact. He took in a deep breath and cleared his mind. He was, after all, a trainee leader of men, chosen personally by this incredible spiritual guide — this powerhouse of mental "muscle". So, what could he do? What skills could he now bring to this arena of devout followers? He breathed out slowly and allowed his mind to find the answers he so desired.

Then, without knowing exactly why, Warrick made his decision, and he tapped the end of the pen over the signature strip before finally speaking.

'You know, to be honest,' he began, 'I am actually rather disappointed with this final conversation,' and he looked directly up at the tiny woman. The two nearest security guards stood defensively more erect.

The tiny woman frowned.

As if with a heavy heart, Warrick sighed, finding the precise words he needed. 'I'm not going to try and hide it, but this has upset me.' He paused again for dramatic effect. 'I was invited to attend tonight's event at very short notice, not thinking to bring my cheque book with me, for why would I? And now I find that I have been finely selected as The — Chosen — One by your shamanic leader, to be personally trained up under his very wing, and to learn and harness the great skills and wisdom of The Divinities and Shamanism. It's a shock to the system, you know. And one that I will not take lightly. It's an overwhelming and somewhat daunting prospect at first glance — but nevertheless... I do intend to see it through.'

The crowd surrounding him fidgeted with uncertainty.

'So...?' encouraged the tiny woman.

Warrick had to think fast. And then it came to him. 'So, of course, I am going to go to Arizona in August! What an honour such a great man has just bestowed on me!' There was a sudden group sigh of relief. 'But...' again he paused, dragging out the moment, 'I will not be spoken to like this. I will not be bullied into doing something at the drop of a hat. After all, I am The Chosen One and I expected more... more respect for a start.' With the very slightest of confrontation, Warrick stared back at her, raising his eyebrows.

The words had come out of his mouth before he could stop them. The tiny woman looked back in blank confusion. A slight panic stirred within him, and he wondered if he had gone too far.

What a nerve he had to think he could use this unauthorised status to throw back at them. Would they buy it, or would they suddenly baulk at the idea of this sudden, indignant command from a recently appointed nineteen-year-old deity-in-the-making? But he held his position.

Then his question was answered in unison, as both the tiny woman and the four security guards bowed their heads subserviently.

'I'm sorry,' apologised the tiny woman.

'Yes, of course,' agreed one of the security guards, and everyone around him seemed to take a step back, granting Warrick more personal space.

Warrick smiled internally at his own cunning. It had worked — he couldn't believe it. The fools! He'd actually "pulled rank" over the staff; he had somehow taken control of the situation and created a momentary illusion of having total command. This sudden shift to an assumed position of acknowledged authority had thrown them all completely off guard. And they were all now listening to him. He would have made Horus proud.

Moving quickly, Warrick stood up purposefully and smiled confidently.

'So, I look forward to seeing you all in August.' He looked about him at everyone and was met with smiling faces and agreement all around. 'And now I really must go,' he finished, turning back to the tiny woman.

Waylaid by the speed and direction at which the conversation had suddenly veered, she smiled back hesitantly. Then he thrust out his hand before her, and she shook it — almost without thinking. Then he addressed each of the bouncers in turn, and so shook all of them, too, by the hand. Their eyes darted from one to another, all showing signs of perplexed indecision.

Everything was happening so fast. But the handshakes were like a binding agreement, so nobody moved.

Warrick, his intention resolute, made for the front doors, which he was pleased to see were now open. But a sudden firm grip on his shoulder made him freeze. What was it now? Another stop? And he was so close to walking out of this sudden "madhouse".

'I thought you might like these,' said a voice, and Rumi came sharply into view holding up crudely folded pieces of yellow paper. 'It's about you; it's what the shaman said about you. I wrote it all down — well, as much as I could. I thought you might like to keep them.' He beamed, looking pleased with himself.

Warrick ran his eyes quickly over the pencilled notes and abbreviations. 'Thank you,' he answered with a grin. 'This will be a good keepsake,' and they shook hands too. Sumera leaned over and kissed him on the cheek.

'We are going to stay on for a bit,' Rumi continued, 'but I am so pleased you were able to come — I really am. And The Chosen One too — I can't believe it — of all people. It's so exciting!'

Warrick smiled again. 'See you both soon.'

Regaining his momentum, he turned back around and started again — his anxiety beginning to rear its ugly head. He'd shown agreement with their cause and was now above suspicion. It was working, and he was finally on his way. He just had to keep moving.

He kept his pace this time, despite still being approached by other people also wanting to say hello, or to just touch a part of him. It was such an odd feeling, but he found it strangely gratifying and empowering. Just keep walking, he repeated to himself, just keep walking.

~ CHAPTER TWENTY SIX ~

cult or college?

inally, Warrick reached the main front doors of the large house, and was pleased to see that the way ahead looked clear of further badgering. Outside, the wind and rain had abated entirely. It was now calm, so much so that Warrick stared about himself in the extreme silence. He hurried across the gravel drive back towards his car. The twilight evening never looked so inviting or refreshing.

Warrick took in deep breaths of the fresh air, smiling back at the various couples and groups that had suddenly appeared to pause and acknowledge him. But he still did not stop. He kept going right out through the front gates and out of sight of the watching winged serpents until he finally found that he was on his own.

Relief flooded through him, and the anxiety left him with every new step he took. He was out, and he was free and was indeed going home for sure.

It wasn't until he was driving back with the car doors locked that he regained the peace of mind to reflect on the last few hours. It was so surreal: a party of guests, a shaman and a chosen one. What were the odds? And he was the chosen one — and he was different. He was also special — a leader of men.

It was still hard to take in, and he thought of his friends and family, and grinned. "Only you", some would say, whereas others, he was sure, would sneer.

Those he knew who would scare easily would, of course, cry cult or devil-worshipping, and even be petrified of discussing such an event.

They would demand that anyone who came across such a non-standard activity turn and run away. Where would they sit on the ascension pyramid, he wondered? The newspapers, of course, would have a field day — how they would love to twist and manipulate such an event to stir up the unsuspecting public. They would whip up such a frenzy to sell as many of their "newsworthy rags" as possible, which would only reinforce that old adage: that which you do not understand, you fear.

Personally, Warrick liked being different, as it made him feel freer, somehow. In contrast, others appeared to be dependent on what other people said and did, and seemed to rely on social gossip, newspapers, TV news channels, or the government to guide them. They relied so heavily on the system that had been built up around them that he feared they would never wake up from it. Warrick had never liked that. The idea of just agreeing to the conditions being imposed on oneself without question bothered him, as he did not want to feel dependent on anyone else.

What would the average Joe make of such an event, were they to ever find out that this kind of mental and spiritual advancement was possible? They would probably reject it, Warrick concluded. Yet, to be fair, if he thought back again to that intriguing ascension pyramid, then perhaps that was a good yardstick as to what type of personality would strive for such possibilities. It also provided a valuable insight into the mental state and general awareness of the culture itself. After all, the lower one sat on the pyramid, the less one could reach out to such lofty heights of attainment. And conversely, the more buoyant and free-thinking a person was, the easier it was to conceive of such a plateau to investigate. And on that note, it was a good reminder for him to pull up his own mental bootstraps, to embrace life with more abandon.

So, in essence, was it a cult with sinister intent? Was it truly sealed off from the outside world, or simply selective with whom it helped and guided? And more urgently... had he just escaped with his life?

In all honesty, Warrick didn't think so. But he knew others would, no matter the outcome. People were quick to cry "brainwashing" the moment something defied convention. In his experience, even the most intelligent minds could be swayed by ignorance or hearsay.

Irrational fear kept many from experiencing so much of life.

Did this path offer a genuine, if unconventional, route to spiritual fulfilment? It certainly seemed so. There was no denying it now — something powerful stirred within this strange and secretive world. And The Seers College was definitely up there in the running. God only knew what some of these other spiritual movements had in store. It would be fascinating to find out.

Naturally, there would be money needed, Warrick reflected. This was not a charity, and someone had to pay for his bed, board and education — it was only fair. The question was: what were you actually paying for? What were you getting in exchange for the money? After all, there was no such thing as a free lunch. Can you realistically put a price on regaining your integrity, sanity or even a higher level of spiritual awareness? £20,000 may even be too cheap... It was an interesting thought.

Perhaps a more tactful and gentle explanation regarding this new world of hope and spiritual enlightenment would have been a better approach. One could so easily dismiss the message here if the messenger were out of sync with the delivery...

Warrick tried to make sense of it all and felt that, interestingly enough, they were a group dedicated to lifting mankind. As crude as the shaman's methods were, his intentions did appear honourable.

He just wanted to relieve man of his guilt and shame, thus springing him from the traps of his own making. Although an unorthodox approach, it was actually quite remarkable. His sheer bravery and commitment to humanity were truly astonishing.

And the £20,000? Well, surely that was nothing in comparison to the current costs of college degrees or years of academic training in prestigious universities. Or as some would say: "modern indoctrination camps." And whereas college students were studying for mundane jobs that they may or may not pursue, those at The Seers College would be studying the wisdom of the ages. They would learn to control their minds and access inner abilities that they had long since lost and forgotten. Did so little a price cap the pursuit of happiness? Again, he did not think so.

But the main thing, he realised, was that there were men and women and groups out there, clever people and dedicated groups, that could and would help their fellow man if given the chance. If only men everywhere would help one another see a better world, reach out and do something about it, rather than withdrawing and holding one another back. Redirecting blame and shunning accountability appeared to be one of Man's shortfalls, which it must not be.

And Warrick needed to take note of this.

There had been plenty for him to learn from the evening, and he'd be foolish not to take something away from it.

The view that Western cultures had on most things spiritual seemed sadly lacking and had, therefore, a lot of catching up to do when compared to Eastern cultures and beliefs. Without a doubt, social conditioning had played a significant role here. A mixture of both arrogance and ignorance would hinder any growth in such a spiritual direction. But then again, the masses, or indeed, the middle classes, would never expand or become enlightened if they continued to carry such an outmoded or supercilious attitude about things for which they had been educated against. They needed to learn that industrialisation or commercialisation had its uses, but also its limitations. There was room for more than just the material, and the spiritual still had a huge part to play. With that in mind, zealots, too, in both religious and scientific communities, needed to put aside any blinkered differences and realise that there would always be scope for improvement in both, albeit different activities.

Pulling into a lay-by, Warrick took out the small pieces of yellow paper that Rumi had given him. Although crumpled and faintly lined, they were still readable in the dim glow of the car's interior light.

The writing was hurried. Some sentences mainly contained brief concepts and snippets from the shaman's evaluation. And random words had been scribbled down at right angles and placed in empty sections of the first page, where Rumi had rushed to catch the main elements, committing them to paper.

Obscure references to Seth and Osiris — the Egyptian Gods and sons of Horus — seemed to refer to a joint reincarnation, as if Warrick was to either learn from this union of dark and light or reflect back to a segment of his own past. He was also reminded to embrace those about him that had suffered in life, as he would then understand their pain and hardship, and from this learn to love his fellow men and women alike.

There were other disjointed references to Warrick having the innate skills of a writer, wherein words and phrases such as "creativity," "warrior," "knowing one's darkness," "sensitivity," "sexually wise," and "inner poet" were all interconnected by the use of small, flowing arrows. Another section of text, which was much harder to make out, referred to Warrick as having much inner wisdom and being a wise lion. Warrick smiled at this, wondering who in his life would relate to any of this. He knew, hands down, they would all laugh and make fun of the shaman's "ravings". A mental note to never show it to them crossed his mind. There was one small passage that suggested Warrick had considered that he had really sinned, when the truth was, he had not, but Warrick had no idea what that was referring to.

The second page seemed harder to read, as if Rumi had rushed to get everything down quickly enough. At the top of the page, the shaman had referred to Warrick "penning the stones," adding another arrowed note that this was very important. Warrick frowned, not having a clue what it referred to. It also mentioned that he had been many poets in the past and must persist in a writing career. Another scribble suggested that he had the will and wine of a poet — another mystery. Again, Warrick felt amused at this. Oddly, he did have an inkling to approach such a career when he was around thirteen, but it had been so violently crushed out of him by school friends, teachers and his parents at the time that he had quashed the idea. But perhaps he should relook at this.

chapter Twenty Six

The shaman did not seem to miss much, so... _Food for thought_, he pondered.

Scanning to the bottom, the final few points that stuck out were remarks about science not surviving without the aid of spirituality and the arts. That further technology was going to make some much needed giant leaps and bounds.

Cybernetics and holographic TV would merge reality to such a marked degree that people would be unable to distinguish truth from lies. By 2030, a quantum leap in technology would be introduced, and by 2070, the world would be a completely different place. These were bold statements, and only time would tell in the end.

Looking back on his "fifteen minutes of fame", that appeared to pass in a heartbeat, Warrick barely remembered half of what was written here in the notes. The only fundamental elements were that he needed to follow his own path, for only by doing this could he move in the right direction, and that he had to heed his own counsel and keep his circle small. These made sense to Warrick. Other remarks he could take or leave, but all the same, the overall evening had changed him, changed him in a way that would forever alter his path or, dare he say it, his destiny.

Warrick took a deep breath and exhaled confidently. Despite these conflicting thoughts, The Seers College, as alluring as it was, was not his path; he realised this now. A mixture of sadness and betrayal stirred somewhere inside. But there were other paths — the shaman had said so — hopefully more discrete in their delivery of personal home truths.

And if he were to pursue his gut feeling, he was yet to find his... but perhaps this would happen sooner than he anticipated.

Following on from that thought, there were others he had heard of who also spoke knowingly of the mind and the spirit.

And the fact that the media had never been too kind about them spoke volumes to him now. Perhaps it was here that he should next look, or at the very least, see what they had to say?

Nevertheless, he was going to make a difference — he was going to contribute something to mankind. His mind was made up. He was going to fight for a better world or die trying. Finally, for now at least, he had something to fight for.

The End

About the Author

For some, Stephen has lead a fascinating life of deliberate curiosity and of thrilling adventure. He has shared extraordinary true stories, of which, have tended to push some peoples' imagination or believability to their limits. These stories and their retelling, whether in his writings or in general social intercourse, has over the years, lead some into further fascination and wonder of the world about us.

It is not the travelling to far off lands, and in meeting uncultured indigenous locals from where he has gathered such unusual stories, but from the people on the street. Secret groups, spiritual societies, magic circles, the deluded unloved and the gifted unknown, he seems to have met his fair share. He wanted to experience their unordered or unorthodox lives, to experience their unique abilities and to bathe in their magical persistence for living.

"Adventure is all about us, if only we dare to walk its path of unknown possibilities. One has to be brave, to seek out and explore, and to be willing to experience that which is not known."